Advance Praise for

Law and Disorder

"*Law and Disorder* is not only a legal thriller in true Grisham style—it is also an excellent window into the total dysfunction of the Justice System.

I literally couldn't put it down."

—Mark Geragos

Renowned criminal defense attorney and acclaimed author of
*Mistrial: An Inside Look at How the Criminal Justice System
Works . . . and Sometimes Doesn't*

"The multidimensional brilliance of Mike Papantonio shines brightly through this can't-put-it-down legal thriller. For a deep dive into law and politics, power and those who fight it, and the very human conflicts that drive and tear at us all, read *Law and Disorder!*"

—Thom Hartmann

Nationally syndicated talk show host and best-selling author

"Pap has long been known as America's Lawyer. He earned that nickname because not only has he represented thousands of Americans, whether they have been put upon by a drug company, automobile company, or anybody injured through the fault of another, but also because he embodies the traditional values that we know as American values.

Pap has a natural ability to weave necessary social and political awareness in an active, intelligent, and engaging story.

Without having to be asked, the reader connects with Deke's character, both his nobility and his flaws. Knowing that Pap is the genesis of Deke, this reads much less as an autobiography than what it is: an intriguing legal adventure.

He leads us down the highways, the side streets and the sometimes seedy back alleys of where lawyers do their work. While trial lawyers shine in a courtroom, it's only because of the days, nights, and weekends spent digging up evidence, witnesses and legal argument. Through Deke, Pap personalizes the profession: It's easy to forget that lawyers are family men and women; they are churchgoers and are worried about their children and the communities they live in. With Deke we see that and we see his shortcomings, and his fears.

Probably the best compliment I can give this book is that I'm now hooked. I know (or I hope) that Deke is not done— that we have not heard the last from him. I'm waiting for the next one, to see what facet of the American legal system Deke will take on, and how he'll do it. Time to move over, Grisham."

—Mark M. O'Mara

O'Mara Law Group
American criminal defense lawyer and legal analyst for CNN

LAW AND DISORDER

LAW AND DISORDER

A Legal Thriller

MIKE PAPANTONIO

SelectBooks, Inc.
New York

This edition published by SelectBooks, Inc.

For information address SelectBooks, Inc., New York, New York.

First Edition

ISBN 978-1-59079-367-1

Library of Congress Cataloging-in-Publication Data

Names: Papantonio, Mike, 1953- author.
Title: Law and disorder : a legal thriller / by Mike Papantonio.
Description: First edition. | New York : SelectBooks, Inc., [2016]
Identifiers: LCCN 2016000027 | ISBN 9781590793671 (hardcover : acid-free
  paper)
Subjects: | GSAFD: Legal stories.
Classification: LCC PS3616.A587 N66 2016 | DDC 813/.6--dc23 LC record
available at http://lccn.loc.gov/2016000027

Book design by Janice Benight

Manufactured in the United States of America
10 9 8 7 6 5 4 3 2 1

For my wife and daughter,
who have been a part of so many of these plots and subplots

ACKNOWLEDGMENTS

I wish to thank the following people:

Josh Young, a *New York Times* best-selling talent who led the way on this project so many times;

Bill Gladstone, the agent who invented long game;

Dana Isaacson, who has helped improve the career of so many fiction writers;

And all my law partners who every day in courtrooms create endless material for a storyteller of thrillers and suspense.

1

WITNESS FOR THE ANGELS

Momentum is everything when it comes to winning a case. Attorney Nick Deketomis knew this from years of experience handling mass tort lawsuits. "Deke" also knew you didn't just need to be ready for trial. You had to count on your fair share of big breaks to even get a shot at telling your story in front of a jury. Deke needed one of those big breaks today in a critically important pretrial hearing before a powerful and likely adversarial judge.

Lawyers all over the country advertised for the big cases, but then the vast majority of them tried to settle without ever going to trial. It was much less problematic to settle out of court. You avoided the expenses incumbent with a big trial and didn't need to worry about the many potential disasters that could develop in a trial courtroom. But Deke wasn't afraid of the fray. He liked to say, "It's not how many times you get knocked down that count; it's how many times you get back up." There was a certain irony in that quote, Deke knew, as supposedly General George Custer said it not too long before Little Bighorn.

Deke liked to think he'd prepared better for this battle than Custer had for Sitting Bull. You'd better be prepared when your opponent is a giant pharmaceutical company valued at more than fifty billion dollars. The multinational corporation Bekmeyer Pharmaceuticals had seemingly limitless resources, including an army of lawyers. Deke was okay with that, as long as both sides played on a level playing field, but Judge Ronald Beedles wasn't even giving him that. Time and again the trial court judge had made extraordinarily bad rulings to make sure Bekmeyer kept landing on its feet.

Judge Beedles was a conservative appointee of a former Florida Republican governor. What had apparently qualified Beedles for the bench was being born into a wealthy family that bestowed timely political contributions. Before his appointment, Beedles was known to spend a lot more time at the nineteenth hole than in the courtroom.

The court was now waiting for the judge to emerge from his chambers.

"He loves making a grand entrance," whispered Deke's co-counsel Angus Moore. He was seated to Deke's left at the plaintiffs' table. Angus was about as big as Paul Bunyan. He'd used that size to his advantage as the starting center at the University of Florida. Deke loved having Angus in the trenches with him. Many years ago the two of them had started the mass torts division of the Law Firm of Bergman Deketomis.

"Let's hope he's actually spending his time reading Jane's report instead of posing in front of a mirror," said Deke.

Dr. Jane Arash was one of the most respected toxicologists in America. She'd written a forty-page toxicology report stating that Bekmeyer's birth control pill Ranidol had caused the partial paralysis of nineteen-year-old Annica Phillips. Judge Beedles would be making a ruling as to whether or not Dr. Arash's opinion rose to a generally accepted standard of scientific methods for medical findings. If he ruled in her favor, that would allow her to testify as an expert witness in Deke's upcoming trial against Bekmeyer. If the judge ruled against them, it was unlikely his ruling would be overturned by an appeals court. In fact, it was likely the judge would do everything in his power to make the case disappear forever.

To Deke's right sat Annica Phillips. Next to Annica was his daughter, Cara, a recent graduate of the Fredric G. Levin College of Law at the University of Florida. Cara was serving as an intern at the firm while studying for the bar exam. The two young women had grown close during the preparations for trial. They had a lot in common—both were honor students and athletes, or at least Annica had been before Ranidol left her paralyzed.

"How are you doing?" Deke asked Annica.

"I'm okay," Annica whispered.

She didn't look okay, but Deke knew Annica was a fighter. He had cautioned her about attending the pretrial hearing, just as he had warned Annica's parents. Deke had wanted to spare them the ugly underbelly of the law as practiced by judges like Beedles, where ideological rulings typically trumped a reasoned judicial opinion.

Deke put a reassuring hand on Annica's shoulder. It was probably good Annica was here. He wouldn't be able to shield her from the enemy much longer—and make no mistake about it, Bekmeyer was the enemy. Deke looked over at the defendants' table. Bekmeyer's lead lawyer, Wharton Garrison, was surrounded by half a dozen lawyers from the Benton, Craighill & Wasserman law offices in New York. If Deke was lucky enough to get Annica in front of a jury, these thousand-dollar-an-hour billing lawyers would make her life a living hell. Deke had warned Annica that Bekmeyer's sharks excelled at character assassination and would do everything in their power to paint her as a party girl who had slept around and done drugs.

Before taking her on as a client, Deke had asked her to tell him about any and all skeletons in her closet.

"I once smoked pot at a frat party," Annica had admitted. "But I've only had two boyfriends my entire life."

She had said the words wistfully. Annica's medical prognosis wasn't encouraging. Even if her health improved, it was unlikely she could ever have children. And it was entirely possible that she might not live long enough to have a third boyfriend.

The week before the hearing Deke had taken Annica out sailing with his family. It had been a warm day, but Annica had bundled up in the way that the elderly usually did. Although her partial paralysis from the drug-induced stroke limited her movements, the sea air had worked its magic and invigorated the young woman. Cara and Annica had found things to laugh about. For an afternoon Annica escaped the confines of her condition.

It was only after they docked that their thoughts had returned to the case. "You remind me of my daddy, Deke," she had said. "I wish he wouldn't worry so much about me."

"That's what parents do," Deke had replied.

"Look after him, will you?"

"Now you're sounding like a parent."

"He's worried about what the trial might do to me. I told him the possibility of a trial is what's keeping me going. I want to be the poster child for what can happen to women taking Ranidol. I don't want anyone else to go through what I have."

Deke looked at the wounded warrior sitting next to him. Cara was still holding her hand. He hoped his key witness would get her day in court and that the judge would allow her to testify.

At long last Judge Beedles made his entrance into the crowded courtroom. Deke helped Annica get to her feet while Cara helped to
steady her. Deke had seen pictures of Annica before her stroke and
had always been struck by how much she had looked like Cara.
Both of them were tall, athletic young women with dark, glossy
hair and large hazel eyes. Both of the young women were now
united in the same cause: They wanted to prevent other women
from being deliberately poisoned for profit. They wanted Ranidol
pulled from the market forever.

After Judge Beedles took his seat, Deke and Cara helped
Annica sit down. Deke could feel the trembling in Annica's body
but wasn't sure if it was from exertion or nerves. From his position at the bench, the judge straightened a few papers, and then
smoothed a crease on his black robe. Darth Vader also wore a black
robe, thought Deke. The judge looked toward the plaintiffs' table
and Deke didn't like what he saw. He and Angus called it "the
Solomon pose." It always preceded bad news.

With feigned sincerity on his face, the judge began. "Mr.
Deketomis, I have reviewed both the report prepared by your
injury causation witness Dr. Arash as well as her deposition testimony. I have spent hours reviewing the case law on this issue. This
is a difficult decision, but I'm sorry to say her opinions simply do
not rise to acceptable scientific standards in the view of this court."
Judge Beedles continued as if he had genuinely struggled to make
an honest and correct decision. "I have no other option except to
disallow the testimony of Dr. Jane Arash."

Even Annica immediately understood the impact of where the
Bekmeyer judge had left her. Without a witness to establish how
and why Ranidol had caused her ischemic stroke and permanent
partial paralysis, her case was going nowhere.

While Beedles blathered about case citations and precedents, Deke turned to Annica to assure her that he was not out of moves, only to see his client had gone sheet-white.

"We lost?" whispered Annica. Then, in an even smaller and more frightened voice, she asked, "Where's my mommy?"

Deke knew Annica's mother wasn't in the courtroom. It was something Annica knew as well, or should have. Annica's breathing was raspy, and she had slumped down in her chair. She was trying to turn her head, trying to look for a mother who wasn't there, but didn't even have the strength to do that.

As Deke signaled to the bailiff for help, Annica slipped further down into her chair. Both Deke and Cara tried to keep Annica from falling to the ground.

"Hang on, Annica," Deke said, "hang on!"

But Deke knew she wouldn't be able to hang on. Dr. Arash's report had documented how Ranidol caused strokes and embolisms. That was the same report that Judge Beedles had said didn't rise to acceptable scientific standards. Dr. Arash had warned Annica and her parents about the possibility of a reoccurrence of an embolism. Deke knew at that very moment a large blood clot was moving through Annica's body and targeting her lungs. Annica was being struck down in open court.

"Dad!" cried Cara.

His daughter was used to him making everything right; Deke felt more helpless than he ever had before.

He started administering CPR, but knew it was a futile gesture. Annica was dying and there wasn't a thing he could do about it.

2
POSTMORTEM

Many of Deke's cases revolved around wrongful deaths. But he had never held a client as she died.

"What Bekmeyer did to Annica is nothing short of murder," Deke said.

Angus and Cara both nodded. The three of them were sitting at the dining room table of the Deketomis family home in Spanish Trace. They needed to talk out what had happened; they needed a postmortem of the day and to share their feelings about Annica. Seeing Annica die had shaken them all to the core, especially Cara.

"It was a good thing you were there for Mr. Phillips," said Angus. "He was pitiful."

Deke nodded. Annica's father had been so grief-stricken, Deke had been afraid he was going to have a heart attack. "Between tears he told me we needed to keep going to beat those bastards. He also requested an autopsy for his daughter in the hopes it would help our case."

After hearing that, Cara reached for another tissue. Deke took a deep breath and hoped his daughter's tears wouldn't be contagious. "Why don't you get some sleep, sweetie?" Deke asked.

Cara shook her head, and Deke felt guilty for having worked her too hard. She was only an intern, but he had been pushing her like he would have pressured a partner in the firm. Cara was supposed to be studying for the bar; she wasn't supposed to be practicing law. It was only now that Deke noticed how pale she was, which accentuated the bags under her eyes all the more.

The stubborn set of his daughter's jaw looked all too familiar to Deke. Everyone said Cara was a chip off the old block.

"What are we going to do now?" she asked.

"We're going to retrench," growled Angus, "and then we're going back to war. For us it becomes that much more personal. For Bekmeyer a few deaths here and a few deaths there is nothing more than the price of doing business."

"Who wants a protein shake?"

Teri Deketomis stuck her head into the dining room, and Deke was almost able to smile for the first time all day. His wife's protein shakes were the purported cure-all for everything from colds to stress to the rigors of a trial. Deke pretended not to notice Teri's tearstained cheeks. He knew how enamored she'd been with Annica.

Her offer was met with a tired chorus of, "No, thanks." Teri accepted the protein shake defeat, but made the same suggestion to her husband that Deke had made to their daughter. "Don't you think you should be getting some sleep, Mr. Deketomis?"

"In a few minutes, Mrs. Deketomis," he promised.

She squeezed his hand, said goodnight to everyone, and left the room.

"We're not the only ones working late," Angus said. "Threepio just texted me. He and Carol are working on picking out who will be our new lead trial plaintiff."

"Threepio" was the office nickname of Ned Williams. Like the droid from Star Wars, their Threepio spoke a number of languages and seemed to have an eidetic memory. Carol was the office's lead investigator, which all but required her to be a workaholic.

"We're down to five plaintiffs," said Deke.

"Bekmeyer is probably hoping they all go away like poor Annica," said Cara.

It hadn't taken very long in the workplace, Deke thought, for his daughter to get so cynical. Annica's death wasn't only a personal loss. When the firm had filed a mass tort lawsuit against Bekmeyer they had named six plaintiffs. Annica had been their unanimous decision to be the representative plaintiff. Now they'd have to go back to the drawing board and select a new lead plaintiff.

While a mass tort case is a civil action with typically more than a thousand plaintiffs, the Ranidol case was more complex because of the take-no-prisoners mentality of Bekmeyer Pharmaceuticals. Bekmeyer was considered the British Petroleum of the drug industry; everywhere they did business, they left behind a trail of bodies and misery. The powerhouse German company had spread piles of money around to super PACs, well-known politicians, media and advertising departments of every description, university research departments, and even to the regulatory agencies that were supposed to keep them honest. All that well-spent cash guaranteed that the random suffering and body count caused by their products was generally overlooked as "the price of doing business."

"We know Bekmeyer has already circled up the wagons," Deke said. "They're going to do anything they can to protect their cash cow."

"And they'll be able to do just that if dysfunctional judges like Beedles continue to treat Ranidol like a sacred cow," said Angus.

Neither man was overstating their case. Ranidol generated a profit of almost five billion dollars a year, and Bekmeyer used that war chest to do everything it could to protect its venerated product. The multinational corporation combated medical critics and consumer protection groups by relying on selective clinical studies that whitewashed adverse events as being unusual, or as being unrelated to the use of Ranidol. Bekmeyer's spin doctors were the best in the world, using clinical data to their best advantage. Not so surprisingly, much of the so-called clinical data cited had been created through Bekmeyer's own drug trials.

"Who guards the guards?" asked Deke.

Thousands of years ago the Roman poet Juvenal had asked that question. The American public wanted to believe that regulators like the FDA were watching out for them, but that was an ill-placed hope. While the FDA might not overtly be in bed with the big pharmaceuticals, their relationship was certainly a cozy one.

"Annica told me you were her hero," Cara said. "She told me no one else was willing to take her case."

"Yeah, some hero," replied Deke. "A lot of good I did her."

"You're not done."

"That's right," he said. "We're nowhere near done."

After four hours of bad dreams Deke welcomed some early morning quiet time with Teri. Deke and Teri had been married for north of thirty years. He thanked his lucky stars that Teri had agreed to spend her life with him. He was always happy to be in her company, and Teri's charm made most people overlook Deke's prickles.

Even after finishing her cup of coffee, Cara looked exhausted. She had to be more tired than Deke had imagined. Normally she was the bounce-back kid. In high school she'd played two sports and been the captain of her soccer team. He supposed Annica's death had laid her low and that she was grieving in her own way. Deke intended to grieve in another way. He'd make Bekmeyer pay.

"Why don't you take the day off?" Deke suggested.

Cara smiled slightly. "I'll be fine."

"I'll be glad to take the day off," said a male voice.

Deke looked up at his son, Andy. As usual, he was the last one in the family to get up. "Judging by your last report card," Deke said, "you took all of the last semester off."

Teri gave Andy a hug, even though he made the act look like he was a victim of torture. "How about I make you a plate of eggs?" she asked.

Andy made the sign of a cross as if he were warding off Dracula. "I'll have some toast," he told her.

He put in his earbuds and raised his hoodie, Andy's signal that he didn't want to be bothered. Deke gestured for him to remove the earbuds, which Andy did reluctantly.

"What?" he asked.

"Your mom tells me you were chosen to be one of the Three Conquistadors," Deke said.

Part of Spanish Trace's Spring Festival was the historical reenactment of three Spanish explorers landing in Florida in 1539. It was an honor to be chosen as one of the Three Conquistadors, but his seventeen-year-old son acted nonchalant.

"So what?"

"We better get to work, Dad," said Cara. His daughter and wife both acted as peacemakers between father and son. For the past year it seemed that neither father nor son could have a civil conversation with the other.

"That's right, Miss Perfect," said Andy in a singsong voice, "You better get to work."

Deke rolled his eyes and gave his daughter a sympathetic look. Cara was learning that no good deed goes unpunished. Teri offered them both a conciliatory smile. It was her belief that Andy was just going through a phase.

Andy wasn't done. "What do you get when you cross the Godfather with a big mouth lawyer?" he asked with his very best smart-ass edge. When no one answered he said, "An offer you can't understand."

Deke found himself clenching his jaw. Having teenage kids had forced him to develop a fair degree of self-control. When provoked, he had a fierce temper, but around his family he always managed to rein it in. Andy must have decided he'd created enough discord. He put his earbuds back in, raised his hoodie, and left the kitchen, chewing on a piece of toast.

When Deke and Cara commuted to work together his daughter usually talked nonstop, but five minutes into the drive she hadn't uttered a word. At first Deke thought she was preoccupied, but then he heard Cara's heavy breathing and saw she'd fallen asleep. Maybe she'd awaken from her nap refreshed. Normally Cara looked like a knockout, but even her application of rouge hadn't put much color in her face today. Her nearly black hair usually glistened, but now it looked dull.

The sound of a ringing phone came over the car's speakers, but didn't wake his daughter. The display told him his assistant Donna was calling.

"I'm ten minutes out, Donna," said Deke. "What is it that can't wait?"

"I thought you'd want to know that Bekmeyer's settlement counsel has already sent you two separate emails this morning saying that all negotiations are off the table on the Annica Phillips case. The letters were signed by Wharton Garrison."

"I'm surprised he waited long enough for poor Annica's body to cool," Deke responded. "Not that the asshole had any intention of settling anyway. It's easy to look like a legal eagle when you have a judge bending over backwards for you."

Deke often gave lectures at law schools where he quoted H. L. Mencken's definition of a judge: "A judge is a law student who marks his own papers."

If Mencken were alive today he might have added that many judges were owned and operated by corporations, and the laws they were supposedly overseeing were slanted in favor of whoever had the most money.

"Tell me something I haven't heard," Donna replied.

Among her many talents, Donna was great at cutting Deke off mid-rant.

"Did I mention that even if this case goes to trial Bekmeyer is already doing their best to poison the jury pool?" Deke replied.

Bekmeyer was ramping up their advertising all over the Panhandle. They were the helpful neighbor donating to youth sports and community activities. They were like a big brother you could count on. This not so subtle branding made Bekmeyer look like the good guys and infected the jury pool. Those that counted on a jury of their peers for justice were often disappointed by a well long-poisoned by the U.S. Chamber of Commerce and other business lobbyists. Few people realized what an effective lobbying group the chamber of commerce was, and how for years they'd been trying to convince the public that most injured claimants initiating a lawsuit were working a scam. It was because of this brainwashing that instead of being vilified for their amoral practices, corporations like Bekmeyer were actually perceived as being the victim.

Just incredible, thought Deke.

"You might have already mentioned that a few thousand times," Donna answered.

"At least I'm consistent," Deke replied.

That made Donna laugh. "I'll have an espresso waiting for you," she promised.

"Bless you," he said. He looked over at his sleeping daughter. "And if you don't mind, you had better have one ready for Cara as well."

"Like father like daughter," Donna said. "And your employees like to emulate you as well. You want to guess who I found asleep in her office this morning?"

Deke didn't even need to guess. "I think we'd better install a Murphy bed for Carol. Heading the investigation of the Bekmeyer case is as intense as it gets."

"Her husband would rather you pay for a Turks and Caicos getaway for two when the trial's done."

"That sounds good," Deke responded. "Remind me about that when this trial is over."

"For future reference," Donna informed him, "I prefer the Cayman Islands."

"See you in a few," said Deke. He hoped his words sounded more like a pleasantry than a threat.

Deke pulled into the parking lot of the tallest building in Spanish Trace. The Bergman Deketomis law firm took up six floors of the building, dominating most of the office space. On the ground floor was an Italian restaurant and shops; at the top of the building were state of the art broadcast studios.

Most of Deke's time was spent on the fourth floor where the mass torts group was located. The fourth floor exuded a sense of energy quite unlike the rest of the building. It was there that phones constantly rang and litigators always seemed to be on the move. It was the noisiest floor and, from appearances, the most chaotic. Impromptu meetings always seemed to be taking place in its halls. Older visitors said the setting reminded them of bustling newsrooms in the days when daily papers were big and journalists were always scrambling to meet a deadline. Unfortunately, investigative journalism seemed to be a thing of the past. That was one reason that companies like Bekmeyer thrived.

Because Cara was still a bit groggy, Deke had to walk more slowly than usual to the security elevator so she could keep up with him. Normally he was the one who had trouble outpacing his jock daughter. The Bergman Deketomis firm was housed in a secure building. There were cameras everywhere, as well as an armed security guard who made rounds throughout the building. Threats—some serious, some not—were not uncommon against the firm and its lawyers.

"How are you doing, Sleeping Beauty?" asked Deke.

Cara rubbed her eyes as she walked. "Only my prince knows for sure," she said,

"Carol Morris is waiting for us in the conference room," said Deke. "I'd be surprised if Angus and Threepio aren't also there."

His daughter nodded and took a few deep breaths. The two of them took the elevator to the fourth floor and made their way directly to the meeting room. Donna intercepted them in front of the room, a cup of espresso in each hand.

"You are a godsend, Donna," said Cara, taking the espresso.

"Tell that to your father," she replied.

As expected, the usual suspects were waiting for them. Ned "Threepio" Williams was middle-aged but looked much younger. He greeted them with a smile that belied his all-nighter. Angus growled, "Good morning," and Carol looked up from her laptop with bloodshot eyes and nodded. Carol's job as lead investigator required her to work almost as many hours as Deke, especially when a trial was going on. She was an intense, fiftysomething woman with mostly gray hair.

Carol tapped her computer, and a familiar picture showed itself on the conference room's display. Ranidol was an innocent enough looking product. The oval pill was the blue color of a robin's egg. The drug had been created as an oral contraceptive, but its popularity had come about when Bekmeyer began touting its weight loss benefits. What Bekmeyer had failed to disclose to Ranidol users was that in addition to losing weight, you could also lose your life. Taking Ranidol increased the risk of chronic liver damage and had been shown to cause an unusual assortment of crippling, systemic malfunctions of the body's filtration mechanism. In Annica's case, Ranidol had first caused cardiac damage, and then a stroke that caused paralysis. Every day more women were coming forward with new symptoms that manifested themselves in a number of ways.

Carol hit another button and six names appeared on the screen. Annica Phillips was one of those names.

"When we filed suit against Bekmeyer Pharmaceuticals," Carol said, "there were six plaintiffs named in the trial docket. With the loss of Annica, we now have five plaintiffs. We don't have any time to waste in finding Annica's replacement, especially with the next trial due to begin in three months. It's time to pick a new lead trial plaintiff."

Carol didn't need to add, "Or else." Everyone knew the clock was ticking. They were also aware that they'd need to tailor some of their legal strategy around the new lead plaintiff, and that would take time.

"I hope you've narrowed the list," said Deke.

Carol and Threepio both nodded. "Ned and I winnowed it down to three candidates," she responded, hitting another key on her laptop.

On the conference room's big screen monitor a woman's face appeared, and beneath the picture were bullet points. "This is Tricia Baker," Carol stated. "As you can see, she's a recent college graduate. Tricia has a clean personal life, but does have a history of surgeries. She also took some pain pills for longer than was deemed necessary. After being on Ranidol for four months she developed sharp pains under her ribs and believed she was having a heart attack. She also began to suffer from severe nausea after eating. Tricia continued taking Ranidol for two months after her first hospitalization. When she was hospitalized for the second time, she was diagnosed as having transient heart abnormalities. At that time they also found mild liver damage.

"That's when she stopped taking Ranidol. Luckily for her, most of her symptoms then disappeared, and she rebounded quite quickly. Doctors have warned her, though, that she will have long-term liver abnormalities and probably a lifetime need for several medications to keep her heart healthy."

Carol looked up as if expecting questions or comments. When none were offered she gestured to Threepio. The picture on the monitor changed. Months before, in that same room, Deke had seen a photo of Annica Phillips. He tried to put that out of his mind.

"My top candidate has a classic Ranidol profile," Threepio began. "Michelle Rodriguez is thirty-one years old, an avid runner, and single. She's a schoolteacher, which juries usually like. Even better, three years ago she was chosen Teacher of the Year in Jacksonville. Both Michelle and her doctor were squarely on Bekmeyer's targeted marketing list."

"Dosage?" Angus asked.

"Ranidol dosage to the recommended limit, nothing unusual."

When Threepio finished, Carol presented a third candidate. After discussing the pros and cons of each candidate, it didn't take long for the group to unanimously choose Tricia. A key factor in their selection was that the treating doctor seemed to care deeply about his patient. This same doctor had seen several patients with serious adverse events that, according to his records, he believed were related to Ranidol. His differential diagnosis was unequivocal about the relationship between his patients' chronic liver abnormalities and the use of Ranidol as a birth control medication.

"Okay," said Deke, "now it's time for round two."

He turned to Angus. "Where are we with the Bekmeyer documents?"

Angus shrugged. "We're still up shit creek without a paddle," he told him. "To say that Bekmeyer hasn't been forthcoming is a huge understatement."

He gestured to a small pile of red file folders. "That's the extent of the dirt we have on Ranidol. We know Bekmeyer's done a damned effective job of purging their files. The thirty or so documents in these file folders are what we've been able to classify as hot docs, and that's after reviewing thousands of pages of the material we got from Bekmeyer in discovery. They've sanitized everything. All we've got are a few table scraps."

DocuSearch was the company that Bergman Deketomis had under contract for doing intensive computer searches of the Bekmeyer files. What they had was all that was there. But that didn't mean there hadn't been a lot more at one time.

Threepio spoke up. "I asked DS to run an intuitive computer analysis for us with the keyword "Ranidol." They located millions of documents. But what stood out among those millions of documents was the complete lack of any smoking guns. There's no question that Bekmeyer scrubbed clean any file or document with the word 'Ranidol,' along with the other keywords on our search list."

Cara looked at Threepio quizzically, and he quietly explained, "Heart, stroke, liver, disease, death, dying, dead—you get the picture."

Carol added, "It's about as thorough a job of housecleaning as I've ever encountered. They barely left us any crumbs, and what we have won't pose any serious problems for them."

"Anybody in this room think we could go to trial with what we've got?" Deke asked. Heads shook but no one spoke.

"Okay," Deke said. "I'm going to see what I can do about getting us some ammunition we can work with." Under his breath he added, "One man's garbage is another man's treasure."

Deke looked around the room. "If you can clear your schedule, Angus, I am going to need your help today. And everyone else, keep doing what you're doing."

Heads nodded, and Deke made a hasty exit from the conference room. Angus managed to catch up to him in the hallway. "Tell me we're going on a road trip," he said.

"We're going on a road trip," Deke responded.

3

NOT SO HOLY ROLLING

Angela Thorn was excited about watching her favorite TV show's big reveal. *These Holy Times*, the show broadcast from their church starring their own Pastor Rodney, was going to make history tonight.

Wearing an ankle-length, floral print dress and cowboy boots, Angela sat on the couch next to her teenage daughter, Kimberly. Both shared the same shoulder-length blonde hair and ice-blue eyes. Angela—never Angie—taught Sunday school at Pastor Rodney Morgan's Holiness Southern Pentecostal Church, and her husband Ken coached the girls softball team that had gone undefeated the past three seasons.

The team had also become something of a national sensation: The photo of the girls kneeling together and saying prayers before softball games had become an iconic image, captured for a *Sports Illustrated* cover story on morality in sports.

"They were doing a lot of filming at our last game," Kimberly informed her mom. "I wonder if they'll show pictures of me pitching."

"Pastor Rodney said as many as a million people might be watching tonight's show," Angela told her. "That's 'cuz he's talking with a man he says will be our next president."

Kimberly merely nodded. She was more interested in the goings-on of her softball team.

"Maybe we should pray that your daddy gets the praise he deserves on tonight's show. He works so hard at his coaching."

Kimberly didn't look as if she was ready to join her mother in that particular prayer. Given a choice, Kimberly would have wished for someone else to coach the team. Instead of acting his age, her father seemed to think he was a teenager. Kimberly pretended not to hear what some of the girls on the team said about him, just as she pretended not to notice the way her father looked at some of her teammates.

"Ken," called Angela. "Come on out. The show's about to begin."

"In a minute," yelled Ken.

"I'm taping it so you don't miss anything," she yelled.

Ken didn't bother to answer, which wasn't a surprise to Angela. He often didn't bother to answer.

It would have surprised Angela had she known Ken was praying. She was always saying he should pray more, but he never listened. Of course Angela would have been even more surprised at what Ken was praying for. When they'd been filming the team Ken had tried to stay out of the camera shots. He didn't want his face on TV, especially now. Ken much preferred anonymity.

Ken silently pleaded with God. "I'll never do it again," he prayed. It wasn't the first time Ken had made that same prayer, but now, given the latest circumstances, it felt particularly lame.

It's not my fault, Ken thought. I was set up. But even he didn't really believe that.

The Thorn family lived in a ranch style house on a corner lot in the East Hill section of Spanish Trace, Florida. It was a conservative, Southern, middle-class neighborhood, where families had roots in what the locals called "traditional values." Those values meant religion, family, and more religion, in a gumbo stew with guns and racial mistrust to boot.

When the family purchased the three-bedroom house five years earlier, the mortgage had been a stretch, but despite the financial gap they had fit right in with their neighbors. To make the leap, Ken had spent extra hours on the job beyond traveling his sales routes and was eventually promoted to his current role as regional manager for HealthIntuit. Raising revenues in Western Florida, Alabama, Louisiana, and Mississippi had put him in line to become a vice president. Earlier that year the Thorns had replaced their hand-me-down furniture with pieces from Pottery Barn. They'd even gotten a big screen TV and started entertaining more. They had finally made it to the middle class, but Ken was afraid all of that was about to change.

"I'll do anything," he whispered.

Even Ken couldn't be sure if he was praying to God, or trying to make a deal with the devil.

"Honey?" Angela called. Once more Ken didn't answer, and she turned her attention back to *These Holy Times* and Pastor Rodney's guest. Senator Ted Bruce was the junior senator from the State of Alabama. Pastor Rodney called him a "godly" man. The American Conservative Union and the NRA apparently agreed, giving the senator perfect scores. Getting the approbation of Pastor Rodney put the senator in good stead with much of the South.

Pastor Rodney's domain, Holiness Southern Pentecostal Church, was the largest religious institution on the Florida Panhandle and one that held great influence.

Rodney Morgan's weekly television show on the all-talk cable channel WSBD-TV regularly drew a few hundred thousand viewers from northern Florida, southern Alabama, and southern Mississippi—the heart of the Bible Belt. Part reality TV show and part interview format, *These Holy Times* featured "private talks" with impassioned parishioners as well as political and cultural debates over topics like the evils of abortion and the homosexual agenda. The pastor's following was rapidly expanding, not only on television and radio, but also through social media where new followers could connect with online "savior sanctuaries." A recent article in *Trace* magazine named Pastor Rodney Morgan "the most influential figure in the South."

Pastor Rodney was known for his tailored white suits, flashing white teeth, and long, white, leonine mane. Senator Bruce—"Ted" to his friend Pastor Rodney—was equally photogenic, although he wore a dark suit and had dark hair. The senator wore two lapel pins: One was the American flag, the other a cross.

Both men appeared comfortable with the other. Their chat was folksy, even with a huge audience listening in on every word. Each man was an expert at self-aggrandizing. They were doing good old logrolling—each scratching the other's back. Pastor Rodney had another name for it that would have shocked his parishioners. They were doing a mutual tug job. Pastor Rodney's show gave Senator Bruce a great platform to announce his run for the presidency, while at the same time putting Rodney and the Holiness Southern Pentecostal Church center stage.

Both men kept talking and smiling. They were building up to the money shot.

While his wife and daughter watched TV, Ken Thorn retreated to the quiet of his office. Making sure the door was locked behind him, Ken opened up his file cabinet and retrieved the envelope that had arrived the day before.

Shit, thought Ken. Shit, shit, shit.

How the hell had she gotten his name? And how had she known his address? He supposed she'd bribed a desk clerk. After all, the envelope's return address was the Corian Hotel in Mobile, Alabama.

The scene of the crime, he thought. His heart pounded as he pulled out the pictures. There they were. Ken had kept hoping this was all a nightmare and that he'd awaken from the dream. But there was no running away from these pictures.

What's the slut's name, he thought? He usually put it out of his mind. She was just some young tail, after all. But then he remembered: Sunny.

How had the bitch managed to get these pictures of them? Kids and their technology, he thought. He assumed she'd taken them on her cell phone. The shots had been printed out on regular paper, and while the quality of the pictures might not be good there was no mistaking their subject. No wonder Ken hadn't noticed her taking the pictures. He looked awfully busy in the shots. Sunny had probably set up the timer on her phone to take the pictures. The little fool had said she was in love with him. She had probably thought she was documenting her love.

Sunny had told him she just turned eighteen, but her poorly applied makeup, the heavily lined lipstick, and her showy clothes couldn't mask the obvious fact that she was a pretty, young Latina of no more than fourteen or fifteen. On one occasion Sunny had worn a red plaid schoolgirl skirt and matching bows in her braids. Ken had liked that. Sunny was certainly no older than Kimberly or the girls on the softball team, although he'd pretended she was. Her nascent breasts, childish mannerisms, and the similar interests she shared with his daughter left no doubts about her real age. And they hadn't only done it once. They'd done it again and again.

"Sixteen will get you twenty," Ken thought. He'd tried to stifle his urges with that reminder, but it had never worked for him. You could actually get twenty years for having sex with a minor. The shit had truly hit the fan.

"Oh, God," Ken pleaded.

Sunny's mother must have found the pictures on Sunny's phone. And then she'd tracked him down. Along with the pictures, she'd left a short note that he studied once more:

Tell the police or I will. It was signed Lucia Torres.

There was no demand for money—only the directive that he turn himself in, or else. It wasn't the first time his life as a predatory pedophile had caught up with him.

"There has to be a way out," he said out loud. "There has to be."

He needed to formulate a plan in his head. Necessity was the mother of invention, and this was a desperate situation. As he tried to focus on his strategy, his eyes strayed over to the printouts. Whenever they got together, Sunny was putty in his hands. And damn if he didn't look like a stud.

Despite everything, Ken found himself growing hard.

4

WHAT ONCE IS LOST, NOW IS FOUND

The law firm's Citation X jet taxied to a stop at a Teterboro, New Jersey, privately held fixed-based-operator airport. The jet required two pilots, both of whom were on the firm's payroll. Since Spanish Trace is a Navy town, there's no shortage of retired naval airmen who are more than qualified to fly private jets. In addition to being highly decorated aviators, the firm's pilots were two nice guys who had received the best flight training in the world thirty years earlier at a naval air base just outside Spanish Trace.

Some in Bergman Deketomis referred to the company jet as "Aorta Force One," a reference to a case that Deke had championed. The firm had been able to afford the jet after they won a case against Cuore Global, a medical device manufacturer. CG had produced a defective heart monitor responsible for the deaths of hundreds of people, and Deke had done his best to put their feet to the fire.

The case had been anything but a slam dunk for Bergman Deketomis. The litigation had been long and costly. Deke had been lead counsel, and CG had pulled out every dirty trick in the book to prevail in the first three cases. Many at the firm had wanted to drop their litigation of Cuore Global. After all, the first three cases had cost them more than ten million dollars, and some of the partners were afraid any more hemorrhaging of money could cause Bergman Deketomis to implode. But Deke wasn't about to give up. He couldn't allow CG to get away with murder, even when it seemed like the only people in the world who believed in him were his wife and Martin Bergman. Things finally turned around during the fourth case. And then Deke won the fifth case. Suddenly CG agreed to pull all their heart monitors. Suddenly CG was more than willing to settle.

Deke had made them pay. And that's when the firm had bought "Aorta Force One" for eight million dollars. There was a part of Deke that was uncomfortable with the purchase of the Citation. No one had come from more humble beginnings than he had, and the idea of a private jet seemed decadent. But the truth of the matter was that the Citation X wasn't nearly as elaborate as the larger jets owned by many corporate defense firms. And as it turned out, their jet had proved to be more of an investment than Deke could have imagined. It was fast and compact enough to land at even the smallest regional airports, and private air travel saved Deke and his firm time. During a trial there was often no more important commodity than time. The plane comfortably seated eight people, which was often the number of passengers traveling together during important case workups. During this trip he and Angus had worked during the whole flight up to New Jersey, and would undoubtedly work the entire flight back.

As Deke and Angus disembarked from the Citation, a beat-up vehicle pulled up next to them.

"Our chariot awaits," said Angus.

Neither Deke nor Angus were surprised at the appearance of the older model Buick, although Deke had to stifle an urge to write "Wash Me" on one of the dirty windows. The front seat was taken up by two toughs who offered no greeting beyond their frowns. Angus and Deke climbed into the back seat.

They drove in silence for almost half an hour. The driver and his passenger frequently checked their mirrors, making sure they weren't being followed. Finally they came to a stop, pulling up to a second car that was as dirty as the first. Deke and Angus left the first car the same way they had entered it—soundlessly—and got into the second car. The two guys in front could have passed for the first set of muscle. Deke wondered how it was possible to find employees who all looked as if they had come directly from the casting of *The Sopranos*.

The two lawyers endured a second Quaker meeting. Angus shook his head at Deke and looked bemused. His expression clearly said, "Only you would be putting me through something like this."

After a few evasive maneuvers to make sure they weren't being followed, the driver came to a stop at what looked to be the guard post of a military base but without the signage. Fort Dix it wasn't. When Deke and Angus got out of the car, the two toughs took up positions behind each of them, ready to react to any threat. The brick-walled fortress appeared to take up at least two city blocks, and was high enough to discourage looky-loos. Atop the brick wall was a chain-link fence and concertina wire. Within the compound were a series of chimney towers, relics from an earlier era.

With a shake of their heads the two guards motioned Deke and Angus over to the guard post where there was another armed employee.

"Nice talking with you," said Angus.

One of the gorillas spat on the ground.

Deke pulled Angus along with him where they were scrutinized by the guard at the post. "We're here to see the Collector," Deke told him, not offering their names.

"Got an appointment?"

Deke had been jerked around enough. They wouldn't have been picked up and dropped off without an appointment. Deke waved to the not so hidden camera.

The phone rang and the gorilla picked it up. He listened to what was being told to him and finally said, "Yeah." It made him sound absolutely talkative. Then he hung up the phone.

Pointing to Angus, the muscle asked Deke, "What's this guy's real name?"

Deke shook his head. He knew the rules, and answering that question would violate them. To Angus, he said quietly, "It's a trick question." To the guard he said: "When you're here, no one has a name."

The guard nodded, and pressed a button. A door sprang open out of what appeared to be solid brick. The guard said to Deke, "Just you."

"We're together," Deke answered.

"I got my orders," the guard replied, his hand inching inside his coat in the direction of his shoulder holster.

Deke was ready to argue, but Angus intervened. "I'm fine. Just don't come back empty-handed."

This time Deke was chauffeured in a golf cart. During the short drive he saw line after line of eighteen-wheelers, all waiting to unload. This place was supposed to be the end of the line for paper trails; at least that's what its customers believed.

The large, thick man known only as "the Collector" didn't get up to greet Deke when he entered the windowless office. He merely waved him to a seat. This inner sanctum gave the appearance of an aging, poorly maintained pool hall, complete with two billiard tables. On one wall was a signed Eli Manning jersey in a large frame, and in a corner cabinet was a replica of the Lombardi Trophy. A hand-carved wooden sign that bore the words, "Transcorp Shredding" hung above the Collector's rolling office chair. The old man sat at an outrageously cluttered, cheap pine office desk. It was as if he were trying to partially hide behind mountains of paper, old fast food wrappers, and small stacks of yellowing newspapers. He studied Deke while chewing on a gummed-up unlit cigar.

"So what brings Clarence Darrow to my humble cave?"

"The usual drill, but with more urgency this go-around," Deke answered. "I need some paperwork on Bekmeyer Pharmaceuticals."

The Collector looked at his fingers and pretended disinterest. "What kind of paperwork?" he asked.

"Money for you, paperwork," Deke said.

Deke pulled a sheaf of papers from an inner pocket of his suit jacket. "I would like documents that contain any of these terms or key words."

He placed the papers on the Collector's desk. At the top of the list was the word "Ranidol." That was followed by a long list of other words. The Collector studied the page and didn't look surprised by what he saw, which included such words as *fainting, dizziness, liver abnormality, cardiac condition, D.V.T., stroke, embolism,* and *death.*

"What's your budget?" asked the Collector.

"Still five thousand per document, right?"

"Prices are so high these days, Mr. Darrow. You seen the price of a dozen eggs? Of course, an important man like you doesn't shop, but the cost of living has gone way up. Five thousand was the old price."

"I liked the old price. And I'm not the kind of lawyer who thinks he's above the fray. I know where I came from. And I know the cost of a carton of eggs."

The Collector nodded and Deke felt as if he'd passed yet another one of his tests. "Just as long as you're still a cash customer," he said.

"On the barrel," Deke replied.

"How many items are you looking for?"

"Two hundred would make me happy," Deke said, "but I need them to be smoking."

"I ever give you anything less than red-hot?"

"That's why I'm here."

The Collector sorted through the paperwork Deke had brought him. While he studied what was there, Deke took notice of all the closed-circuit monitors the Collector was able to view. Truck's crisscrossed the compound's series of nearly identical buildings. From client companies all over the United States and beyond, trucks brought documents to be unloaded and sent to massive shredders. From there, all the paperwork was supposed to be rendered into thin, unreadable strips and then compacted into individual bricks. But now and then an arriving truck was sent in a different direction, ending up at a warehouse with barred windows. A pair of armed guards stood outside the only entrance to that building.

"So what the hell is this Ranidol?" the Collector asked, chomping on his rank looking stogie.

"A birth control pill, but Bekmeyer also tells women it will make them skinny and beautiful. It has a secondary effect though.

Every year it's killing about a hundred young women. That's the reason I need your best material on this one."

While the Collector continued to go through the documents, Deke snuck a look at the group of monitors closest to his desk. These monitors didn't show the movement of trucks, but of women sorting and scanning paperwork. There was row after row of Hispanic women sitting at tables busy at work. This was the most lucrative part of the Collector's business, and the riskiest. Deke knew all these documents were stored in an encrypted server that even the NSA wouldn't be able to hack.

To a tiny number of mass tort attorneys who sued major corporations, the Collector's massive e-library of scanned documents was a virtual goldmine, a way of recovering memos, letters, internal directives, and the results of testing by a company's own scientists. A single document of the Collector's had been enough to change many a trial's outcome, all the while leaving corporate management bewildered about how something they were certain had been destroyed could have fallen into the plaintiffs' hands. The Collector had developed a foolproof system for covering his trail. To most observers, it appeared that an angry whistleblower or unsuspecting subcontractor was the source of the embarrassing document dump.

The Collector finished with his scrutinizing. "Okay, we'll get you what you need, Clarence. You got what I need?"

Deke nodded.

"Better go join your friend before he gets too lonely. We should have you on your way in about two hours. And then you can go save the world. That's what you do, isn't it?"

"More or less," Deke confirmed.

"I guess that puts me on the side of angels. Who would have ever believed that?"

5
PLAYING POSSUM

Ken plotted while his wife and daughter slept. He knew that in order to get his wife in his corner he would have to do something drastic. There were some things even Angela might not forgive, and Ken couldn't have that. He didn't yet know how he'd escape the noose that came with those pictures of him with Sunny, but he did know there was no chance of that without Angela at his side. He needed a Tammy Wynette big time: Stand by Your Man. Everything else had a chance of falling into place after that.

Over the years, Ken had mastered the art of manipulation by practicing on Angela. He could usually play on her guilt. His wife was a devout Pentecostal who believed in forgiveness. That meant if he made her believe he'd repented his sins, then she was all but obligated to forgive him. It also helped that she believed the husband was the head of the family, and that it was the wife's duty to obey. Pastor Rodney had Ken's back on that one. It was one of Rodney's favorite things to spout from the pulpit. There were also a few biblical passages Ken used on her to good effect.

Ken hoped all that would be enough. He wasn't quite sure how old Sunny was, but he doubted she was older than fifteen. If Ken could show Angela how truly sorry he was, the chances were she'd play ball. Maybe he could even get Angela to talk to Sunny's mom and try to make things right. His wife had helped him out of other situations in the past. Now, more than ever, he needed her to be dutiful.

Ken silently got out of bed an hour before Angela usually got up. He picked out the dosage he wanted from a medicine cabinet full of pills, almost all of which he'd pilfered from work. From his years on the job Ken knew which pills did what, and how many he should take. He wanted a Goldilocks porridge that would be just right. Too many pills and he might die for real; too few and he'd look like a fraud.

Ken carefully staged his suicide scene. He left the bathroom door slightly ajar. Then he placed two R-rated pictures of him and Sunny on the bathroom counter. It was better that Angela didn't see the really bad pictures, but just a few tittie shots showing the two of them naked. He also left out Lucia Torres's note that she'd written on the Corian Hotel letterhead telling him he had to go to the police.

That should do it, Ken thought, making sure he hadn't forgotten anything. Then he chewed a handful of pills, and spit some of them out on his shirt. He swallowed the rest of the macerated pills, and then downed a few more with a glass of water.

He had thought about lightly cutting his wrist in a few places, but had decided not to. Ken hated the sight of blood, especially when it was his own.

It wasn't long before he began feeling woozy. He'd been afraid he would have to fake being out of it, but no longer had to worry about that. Ken was ready to sleep. He reached for the shower curtain and pulled. It didn't come down, so he gave it a harder yank. This time it came crashing down. It was important to stage everything right.

Then Ken crawled into the tub. In less than a minute he was fast asleep.

Angela was usually up before Ken. She considered it her duty to have breakfast waiting for him, even though half the time he went without. It was a shame Ken hadn't been featured on *These Holy Times*. They'd had some good shots of Kimberly, though, and her teammates. When all the girls had kneeled together they looked like angels.

The first thing Angela noticed when she opened the bathroom door was the shower curtain on the ground. And then she began screaming. Ken was sprawled in the tub. Had he fallen? Had he had a heart attack? Or stroke?

Her screams abruptly stopped when she noticed the pictures and note. Horror combined with fear. Ken was pictured with a naked girl. That's why he'd killed himself. But no, he wasn't dead. Angela could see he was still breathing. Down the front of his shirt she could see chewed up pills that he must have thrown up.

"Ken!" she yelled, "Ken!"

He didn't respond, but Kimberly did. She'd heard Angela's screams and came running. Angela blocked her entry to the bathroom. She didn't want Kimberly seeing her father. And even more than that, she didn't want Kimberly seeing the pictures of her father with the naked young woman.

"Call 911!" Angela shouted, and Kimberly rushed down the hall to the phone.

Angela needed to hide the filth while she could. She didn't care about the open pill bottles. The world could see those. What she couldn't let her daughter, or anyone else see, were those pictures and that note. Angela folded up everything and slipped them into her robe.

That's when Kimberly appeared in the doorway. "They're coming! The ambulance is coming!"

Angela merely nodded.

Kimberly looked past her mother and saw her father on the floor of the tub. "Is Daddy okay, Mom?"

"Go to the front yard and wait for the ambulance," Angela said, her voice oddly composed. "It ought to be here any minute. You'll need to direct the EMTs up to the bathroom."

After Kimberly left, Angela stared at her husband. Normally she would have prayed, but at the moment Angela wasn't sure if she would pray for her husband to live or pray for him to die. Once, and then a second time, Angela tried to pray, but it was the first time she couldn't talk to God. Maybe she was afraid of what she might say.

The stomping on the stairs alerted Angela to the presence of others. And then the paramedics came running into the bathroom. What shocked Angela was that she knew one of the men. His daughter played on Kimberly's softball team, the same team that Ken coached.

Angela had to stifle her laughter. What kind of cosmic joke was this? But everyone assumed her laughter was crying.

"Is he okay, Mr. Barry?"

Kimberly asked the question of the paramedic, the father of her teammate. "I think Coach will be fine, Kimberly, but why don't you go downstairs for now?"

Her daughter did as directed, and Angela watched as both paramedics began treating her husband. They lifted him out of the tub and hoisted him onto a gurney.

"Coach, how are you?" the paramedic asked, taking Ken's pulse. "I'm Jack Barry. My daughter's on your softball team. And don't worry about the guy holding your hand. That's Charlie. We're both here to help you out."

Ken began to mumble, but Angela cut him off. "It's my fault . . . I'm so sorry," she said, speaking not to her husband, but to the paramedics. "I think I accidently put some prescription pain pills in the same vial as Ken's allergy pills."

"Don't worry about that now, ma'am," Jack told her. "Plenty of time to get those details later. Right now we got to get our favorite coach to the hospital so they can check him out."

Angela was already regretting her lie. How was it that Ken always brought out the worst in her? But Jack assumed she was worrying about her husband.

"Don't worry, Mrs. Thorn," he said. "I'm pretty sure this is all going to work out just fine."

He was talking about Ken, but that's not what Angela was thinking about. She was thinking about those pictures and that note. And that was enough to make her think that everything was not going to work out just fine.

Angela Thorn didn't race with her husband's ambulance to the emergency room. In fact it was almost three hours after he'd been admitted that Angela finally began her drive to the hospital. She had gotten Kimberly settled down and taken her to school. And afterward she'd spent the time thinking, and looking at the pictures of her husband and that girl.

How could she ever get those images out of her head?

She reached for one of the preset radio buttons programmed in her ten-year-old Camry. Living by the mandates of her church, Angela avoided listening to any program that did not focus either on a religious message or local news. She found a news station and started listening, even if most of what she heard was just background noise for her jumbled mind.

"Flamboyant attorney Martin Bergman," a female reporter informed her audience, "says he will raise however much money it takes to get community activist Lumon Maygard elected to the Florida State Senate. Here is what Bergman said last night." A deep gravelly voice came on the air. "Our firm helped get our founding law partner Rubin Askew elected as governor. Now we're going to help Lumon Maygard beat Darl Dixon."

Angela recognized the name of Darl Dixon. He was a longtime member of her church, as well as being the county prosecuting attorney. Pastor Rodney even talked about Darl from the pulpit. He'd told the congregation they should vote for him for state senate.

Maybe Pastor Rodney could talk to Mr. Dixon about Ken's . . . situation. Angela found herself sighing. Why did Ken always drag her down into the pitch? But if she didn't do something, they'd all suffer. She didn't want Kimberly to pay for the sins of her father. Her church preached forgiveness, but many of its members weren't forgiving sorts. Angela had heard nasty whispers about others in church who were much less sinful than Ken but had been made to feel like they were pariahs.

If the congregation ever found out about Ken and his young girlfriend, there would surely be hateful talk. Angela knew there would be many who blamed her, finding her somehow responsible for Ken's transgressions.

Another news story came over, but Angela was worrying too much to take notice. And then a sudden realization caused Angela to turn off the radio. If she didn't do something, Ken's sins would become part of the news. She couldn't have that happen, she just couldn't.

After parking, Angela went in search of Ken. The receptionist told her he was out of the ER and directed her to his room.

Angela was glad to see there was no one in the room with Ken. What she had to say no one could overhear. This wasn't a case of her finding his pornography, as she had on too many occasions. Her husband was part of this pornography. And Angela wasn't going to be dissuaded by Ken telling her that Scripture said it was her duty to listen to him. When he tried to do unnatural things with her in the bedroom, that's what he always told her. But all her righteous indignation vanished when she first caught sight of Ken. He looked so frail—so sad.

"All this time I've been praying for you to forgive me," he whispered.

In her mind Angela had rehearsed what she was going to say. She opened her mouth to speak, but Ken spoke before she could.

"And while I was praying," Ken continued, "I felt the spirit of the Lord. I felt His forgiveness. And God told me to beg your forgiveness. More than anything, I want to be right with you, and right with God."

Angela could feel some of her resolve melting. "You've sinned terribly."

Ken hung his head. "I know it," he whispered. "And I've promised to God that I'll never do anything like that again."

He raised his head and looked at Angela. There were tears in his eyes. "And I make the same promise to you."

Angela started crying. Maybe they could work things out. "We can go to Pastor Rodney," she suggested. "He might be willing to help us."

Ken nodded, pretending to be grateful. He was glad Angela had come up with that one on her own. There was no way old Rodney would want his church tainted by the association of a softball coach sleeping with an underage girl. And the pastor would surely fear what else might be revealed. But he couldn't be more afraid of that shitstorm than Ken already was.

"Can we pray together?" Ken asked.

From the day they'd first married, Angela had been waiting to hear those words. She hurried to her husband's side.

6
THERE'S NO PLACE LIKE HOME

The most important thing of all to Deke was home and family. Having grown up with neither, Deke was more grateful to Teri and the kids than they'd ever know. He only wished he could carve out more hours in the day to be with them.

But after securing the Collector's papers in the office safe, Deke had gone to the building's upstairs TV studio. By satellite he'd appeared as a guest on the national TV political talk show *The Big Picture*. It was almost nine o'clock when Deke arrived at his home.

Having grown up dirt-poor was something Deke couldn't forget, and didn't want to forget. Deke knew it was nothing short of a miracle that he'd succeeded and that there were any number of instances when he could have, and should have, fallen through the cracks. When Deke saw the destitute, the homeless, and the incarcerated, he often found himself thinking, "I could be one of them."

That's what drove his progressive politics. That's what motivated him to take cases that other lawyers wouldn't. He wanted to give voices to the voiceless. He wanted to give the disenfranchised a place at the table.

His television and radio appearances had made Deke a national figure. He was well known in Spanish Trace, if not well regarded. Jesus had hit the nail on the head when he said prophets don't have any honor among their own people. Spanish Trace was mostly a conservative military town. Travel magazines touted it as a great place to retire. Those same travel magazines neglected to talk about the environmental degradation taking place in and around Spanish Trace, the strained race relations, and the decline of the public schools. It didn't make Deke any more popular when he brought up those issues on television or radio, or when he wrote rebuttal editorials in the right-leaning *Trace Journal*. The tea party, popular in Spanish Trace, had hung Deke in effigy more than once. Deke was actually happy they spent so much time pillorying him. If the teabaggers were occupied with him that gave them less time to undermine the Constitution.

Deke parked in the garage and heaved a sigh of relief. After a long day he was back at home, sweet home. Teri was waiting for him in the kitchen. "Did you eat?" she asked, taking him in her arms.

"Pizza and beer," Deke answered, hoping to get a rise out of her. But when Teri didn't bite he admitted, "I called out for chicken breast and asparagus."

Under Teri's tutelage, Deke had been eating healthy foods for many years. He had learned it was especially important to do so during trial.

"Good boy," she said, and gave him a kiss. Her nose alerted her to something and her eyes confirmed what her nose had smelled. "You're still wearing your makeup," she let him know, "complete with citrus-scented foundation."

"It's been one of those days," he told her.

"After you shower you can meet me on the balcony and we'll talk about it."

The night was warm enough for them to be out without a coat. Teri was dressed in her usual simple style: jeans, sandals, and a lightweight burgundy V-neck sweater. Her beautiful, shoulder-length dark hair was pulled back in a ponytail and her large hazel eyes sparked with pleasure at having her husband to herself for a while. After showering, Deke had put on sweats.

Teri handed Deke a glass of merlot, and then the two of them clinked wineglasses. There was nothing they enjoyed more than sitting together on their terracotta terrace. It was private and comfortable, and a place for them to be together. During the daylight hours their special spot afforded them an unobstructed view of the inlet of the Gulf of Mexico. And on quiet nights like this they could hear the waves breaking on the shore.

"So how is Spanish Trace's most dangerous man?" Teri asked.

That had been the headline in the latest issue of *Trace* magazine. "Consider the source," he replied.

"I caught the tail end of your show," Teri informed him. "If I didn't know you were a pussycat, I might believe you were dangerous."

"Since when did it become dangerous saying that if you want solid bridges and a functioning fire department well, then you have to pay for it."

"Only you could make infrastructure sound sexy," said Teri.

"Roads," he whispered, "sewer connections."

"Quit with your dirty talk," she said. "I can't take any more."

They both laughed and then kissed. "We wouldn't happen to have the house to ourselves, would we?" asked Deke.

"Cara's at her apartment," she said. Their daughter had her own apartment in Spanish Trace, although two or three nights a week she still slept in the house. "But Andy's in his room. When I checked in on him he said he'd already finished his homework."

"Likely story," said Deke.

"I agree he's not as studious as Cara was, but at least he's getting passing grades."

"Barely," replied Deke. "He doesn't apply himself."

"You ever stop to think he's as oppositional as he is just to get your attention?"

Deke made an unimpressed sound.

"He reminds me of you," Teri responded.

"What?" Deke couldn't believe she'd said that.

"You were a rebel with a cause," she replied. "Right now Andy is just a rebel. But mark my words, he'll find his cause."

"I hope you're right."

"Yes, Andy's different from Cara," Teri said, "and he won't ever be a lawyer. But I'll bet one day soon he'll surprise you in a good way. Just don't underestimate him."

Deke found himself nodding. No one had believed in him when he was young. No one had ever thought he would amount to anything. As annoying as Andy could be, Deke still needed to show he believed in him.

"Did Cara stop by tonight?" Deke asked.

Teri shook her head. "She called earlier this evening. Why?"

Deke decided it wouldn't do to worry his wife. Cara's exhaustion was probably just a one-day thing. Tomorrow morning she'd show up to work with her usual vim and vigor, he thought.

"It's nothing important," he replied. "It's just a work thing."

7

1–800–DOGFIGHT

Deke left for work early, taking with him a thermos of Teri's protein shake. He knew her shake was full of vitamins and nutrients. Most of all, it was full of love.

As usual, Deke arrived at the Bergman Deketomis building even before most of the junior partners. He told Donna to put out the call to his team to meet in the conference room at nine, and then closed his door behind him. In the privacy of his office, Deke put up a special picture. It was doubtful that anyone outside their office would ever be able to identify the person in the framed picture, but Deke didn't care. He had been with Annica Phillips as she took her last breath, and he would never forget her.

The wall of pictures showed Deke with a number of politicians, including two presidents. There were also photos of Deke amidst movers and shakers, athletes, and celebrities.

"I'm sorry," Deke whispered to Annica. "I'm so sorry."

He didn't linger over her picture for very long. The only way Deke was going to get justice for Annica would be to make sure her case was heard in court. He unlocked his office safe and removed the sheaf of papers he'd been given by the Collector. During the flight home he and Angus had begun sorting the documents. Now Deke continued that work.

He scanned the paperwork and made some copies. Deke didn't want to involve anyone else. He would have preferred not having to fight fire with fire, but Bekmeyer hadn't given him a choice. They thought they'd hidden their figurative and real bodies; Deke had done the spadework to uncover them. What he'd done wasn't strictly legal, but it was a minor peccadillo compared to Bekmeyer's sins.

At nine o'clock Deke entered the conference room. As he walked around the table he handed different folders to all those he'd summoned.

"It's a whole new fight," Deke announced. "Bekmeyer thinks we're down for the count, but after you look at these documents you'll see that we not only have a pulse, but we're ready to come out swinging."

Deke's attitude brightened the spirits of everyone in the room. It even brought a smile to the pale face of his daughter.

"I'd like everyone to read through this paperwork, and tomorrow we'll gather for a strategy session. We'll also be looking to bolster the troops. Today Angus and I will be calling firms around the country trying to enlist them in a mass tort against Bekmeyer. The more dogs we get in this fight, the better it will be for us."

Deke looked around the room. "Questions?" he asked.

No one said anything. "Great," Deke announced. "Go get 'em."

Deke caught up with his daughter outside of the conference room. Not only was she moving slower than usual, but her breathing seemed labored.

"How are you doing?" asked Deke.

"I'm fine," Cara replied.

She saw her father looking at her skeptically. "All right, I guess I have a touch of the flu."

"Then you should really go home."

"Do as I say," Cara said, "not as I do? Remember a couple of months back when you had walking pneumonia and you were still working twelve-hour workdays?"

"You're a lot smarter than your old man," Deke told her.

"I'll leave early today."

"Promise?" asked Deke.

"Promise," she answered.

Both went their separate ways. As promised, Deke kept his word and started making calls, most of them to the billboard variety. "Billboard lawyers" were those that advertised with 800 numbers. Their ads usually showed someone in a bad way often caused by an on-the-job injury, or affected by some man-made disaster. Most of those Deke was calling were people he had only a passing acquaintance with, if that.

"Tim, it's Nick Deketomis and I need your help with a case."

Dallas-based attorney Tim Crum tried not to sound surprised even though it wasn't every day he received a call from the likes of Nick Deketomis. "Sure, Nick, what can I do you for?"

Although Deke didn't really know Tim Crum, he knew many lawyers like him. Crum had spent his first twelve years in practice settling low-end, local personal injury cases. Over time he'd been able to negotiate a few low two-comma settlements. Crum had been in a courtroom trial setting only two times in his entire career. Deke estimated that put him on par with the vast majority of advertising lawyers. The economics of a lawsuit usually forced them to fold before they would have liked.

Most non-advertising lawyers complained that advertisers like Crum gave lawyers a bad name with their loud and lurid TV ads.

Deke had a different point of view: He felt these attorneys provided a vital service to American consumers. Deke knew it was advertisers like Crum whose commercials warned the public that the pills they were popping like chocolate bonbons might shut down their livers, cause heart disease or leukemia, or worse. It was often the Crum-level advertisers that were the first to disclose appalling truths that drug manufacturers worked hard to keep secret.

Deke believed that Tim Crum and those like him were unsung heroes. Personal injury cases in the State of Texas had become more difficult to win and nearly impossible to uphold on appeal, even if there was a rare claimant's victory. In the face of changing laws, along with the packing of the courts with regressive and highly conservative judges, if someone had the misfortune of being injured or killed because of corporate negligence or indifference in Texas, their chances of prevailing against that corporation was somewhere south of one in ten.

Because of that daunting reality, Deke suspected Crum and others like him would be eager to move into the mass tort arena. It was Deke's goal to handle other Ranidol cases across the country by teaming up with a collection of out-of-state co-counsels.

Deke knew that while Crum wanted to expand his practice, he also didn't know how to try or settle the truly big cases yet. The battle with Bekmeyer could be a teachable moment for him.

"Tim, we are putting together a case against Bekmeyer Pharmaceuticals because their product Ranidol is killing scores of women. The documents we are already seeing lead me to believe that Texas doctors in particular are handing out Ranidol pills like candy. As your backyard appears to be a Ranidol salesperson's paradise, it will be an important part of this project because you have so many cases right around you."

"Ranidol?" asked Tim. "I think I heard my daughter-in-law talking about all sorts of weight she'd lost with Ranidol."

"Then right after we get through talking you better give her a call and tell her to throw every last pill out," Deke replied. "But before you do that I just want to talk for a minute and walk you through the case to see if you'd be interested in putting together an ad campaign that tells people all the disgusting facts about this drug. I really believe this is an incredibly important project, and if it's handled right, it could be a solid business decision for you."

Like most in his position, Deke knew at that moment Crum was probably trying to calculate how much money he stood to make. To help him out with those calculations, Deke explained his firm would pay Crum 40 percent of the net settlement for the first five hundred Ranidol cases that Crum dug up, and 30 percent for each case beyond that.

"Don't get me wrong, Tim, this is going be a dogfight," Deke said. "It's a complicated action and Bekmeyer is the true evil empire of the drug industry. They'll outspend us, and they'll try to out-PR us and out-politic us. Expect that they will pull out their entire rancid bag of putrid tricks. So you have to be up for it."

Deke listened to Crum's answer. "Well, I'm glad to hear that, Tim. And like my legal mentor, Martin Bergman, always tells me, 'It's not the size of the dog, but the fight in him.' And this dog is ready to fight."

He heard Crum laugh and then told him, "Now I want you to call that daughter-in-law of yours. Ranidol is no laughing matter. It's poison and she needs to get rid of it now."

8
CIVIL AND UNCIVIL LIBERTIES

For years Deke had been doing both local and national radio shows. It was his friend Robert F. Kennedy, Jr. who had encouraged him not to overlook the goings-on in his own backyard.

"All politics is local," Kennedy had reminded him.

That's why he was doing yet another local radio broadcast. Jackie Farron was a tireless twentysomething who ran the show like a veteran news producer despite the fact that this was her first job out of college.

Lumon Maygard was that night's guest. "May" was an African American community activist who just might give good old boy prosecutor Darl Dixon a run for his money in the upcoming election for state senate.

Jackie did her countdown, and then Deke opened the radio show by saying, "Don't blame Christ for Christians."

Subtlety was not one of Deke's strong points.

"I'm wondering if so-called men of God like Pastor Rodney Morgan have even read the Bible. Or have they conveniently forgotten the parts where Jesus took on the moneychangers and went out with the unwashed and unholy to preach love and forgiveness? So explain to me how it is that Jesus suddenly became conservative? When did he start hating gay people? When did he advocate a huge buildup of our military? Does that sound like Jesus?

"Every year taxpayers allow church organizations to avoid paying almost one hundred billion dollars in tax revenue to the federal government," Deke said. "The idea originally behind that is that by giving those huge tax breaks to church organizations, it was hoped society would benefit from extensive charitable work and the trickling down of a whole host of positive social initiatives. Sometimes that theory plays itself out perfectly. But lately, on Sunday morning folks around here are more likely to be forced to listen to something that more closely resembles the rants of the KKK than the lessons of Jesus Christ.

"This country was built on the separation of church and state. The Founding Fathers understood that the religious and the secular should not be intermingled. But from pulpits all around the South many pastors are telling their parishioners how to vote, and who to vote for. They are saying this is the candidate Jesus would like. What would Jesus do? I can't tell you that. No one can. But I doubt Jesus would be going around goose-stepping in jackboots.

"Pastor Rodney Morgan told his congregation that my next guest is a 'welfare socialist.' Then he encouraged his many parishioners to vote for Darl Dixon. So is it right that preacher Morgan and his tax-free institution tell us how we should vote?"

Deke paused to take a breath, and let his diatribe sink in. "After a short break, we will be back with Lumon Maygard."

Lumon Maygard entered the broadcast room looking like a movie star. "Is there anyone you didn't insult?"

Both men laughed. "I guess I had an edge on," Deke confessed. May whistled.

"I always say this show is about having fun and annoying people for the right reasons," Deke told them.

"That sounds good to me," May said.

Jackie signaled from the control and Deke took his place at the microphone. May sat across the desk from him. Jackie gave a five count and cued Deke.

For fifteen minutes Deke asked May about a variety of topics. Instead of offering up rehearsed one-liners, Maygard tried to provide thoughtful answers. He pointed out how he differed from his opponent, Prosecutor Darl Dixon, but did so without taunting or smearing. In fact he was so even-handed that Deke felt it necessary to point out Dixon's failings as state attorney, including how he'd failed to prosecute half a dozen cases of police brutality even after special grand juries had recommended indictments, and how he'd passed on prosecuting British Petroleum for their environmental crimes wreaked upon Spanish Trace.

Deke closed the show much as he'd begun it, talking about the demagogues who wrapped themselves in the American flag.

"Yes," said May, "I've heard those same people talk about how school prayer is good, but school lunches for the poor are bad. And I've heard them say if you are for the environment, you are against jobs. Instead of bringing people together for the common good, they divide people by exploiting their differences. Northern Florida is nearly overwhelmed with that type of demagoguery and that kind of policy and rhetoric takes us backward, not forward."

"On that note," Deke responded, "I think I'll open up the program to callers. If you'd like to talk to Lumon Maygard, please call now."

Deke expected that the floodgates would open with vitriol, but was surprised at the reasoned tone of the first two callers, both of whom wanted to know May's stance on different local issues.

The third caller, a man who identified himself as Lee, started in by asking, "What kind of name is Lumon Maygard?"

As May tried to explain, Lee interrupted him. "So you're saying this is like your Kunta Kinte name, is that it?"

"It's the name my parents gave me," May said.

"It sounds like the name I'd give to my porch monkey."

"You have a question, Lee," asked Deke, "or do you just want to sing *Deutschland über alles?*"

"Yeah, I got a question Mr. 'Dickemotis.' Why is it that bloodsucking parasites like you hate America?"

"I love America, Lee. And if you claim to love America then you had better pray that our country always has bloodsucking parasites like me to protect it.

"It's because of shysters like you that the barbarians are at the gate," Lee said.

"If those barbarians are where you say they are, then I am convinced of this: Protecting our civil liberties will keep us safer as a nation than building up walls and gates."

"Is it hard protecting liberty while chasing an ambulance?" the caller asked.

"Yes it is, Lee," Deke answered, "yes it is."

9
THY WILL BE DONE

Across town, Pastor Rodney Morgan finished listening to Deke's radio show. He knew that Deke's local audience was miniscule compared to his own, but that thought didn't ease the state of his temper.

That infidel, that Judas, had dared to call him out. He'd even threatened the tax exempt status of his church, by far the biggest and grandest in all of Spanish Trace.

Pastor Rodney wasn't used to being attacked. He was used to being respected as a man of the cloth. He was used to others doing what he advised. That lefty lawyer had no sense of propriety. He was a bull in a china shop. He was a bull who needed to meet a matador with a sharp sword.

Hardly anyone listens to that godless charlatan, Rodney told himself, but he was still unsettled. Deketomis was like one of those inflatable punching-clown toys. You hit him, and hit him, but he kept coming back up for more. Deketomis had seen Florida turn into a red state that was run from top to bottom by the Republican machine, but that hadn't stopped him from backing losers like this latest Uncle Tom of his. State Prosecutor Darl Dixon should make mincemeat of this Lumon Maygard character, but the pastor knew he couldn't take that for granted. A Dixon victory would mean that Pastor Rodney and his expanding church empire wouldn't have to worry about scrutinizing eyes. Dixon was a deacon at the church, and would be a good friend to their mutual interests.

It bothered the pastor that Deketomis wasn't willing to accept the inevitable. On a few occasions he knew the lawyer's candidates had beaten the odds and actually won. That couldn't happen this time. Deketomis might have some money and power of his own, but it was nothing compared to that of the Holiness Southern Pentecostal Church.

The intercom on the pastor's monstrously sized desk buzzed. Pastor Rodney's chair was in keeping with his desk. Visitors were forced to look up at him when they visited him in his office.

"Angela Thorn is here," his secretary announced.

Earlier that day Pastor Rodney had agreed to see Mrs. Thorn. She hadn't specified her reasons for wanting to see him, but had told his secretary that it was a private matter that involved her husband who was apparently the softball coach of the church team. His secretary had learned it was a "delicate situation." That had been enough to make her defer the matter to her boss.

Angela Thorn was dressed in drab grey, a contrast to the pastor's ornate office with all its finery. She was trembling as she entered the office and made no effort to hide how troubled she was.

"Pastor Rodney, thank you so much for seeing me," she said. "I didn't know where else to turn."

Pastor Rodney was good at reading people. Even if he hadn't been, it would have been obvious to anyone this woman was at her wit's end.

"I am here to help," he told her.

"It's about my husband, Ken," she began. "You probably know him as Coach Ken because he coaches the softball team."

As the woman began to cry the pastor was ready with a box of tissues. Between her crying, snorting, and wailing, the story came out. What Angela didn't tell the pastor was that Ken had coached her on what to say. He had wanted her to emphasize what might happen to the reputation of the church if the story of his being with an underage girl was to surface.

"He's truly repentant," Angela explained. "He swears it will never happen again. He would have come with me, but he's still weak—he tried to kill himself. I came upon him just in time."

What was good timing for Ken, thought the pastor, was bad timing for him and his church.

"Ken says he'll do anything you want."

Pastor Rodney was no fool. Where there was smoke, he knew there was invariably fire. And it was the church's fault that they'd let this pedophile coach the girls. It wouldn't have been so bad if the softball team hadn't caught on with the country, but now the girls were minor celebrities. The public was quick to build something up, but even quicker to tear it down. The pastor wasn't a betting man, but if he were he'd be willing to bet every last dollar that this wasn't the first minor Ken had been with. Had the fool diddled any girls on the team? If the pervert was arrested for being with this girl, then surely there would be an investigation—and the last thing Pastor Rodney wanted was for his church to be scrutinized under some magnifying glass.

"Let us pray," the pastor recommended.

He was amazingly good about being able to compartmentalize. As a long prayer came off his lips, Rodney considered the problem that had been presented to him.

"Man is weak, Lord, that we know. Was not King David weak? Flesh is fallible. Give comfort to our good sister Angela, dear Lord, and show our brother Ken the sins of his ways. Bestow your grace upon our poor sister and help her through these most difficult travails. Amen."

They'd have to find a way to sweep all this under the rug.

He needed to make sure of that. "Now that you've shared your troubles with me, Sister Angela, I don't see any need for you to talk about this matter with anyone else. But of course I'll need to talk with your husband. I'll need to be sure he's right with the Lord."

And I'll need to make sure he doesn't get anywhere near the girls on the softball team from this day forward, the pastor thought.

"Try and be at peace, Sister Angela," Pastor Rodney continued, "and go home and minister to your husband. In the meantime I'll pray on this matter."

Angela thanked Pastor Rodney before stumbling her way out of his office.

10
THE SLEEPER HOLD

As Deke, Threepio, Carol, and two paralegals rushed across the tarmac in St. Louis, there was something about the purposeful way in which they moved that made them seem more like a commando team than a legal team. Two black SUVs waited for them with their engines running.

Within thirty minutes of their jet touching down, Deke and his colleagues had arrived at a plush-looking downtown office building. They rode an elevator to the sixteenth floor, which housed Benton, Craighill & Wasserman's St. Louis satellite office. The firm's Mergers & Acquisitions Department had recently helped cobble together a multibillion-dollar deal between a beer giant and its chief distributor and were now reaping the benefits of that hourly billing goldmine.

In the reception area, the Spanish Trace legal team was greeted by a waiting paralegal. The firm's décor of dark walnut walls, steel grey carpet, and walnut-accented chairs spoke to massive corporate money. In one corner sat a seven-foot-tall beer can, a reminder of the golden goose.

The paralegal escorted Deke and his team to a conference room. A contracted IT team was waiting with two video cameras and a locally hired stenographer. Today's sole witness, Bill Persons, was seated at a long walnut table. He was flanked on each side by lawyers. There were several bottles of water and a few soft drinks on a credenza against one wall, and a lonely silk ficus tree gathering dust in the corner near the window. Deke found most corporate defense law offices reflected the personalities of its lawyers. The fake tree had a spiritually deadening effect.

At their entrance into the conference room, the two young lawyers from Benton, Craighill & Wasserman jumped from their chairs. The one wearing an officious-looking, bright red bowtie extended his hand to Deke and introduced himself as Tom Golnick.

"Nice to see you Mr. Deketomis. We didn't expect you. Your name wasn't listed."

Deke shook his hand and replied, "Yeah, I'm in town giving a speech, so I thought I'd kill two birds with one stone and save myself the expense of flying one of our lawyers up here."

Golnick seemed satisfied with the answer, but his colleague in the three-piece suit tapped him on the shoulder. "Excuse us for a minute," he told Deke.

The two lawyers moved into the hallway. Deke knew they were discussing whether or not to call their boss and let him know about their unexpected guest. The young lawyers were correct to be concerned, but Deke hoped they'd decide to handle the situation themselves. Deke also hoped neither one of them had read his trial lawyer handbook *The Last Battle*. If they had, they would have read a chapter devoted to a tactic devised by Deke and his partner called "the sleeper document bounce," or as Deke affectionately called it, "the sleeper hold." When applied correctly, it was night night.

It was a simple strategy based on the practice of low-level corporate associates representing their firm during what was assumed to be a routine deposition. During a "sleeper document bounce," few substantive questions were asked of the witness. Instead, the true purpose of the deposition was to bounce off the most incriminating documents that had been created by their corporation. Emails, corporate marketing files, and clinical trial memos that management maintained had never existed became the main focus during the entire deposition.

In a typical mass tort case, millions of documents are produced. Out of those, there will always be fifty to a hundred that reflect the true corporate culture. Shakespeare had written, "The truth will out." Deke did his best to make that so. He wanted to show the darkness of Bekmeyer's soul, and to that end there was no better way than to use their own words—words they thought were no longer around to haunt them.

Deke had fifty documents he had paid big money for, and this was the day they would be used to inflict some serious harm to Bekmeyer. The ultimate goal of the document bounce deposition was to videotape a low-information employee's real-time response to incredibly hot documents created by the employee's own corporation. In most instances, the employee witness has no idea what the documents are, and, more importantly, the witness has never been shown the document prior to deposition.

Over the years Deke had seen employee-witnesses responses from a document bounce that ranged from, "Oh my god!" to "No way my company did that!" In most instances the younger associate lawyers defending the witness never saw the danger in the documents being introduced, because corporate "need to know" had left them in the dark. Most of the lawyers didn't know such documents even existed.

The *gotcha* point would come later at trial: Generally all the documents used in the deposition would be admitted as evidence against the corporation if it could be shown before trial that they came from the corporation's own file cabinets.

When an inexperienced employee and his or her minimally experienced lawyer were confronted with a fast-paced barrage of very hot documents that they have never reviewed, it becomes virtually impossible to explain them away with any degree of credibility. A well-edited videotape of the bounce deposition almost always ended badly for a corrupt corporation in a jury trial. Deke and Martin Bergman had often made bets on how long it would take before a corporate defendant wised-up and sued his or her silk-stocking corporate defense firm for what amounted to nothing short of corporate defense malpractice.

When Golnick and his colleague returned to the conference room, Deke and Threepio were sitting at the table across from the witness, Bill Persons. Like old buddies in a bar, the three men were yukking it up about the St. Louis Cardinals' pitching rotation.

With the St. Louis attorneys' go-ahead, Deke started the deposition, first asking the bespectacled salesman a few basic background questions. Everyone got to hear how Persons had been with the company for eleven years, and how Ranidol was one of his "big sellers."

"Every day I meet with doctors," said Persons. "My job is to convince them that Ranidol is the birth control of choice, and try to get them to prescribe it as much as possible."

Deke encouraged Persons to speak by using nods and smiles, and the occasional nonthreatening question. But fifteen minutes into the deposition, Deke asked the salesman a question that didn't seem quite as friendly:

"Do you happen to have a personal lawyer here today, Mr. Persons?"

The witness gestured to the two surprised looking Benton, Craighill & Wasserman attorneys. "Aren't they my lawyers?" he asked with a nervous chuckle.

Deke didn't answer. "Prior to coming here today, Mr. Persons, has anybody explained to you that you personally, along with your company, are operating under special performance guidelines laid out in a Corporate Integrity Agreement?"

In addition to the array of documents Deke had gathered showing Bekmeyer's criminal level of reckless indifference for safety, the company faced another potential minefield in the form of its Corporate Integrity Agreement. That agreement had resulted from Bekmeyer's longstanding violations of the government's regulatory rules. In essence it was a sanction that subjected them to fines in excess of $20,000 a day for each incident where the corporation violated compliance with the regulatory standards in their process of manufacturing and selling drugs.

Bekmeyer had "earned" this designation when one of its drugs used to help promote blood clotting in hemophiliacs was found to be contaminated with the HIV virus. In its haphazard process to manufacture the drug, the company used blood collected inexpensively from plasma centers located in big-city drug war zones where the risk of donors being infected with HIV was astronomical. Their blood-bonding product was never tested for HIV before Bekmeyer placed it on the market.

As if that wasn't bad enough, even after Bekmeyer knew the state of its infected batches, they still turned around and sold them in less regulated markets throughout Asia and South America. It was only after another class action suit that Bekmeyer finally destroyed its infected blood-bonding supply. But the most important part of that second class settlement was that in the end the company was required to operate under the Corporate Integrity Agreement.

Deke knew that Bekmeyer had violated its Corporate Integrity Agreement with the sale and distribution of Ranidol, and hoped that the threat of huge potential fines would be the leverage he needed to get them to pull the drug from the market, as well as adequately compensate its victims.

Persons looked mystified at his question. "No, I never heard of any Corporate Agreement or whatever you called it. My job is to sell Bekmeyer's products."

Deke nodded, as if he approved. "Okay, Mr. Persons, let's read this first document together."

The document in question appeared on the video screen set up in the room and Deke began reading, "Ranidol was—" He stopped because the witness did not read along. Most likely, Persons was still trying to understand why he had been asked about a personal lawyer and a technical agreement of which he had no knowledge. "Mr. Persons?" Deke prompted.

"Oh, sorry," the witness said, and then began reading aloud as Deke sat quietly. "Ranidol was approved in May 2002 only for the prevention of pregnancy in women who elect to use an oral contraceptive. Ranidol was not approved for off-label use." Persons continued reading the next slide about restrictions on the use of Ranidol. When he finished, Persons shifted in his chair, not entirely sure what he had just read.

It was a warning letter from the FDA advising Bekmeyer not to advertise or promote their product for anything except birth control. This FDA threat letter had then been incorporated into an in-house memo. Unknowingly, Persons had likely introduced the document as evidence in an upcoming trial.

"Okay, let's read something else," Deke said.

Another document with CONFIDENTIAL stamped across the top appeared onscreen. Persons adjusted his glasses and began to read: "The market for the approved indications of birth control pills is too limited to create a new blockbuster drug. We must expand the market for Ranidol by having our sales force push off-label use for weight control and acne control. Our marketing department can create a series of ads with the tagline 'Ranidol: The Only Birth Control to Make You More Appealing.' According to our internal estimates, by employing this strategy sales of the product will increase twentyfold."

When the witness reached the end of this document, the two defense lawyers waited for Deke's question. Both of them were ready to voice their objections, but instead of giving them an opening Deke only asked Persons if the attorneys in the room had ever shown him the document.

Clearly bewildered, Persons shook his head and replied, "No."

An affable Deke nodded his head and said, "Let's read another."

"Excuse me," the three-piece suited lawyer interrupted. "Can we take a ten-minute break to confer with our client?"

"Certainly," Deke answered.

The two Bekmeyer lawyers and Persons hurriedly left the conference room. Deke was confident that no last minute coaching by the inexperienced Bekmeyer legal team could prepare the poor witness for what was ahead.

A few minutes later, the Bekmeyer lawyers led the witness back into the deposition. Everyone took their seats, and Deke plunged back into his document bounce routine. When another document appeared on the screen, Deke again asked the witness to read it.

"Ranidol has not been evaluated for the treatment of weight loss," he read, "but it seems to be the factor that is attracting our customers, so life is good."

"And what name is on that document?" asked Deke.

"It's signed by Ronald Davidson."

Deke knew that Davidson was Bekmeyer's marketing guru, but Persons clearly had no idea who he was.

"Prior to your coming here today, Mr. Persons," Deke asked, "were you aware that your company had made a decision to outright ignore FDA regulations?"

Golnick objected, and Deke demurred. It was better not to push too hard, better to let the opposing counsel think they were doing a good job.

Deke pressed on. "Mr. Persons, were you aware that your company had you selling Ranidol for health issues it had never been approved for?"

The lawyers objected at the same time. In unison they instructed Persons not to reply even though it didn't matter to Deke whether or not the witness answered. Persons was only there as a vehicle to bounce documents into evidence that a jury would later read word for word. The poor guy now seemed more befuddled than ever about why he was reading aloud documents that he had never previously seen.

"Let's continue Mr. Persons," Deke instructed. "Please read this next one." At the top of the document again were the words CONFIDENTIAL: FOR IN-HOUSE EYES ONLY.

Persons began to read the document. The letter had been drafted by Bekmeyer scientists who were questioning the validity of clinical data that had been used in communications with the FDA, as well as with doctors and patients. In a nutshell, the concerned scientists said that portions of the data had been "hustled," and the company might have a "dangerous drug on the market."

The deposition had introduced this sleeper document, and it should be enough to get Deke his date in court.

And that's where I'll put the sleeper hold on Bekmeyer, vowed Deke.

On the way back to the airport, Deke and Threepio rode together in the backseat. "Did that really just happen?" asked Threepio.

"It did," Deke said, "and if we're lucky we can get two more similar depositions under our belts before Bekmeyer realizes what we've done."

The Bekmeyer St. Louis lawyers had assumed that their lead counsel Wharton Garrison already knew about the documents that Deke had introduced. These were the same documents the lead counsel would assume were long buried. Now Deke wanted more of those "buried" documents introduced through other depositions. Bekmeyer was huge, but sometimes size could be a disadvantage. At the moment, one hand didn't know what the other was doing.

11

MAKIN' BACON—AND SAUSAGE

Pastor Rodney had driven one of the unmarked church vans to the parking lot of a restaurant called Makin' Bacon. The exterior of the restaurant had a number of signs featuring pigs that appeared to be dancing and playing an assortment of musical instruments. Pastor Morgan had been a regular at the fifty-year-old restaurant much of his life, and often found himself over-analyzing the irony of the dancing pigs and the tons of sausage that had been gobbled up for decades right on the other side of those peculiar signs.

Darl Dixon appeared at the passenger door. Instead of just opening the door and getting inside, Darl knocked.

"Get in," said Pastor Rodney. The longer the fool stood out in the parking lot, the more likely he was to be noticed.

Darl took a seat. "How are you doing today, Pastor?"

Rodney dispensed with the pleasantries. "What do you have?" he asked. The pastor had already briefed Darl on how Ken Thorn hadn't been able to keep it in his pants with a minor.

"The girl is named Sunny Torres," answered Darl. "She'll be fifteen in two weeks. The woman who wrote the 'or else' note is her mom, Lucia Torres."

"Sausage making," said Pastor Rodney, thinking how distasteful the whole thing was.

"Say what?" asked Darl.

"Can you make this problem go away?"

Darl winked at the pastor, something Rodney could have done without. "The mom—this Lucia Torres—is a hooker."

"So was Mary Magdalene," Pastor Rodney said. "How is that to our advantage?"

"In addition to being a hooker," Darl told him, "Lucia is also an illegal. With the right phone call to the right person I could get her deported."

"Then make that call."

"I'm not so sure I should. Lucia might be able to raise more of a stink after she's been deported and has nothing to lose. I'm thinking it would be better to control her by stringing her along at first. I can tell her that I'm building a case against Ken Thorn. And then down the road we can either buy her off, or tell her *hasta la* bye-bye."

Pastor Rodney thought about Darl's plan. "Okay," he said at last. It was as much of a blessing as he wanted to offer.

"What about your part?" asked Darl.

"Your campaign contribution is in that sack," the pastor said, signaling with his eyes.

Darl reached for the bag, and then opened it and looked appreciatively at all the money. "I'm going to need this," he told him. "That SOB bloodsucker Nick Deketomis has been shaking down his lefty friends to contribute to the Lumon Maygard campaign. I'm not going to let that bastard beat me again."

Two years earlier Darl had run for state senate, and Nick Deke-tomis had successfully championed the campaign of his opponent. The thought of losing still rankled Darl.

"Deketomis is no friend of the church either," Rodney said with some authority. "And that's why you need to make sure that money can't be traced to either me or the church."

That was the wonderful thing about being a tax-exempt insti-tution, the pastor thought. Skimming money was easy to do, and would continue to be so, unless people like Nick Deketomis brought the IRS into the picture.

"What are we going to do with this Thorn guy?" asked Darl. "From what I've been able to dig up, he's a real creep."

Pastor Rodney wasn't quite ready to tell Darl his plans, but he did say, "I believe Mr. Thorn was sent to me to serve the Lord's purpose and, not coincidentally, our own."

"That sounds good to me," Darl said.

"In the next day or two I am going to have you personally counsel him," Pastor Rodney informed Darl. "Before that meet-ing the two of us will discuss how he might best serve us. It goes without saying that your help in this matter will mean more for your political coffers, *Senator*."

Darl couldn't help but smile. Just the sound of "Senator Dixon" was enough to make him happy. "Are we done?" Darl asked.

"For now," Rodney answered.

Darl shifted his girth out of the car, and Pastor Rodney was struck by how similar the porcine faces at Makin' Bacon were to Darl's.

Making sausage, he mused, and then started up the van.

12
THE POISONED WELL

In the days following Deke's deposition of Bill Persons, he was able to send out two other lawyers from the firm to depose other Bekmeyer employees. Deke had opted not to personally conduct the other depositions, because he knew there was no way Bekmeyer's legal team wouldn't have grown suspicious at his involvement. The Bergman Deketomis lawyers had successfully used the sleeper document bounce, and managed to get more Ranidol documents entered as evidence.

Because others in his firm were doing the necessary Ranidol groundwork, Deke was able to spend time on what he called the Poisoned Well case. Deke had first become interested in initiating the lawsuit after getting a call from Clem Walters, an old-time country lawyer who lived in Southeast Texas.

At the onset of their conversation Deke had learned that Clem wasn't one for small talk or pleasantries. "I don't know you, Mr. Deketomis," said Clem, "but I've heard you talk a time or two and I think you might be able to help my client. Now, first thing you need to know is that she don't have a pot to piss in, but that's not exactly her fault. In fact it's sort of becoming a common story around here. My client and her husband used to have a farm that they did well enough by. But then both of them got sick. Last year her husband died and right now my client's not doing too well herself. I think she's holding on out of spite and gumption. According to her, she and her husband were healthy as all get-out until their land got slowly poisoned by an old oil refinery."

"That's a hard claim to prove," Deke had said.

"It would be," agreed Clem, "if the local town council hadn't paid a firm to come in to sample the air and water. What they found was a horror story."

"Any way you can email me a file of that report?" Deke had asked.

"The office scanner is busted," replied Clem, "but I can put a copy of the report in tomorrow's mail. One thing I need to tell you, though, before you get all fired up."

"And what's that?"

"The oil refinery is called S.I. Oil, but locals call it 'the Swanson field' on account that it's owned by the Swanson brothers. I'm betting those two brothers don't even know they own S.I. Oil, even if it does produce a hundred thousand barrels of oil a day. For them, that's a drop in their big bucket. But there's no way any lawyer in this state wants to take on those hombres."

Kurt and Anton Swanson were unapologetic billionaires. One of their unadvertised businesses was the buying and selling of elections which they did with regularity on both the local and national level.

"Do me a favor, Clem," Deke said. "From now on I better never hear you call me Mr. Deketomis. I'm Deke. And I need you to do me a second favor: Overnight that report to me."

The next day the report landed on Deke's desk and proved to be everything that Clem Walters said it was and more. S.I. Oil was more a toxic waste dump than it was an oil refinery.

At the firm's behest, Carol Morris took a trip to Southeast Texas and surreptitiously dug up everything she could. After being away for a week she showed up again in Deke's office. "How was your vacation?" he asked.

"Next time send me to Siberia in winter instead."

According to Carol, matters were even worse than the thirty-page toxicology report that had been sent to them indicated. "If there was a bigger population base," she said, "I think this would be another Love Canal, or worse. No one has documented it yet, but the area is a cancer cluster. The poison coming out of S.I. Oil is killing both farms and people, so the area is getting even more sparsely populated every day. Most of the locals are suffering. The only person who seems to be doing well in the area is the owner of a local cemetery. In fact business is so good he joined a country club and took up golf."

"This is for you," Carol said. She handed Deke a fat report documenting her findings.

Deke thumbed through the pages. With even his cursory look Deke could see Carol had managed to get the dirt. She came across as middle-aged and nonthreatening, a friendly woman who managed to get people talking. That was how she drew out information that most investigators would never have been able to uncover.

"The plant is old and ugly," she explained. "It's more than half a century old, and looks it. There are cement smokestacks everywhere spewing out filth night and day. And what you can't see is how the plant has destroyed the aquifer, filling it with toxins. That's what's killing all the farms, and the farmers. For years people were drinking this poison that even plants can no longer tolerate."

"I think we need to get the Swanson brothers drinking from those same poisoned wells," Deke said.

It took several weeks, and Deke's considerable persuasion, to get the partners at Bergman Deketomis to want the same thing for the Swanson brothers. While the partners loved Deke's passion, they frequently had to remind him that his tilting at windmills came at considerable cost. The Swanson brothers hadn't become billionaires by giving their money away. It was a foregone conclusion that they would spend umpteen millions in legal fees, and force opposing counsel to spend the same. Big game came at big cost, and it went without saying that the Swanson brothers had much deeper pockets than the Law Firm of Bergman Deketomis.

There was also worry about Deke overextending himself. Taking on Bekmeyer was a huge responsibility by itself, and there was worry that S.I. Oil could be the straw that breaks the camel's back. Those in the firm often had to temper Deke's desire to help the underdog. The partners were forever reminding Deke that they could only effectively handle a certain number of cases. Some people can't go to an animal shelter without wanting to adopt every animal they see—Deke had the same problem saying no to good people put in bad situations beyond their control.

Instead of declaring open war against the Swanson brothers, Deke agreed that they would initially conduct a stealth campaign against them. He enlisted Clem Walters and others to help him build his case while he spent most of his time preparing for Bekmeyer and Ranidol. Juggling lawsuits was nothing new to Deke.

"So many bad guys," he said to himself, "and so little time."

Deke put aside the latest reports on S.I. Oil, and dialed his daughter's extension. "Hi, Dad," she answered.

That meant no one was around her. Like everyone else at the firm, Cara called him "Deke," or at least she did in the presence of others.

"I was wondering if you wanted to go out to lunch with your old man," Deke said. "Then you can report to your mother that I dined on carrot juice and tofu."

"Mom wants you to be healthy."

"And to that I say bless her. But I also have a hankering for a burger. What do you say?"

"I'm kind of busy, Dad."

"You need to eat. That's your boss talking, not your dad."

"To tell the truth, I'm not very hungry."

Deke tried to hide the worry in his voice. "I think you need to see a doctor, sweetie. You can't seem to shake this flu."

"I made an appointment," she admitted, "but my doctor can't see me until the day after tomorrow."

"You could go to the emergency room."

"I don't need to go to the emergency room. It's a case of my get up and go got up and left. I am sure it's a virus and they can't prescribe anything for that. If I wasn't worried about getting you sick I'd go to lunch with you, but I don't want you to get this bug."

"I'm glad you're finally seeing a doctor."

"Go eat your burger, Dad. Don't worry, I won't tell Mom. But I hope you plan on eating nearby."

"Why's that?"

"You don't know? Pastor Rodney and his Holy Rollers have Spanish Trace pretty much closed down. Protestors have positioned themselves at the bridge and all the major intersections in town. They're calling it a 'Prayer-In' for the unborn. If you go up to the top floor of the building you can see them demonstrating."

"I'll pass," said Deke. And then he told Cara, "I love you."

"I love you too, Dad," she said.

Deke didn't want to deal with the crazies, so he decided to have an apple and crackers for lunch. He had finished both, and was debating raiding the snack machine for a candy bar, when his door flew open. Donna was wild-eyed and breathing hard. Normally his assistant was unflappable.

"What?" asked Deke.

"It's Cara," she told him. "She collapsed, and she's not responsive. We've already called 911. An ambulance has been dispatched."

Deke was already out of his chair and sprinting past Donna down the hallway. He found Angus administering CPR to Cara. Helpless to do anything, he was forced to watch. The fourth floor, always so busy, always so chaotic, was suddenly deathly still. Everyone wanted to help, but no one could.

"Where are the damn EMTs!" screamed Deke.

Donna pulled out her cell phone and had a hurried conversation. She shouted, "The ambulance is on the way and should be here soon. But response time is longer than usual. Pastor Rodney's 'Prayer-In' has traffic backed up around the city."

With trembling hands, Deke covered his face.

13
DOWN THE RABBIT HOLE

At periodic intervals, somber looking doctors came out to the waiting room and reported on Cara's condition. No one would tell Deke or Teri whether their daughter was going to live or die.

Finally a cardiologist appeared before them. "We've determined Cara has suffered heart damage," he said.

"How is that possible?" asked Deke.

Deke didn't know much about his own biological family, but he had never heard of anyone having a history of heart disease. And Teri's parents were still going strong in their eighties.

"We haven't been able to establish cause," the cardiologist replied. "I can only tell you that there's been some blood leaking through her heart valves. Because of that, I recommend that we operate."

"What are Cara's chances?"

The doctor shook his head and refused to answer. One of the first things they teach in med school is to never venture an opinion to a lawyer.

Teri intervened. "Will my daughter be all right if she has this operation?"

The mother's tears moved him to answer. "She will have a much better chance of a full recovery if she does have the operation than if she doesn't."

"Then I want you to operate," Teri said, speaking for both of them.

While their daughter was being operated on, the Deketomis family huddled together. Neither Teri nor Andy had ever seen Deke so distraught.

"I wish it was me," he said. "I wish I could do something."

He shook his head and looked lost as he thought of his own childhood.

Things had gotten so bad between his parents that at twelve years old Deke ended up in the foster care system. Before aging out as an eighteen-year-old, Deke was taken in by several foster families, but not for altruistic reasons or love. Taking in a foster kid meant the families got a badly needed monthly check. When he resumed his conversation, it almost seemed like he was speaking out loud to himself.

"Because of my crappy upbringing, I was afraid I'd be a bad husband, and a worse father. But the husband part proved easy. How could I not love Teri? But when Teri told me she was pregnant, I was terrified. There was this—thing—coming into our house that I wasn't even sure if I was capable of loving. That was before I saw her in the delivery room. One look was all it took. I was crazy in love with my little baby. And that never changed in all these years.

"The same thing happened the second time Teri announced she was pregnant. I pretty much had a panic attack. I didn't think there was any way I could love the second baby the same way I had the first. But the same thing happened when I saw Andy. I was so proud I thought my heart would burst. And that's how I feel to this day.

"And that's why I feel so damn helpless."

Teri and Andy took turns hugging Deke, and then the three of them waited. Never was a wait so hard.

* * *

Later, with the breath of each family member held in suspense, they heard five words uttered. They were the most beautiful five words the Deketomis family had ever heard: "The operation was a success."

And they offered thanks to God, and hugged one another, and laughed. But Deke had to see his baby with his own eyes to make sure she was all right. "When can I see her?" he asked. "When can I talk with her?"

The next day, Deke got his wish. Cara asked to see him first, saying there was something she had to discuss with him. And though the doctors assured Deke that Cara would completely recover, when he walked in the room he was taken aback by how fragile she looked.

Deke came and sat at her side. "I should have told you," whispered Cara.

"You told me that you loved me," he said. "That was the last thing you said to me. I was afraid those were your last words. But at least I had that much."

Cara shook her head. "I know why I got sick."

Deke didn't understand what she was trying to say. "The doctors tell us it could have been any number of things," Deke told her. "They say it could have been a virus, or . . ."

"I took Ranidol for fifteen months," whispered Cara. "It was only when you took the case against Bekmeyer that I went off of it. And after meeting Annica, I was so glad that I did. I thought I'd dodged a bullet, but I guess I didn't."

Deke's mouth opened. He had never been short of words, but now he was speechless.

"I didn't want to tell you I was on birth control," she said. "I didn't even tell Mom. It was just one of those things."

Deke nodded.

"When I was taking Ranidol, it seemed too good to be true." I had gained some weight in law school, and the pounds just dropped off."

The pounding in Deke's head made it hard for him to think. His precious, precious girl had almost been taken from him because of a company's greed. The veins on his forehead throbbed.

"I am going to destroy those bastards," said Deke.

"Dad . . ."

Deke remembered where he was. He took a few deep breaths.

"Talk about weight loss," he told her, "when the doctors told me you'd be okay, when they told me you were going to live, it felt like all the weight in the world dropped off me. I felt like that phoenix rising from the ashes."

Cara gave him a smile, and Deke smiled back. He'd been given the greatest gift—Cara was alive.

But he was still going to make those bastards pay.

14

DOUBLE-TROUBLE

It had been a long fall from grace for Senator Roger Dove. Once upon a time he'd been a respected US Senator from the State of Tennessee. Then there had been a bit of a scandal, and the voters of the Volunteer State had sent him packing. Gone were the perks, and gone was the respect. All he had left was some vestigial pride. And the Swanson brothers weren't even content to leave him that. He was their beggar dog, and they made him beg for scraps.

It was Senator Dove's job to watch out for the Swanson brothers' interests. He kept his ear close to the ground, alerting them to anything that might impact their empire, but his main job was heading up STARS, a right-wing political PAC. It was the Swanson brothers who bankrolled STARS and the candidates who took the STARS money knew that it came at the price of serving their interests.

Because of STARS money, the political map was rapidly changing. With a Republican majority in state legislatures, redistricting was happening all over. This gerrymandering meant that

Republicans now had a lock on these congressional seats well into the future. The Swanson stranglehold was working on both the local and national levels. Senator Dove's job was to find subservient Republicans who were blindly loyal to the Swanson brothers, and then make sure they got elected. These political lackeys were especially important in the areas of oil and gas drilling. The Swanson brothers didn't want anything impeding their business, and that included fracking, offshore oil drilling, and minimal refining regulation. To get and maintain this favorable kind of business environment, the brothers regarded no elected office as being too insignificant to own.

As beholden as he was to the Swanson brothers, Dove loathed them. They were arrogant and entitled. Though they had come from inherited wealth, neither Anton nor Kurt Swanson ever acknowledged this, and embodied the observation: "They were born on third base and grew up thinking they'd hit a triple."

The two brothers liked to make Dove feel like he was their errand boy. And that was the rub, thought Dove. He was their errand boy. The brothers had combined assets north of $90 billion. Their funding allowed Dove to be considered an extremely important political operative. Without it Dove would be just another washed-up politician turned lobbyist.

The Swanson brothers lived for most of the year in adjacent massive estates just south of downtown Palm Beach. For the past month Dove had been trying to arrange a meeting with them, citing some important information that he'd come across. They'd finally agreed he could "stop by the house." His transportation, Dove had been informed, had been arranged. Dove was now standing outside his hotel waiting for that ride. Another limo pulled up, but it wasn't his.

Dove continued to wait. It wouldn't have surprised him if the Swanson brothers were purposely making him wait. He looked hopefully at another limo driver, but he was dropping off a passenger and not making a pick-up.

"Mee-stah Dove?"

Dove turned towards the voice. A thirtysomething Hispanic woman was calling his name. She was standing outside a faded red Kia that might charitably be described as a junker.

"I'm *Senator* Dove," he said.

"They tell me to pick you up, Mee-stah Dove."

Dove tried to hide his mortified expression. He should probably be grateful that a clown car hadn't been sent to pick him up. The Swanson brothers had what was described as a "peculiar" sense of humor. Dove was willing to bet that as boys they had probably spent many a day pulling the wings off of flies.

"Sorry everything such a mess," apologized the woman. "I told the Mee-stahs that but they said it was all right. I am the Mee-stahs housekeeper Sancha."

Don't blame the messenger, thought Dove. Don't blame the messenger.

"Thank you for agreeing to drive me, Sancha," he said.

"I hope your seat is no dirty," Sancha warned. "I just drop off my little girl at daycare. She eat a burrito on the way."

Dove pulled free the handkerchief out of his Hickey-Freeman suit, applying it to the front seat. He couldn't see anything there, but didn't doubt a landmine was waiting for him.

His conversation with Sancha during their drive, Dove knew, was far nicer than what he could expect from the Swansons. The brothers' estates were hidden behind fourteen-foot walls that were covered in bougainvillea that bloomed year-round. Combined, the brothers enjoyed a half mile of oceanfront, the area's longest private stretch of beach. Sancha pulled off the A1A into a drive, and smiled at the uniformed security man in the small guardhouse. He glanced at Dove and then waved them into Xanadu.

Sancha drove her car past the giant children's playground between the two houses. The brothers had purchased the mansion between their properties and demolished it. On the former site of a $35 million mansion they had built a paradise for their grandchildren, nothing less than a year-round carnival. The little darlings could play whack-a-mole, drive bumper cars, and climb on wooden jungle gyms and swing sets before they took a ride on the backs of giant sculpted dinosaurs on a musical carousel. Two moon-bounces were hidden by palm trees, and beyond that was an elaborate hide-and-seek maze with eight-foot hedges. Dove saw the trio of huge nude Botero sculptures he knew the Swanson grandkids liked to climb on and try to push over.

Even though he had served in the US Senate, this was truly the most dysfunctional group of crazies Dove had ever been around. During his last visit one of the Swanson granddaughters had bitten him on the arm and actually drawn blood. Anton had just about lost a lung, he had laughed so hard. It had taken all of Dove's self-control to not ask if the girl was up-to-date on her rabies vaccine.

"The Mee-stahs tell me to bring you in the back way," explained Sancha. "That where I park."

Dove would be entering the house through the help's entrance. "Thank you, Sancha," he replied.

Kurt's house sat to the south and was twenty-eight thousand square feet, while north of the kiddie playground Anton's mansion was similar in layout though slightly smaller. The residences contained every conceivable luxury, from movie theaters to indoor pools and bowling alleys. Kurt's had a walk-in wine humidor equipped with a push-button retrieval system. Anton's bragging room was his ocean-view bar; the crystal glasses and stemware had at one time belonged to Benito Mussolini. The walls in that room, just off his massive office, were covered with enough Picasso sketches to fill a small museum.

Dove was kept waiting for twenty minutes in Anton's freezing office. He heard laughter from behind the door to the bar but didn't venture to look. Instead, he took his time admiring the room's exquisite artwork. There was a Modigliani oil of an elongated nude woman and a Sargent portrait of a little boy. Dove's art appreciation was interrupted when a small flaxen-haired girl peeked into the room. He couldn't be sure, but thought it was the little demon cannibal who bit him during his last visit. She made a face at him, but apparently had already eaten, and scampered away.

Finally the two brothers entered from the bar. Anton Swanson, the more spiteful of the two, was generally the one in charge. Both men sat down, but this time it was Kurt who spoke first.

"You've been trying to bend our ears for some time, Senator Dove. What is so important that you had to speak to us personally?"

"Why do you call him *senator*?" asked Anton. "The people of Tennessee turned out in record numbers to kick him out on his ass. No one ever thought Tennessee would elect a Democrat, but this one managed that."

"Once you're a senator," Kurt informed his brother, "you're always a senator. It's like being the president, or being a judge, or being a cardinal."

"Like being a cardinal?" asked Anton. "Should we kiss his ring?"

"I think the senator would rather we kissed his ass."

Anton puckered his lips and his brother laughed. "You ever hear the definition of an honest politician, Kurt?"

"I can't say I have."

"An honest politician is one that when he's bought, he stays bought."

"If that's the case," Kurt said jovially, "I think Senator Dove is an honest politician."

"Talk to us, Senator," Anton said. "What's so damned important?"

Dove licked his lips. Whenever the Swanson brothers looked at him, he felt like a butterfly pinned to a page.

"I have a contact in Kinkade County, Texas. He alerted me to an action being directed your way. The word is that Nick Deketomis is going to try and blindside one of your holdings, S.I. Oil. There's talk that he'll be trying to make this a RICO action."

Dove looked from brother to brother. Neither of their faces gave away anything. The senator had thought they would appreciate being forewarned, but he was mistaken.

"So this Greek-o wants to get us on a RIC-O," Kurt commented.

"Cousin Tim's daughter Susan married a Greek boy," Anton said. "She thought she was marrying a Greek god, but now she says she married a goddamn Greek."

Kurt slapped his knee at that one.

"Deketomis is dangerous," Dove added.

What the senator didn't tell them was that in his last, losing political campaign, Deketomis had done fund-raising for his opponent, and had used the airwaves to mock him. It wasn't something Dove had forgotten. In the years since his defeat, he'd made a point of keeping tabs on Deketomis. That was how he'd heard the hush-hush story of what was going on in Texas.

"He's a mass torts lawyer," Dove continued. "And he's got a national radio show with one of those Kennedys. And he's always appearing as one of those talking heads on television shows."

"You scared, brother?" asked Anton.

"I'm quaking in my boots," answered Kurt.

Dove wiped a trickle of sweat from his face. This wasn't going as he had hoped. "Deketomis is also trying to derail one of the candidates we've earmarked for the Florida Senate. We've managed to get a majority in the senate, and don't want that to change. This seat is important. I know you want Florida to be a stronghold."

Controlling Florida politics would be beneficial to the Swansons' chemical and petroleum industry business plan. If the brothers could externalize all cleanup costs and transfer all health costs to the taxpayers, their profits would soar. To Dove, Anton Swanson had once characterized that hoped-for outcome—tongue in cheek, of course—as "corporate socialism."

"I know you hope to ramp up fracking operations in North Florida," Dove said, "and not have to worry about the cost of cleaning up the freshwater aquifers. I am working to get you the right foot soldiers to do your bidding on that front, as well as with your offshore drilling concerns."

That's why the Florida Panhandle was important to the Swanson brothers, and to Dove. If they were to have unimpeded offshore drilling, they'd need to win elections in the area. Getting Darl Dixon elected would make Dove's overlords happy, and even more important, it would be a chance for the senator to spit at Nick Deketomis.

"This Deketomis hustler shouldn't be underestimated," Dove reminded him. "Mark my words when I say that he'll be coming after you. Deketomis has won some huge settlements."

"Is that your big news?" asked Anton. "What a waste of our fucking time. And I most definitely don't like wasting time. Maybe you've heard I have cancer."

Dove knew better than to say anything. Now it was Kurt's turn to lecture him.

"If this ambulance chaser tries to take us on," he said, "then we'll beat him to a pulp in the courtroom. But we don't want to hear the sky is falling when it comes to an oil refinery deep in the heart of Texas. That's chickenshit, Chicken Little. We all but own that state."

"Senator," said Anton, "we're paying you way more than you're worth to keep the regulators, the EPA and the DOJ, off our backs. And most of all we're paying you to see that our hired help gets elected. Do your job and don't bother us."

Dove understood he was being told to leave. He stood up, tried to smile, and said, "I'll be off then."

Anton decided to get in the last word. "While we're on the topic of hired help," he added, "you better call Sancha to give you a ride."

As Dove took his leave of the room he pretended not to hear the brothers laughing, just as he pretended not to see their smirks.

15
DOMESTIC TERRORISM

This time Pastor Rodney arranged to meet with Darl Dixon in a strip mall. The pastor was in a foul mood and didn't try and hide it, laying into Darl the moment he seated himself in the van.

"Do you know what that spawn of Satan Deketomis has done?"

It was the rare person in Spanish Trace, or even Florida, who hadn't heard about the lawyer's latest lawsuit.

"I guess he's suing you and the church," Darl replied.

"In his lawsuit he is claiming that the Holiness Southern Pentecostal Church is guilty of committing domestic terrorism."

Pastor Rodney's outrage was real, and Darl had to make sure not a hint of his smile showed through. It was kind of funny that Deketomis was trying to link the church with the likes of terrorist groups like Al-Qaeda, ISIS, and the Taliban.

"Our citywide 'Prayer-Ins' were protesting the disregard for the sanctity of life," said Pastor Rodney, "and for that this miscreant has suggested that our actions caused the shutdown of government and essential services, making us a terrorist organization."

"I guess his daughter had a seizure or something," Darl said, "and her ambulance was delayed. And now he's advertising for others who were adversely impacted."

"It's a hateful publicity ploy," agreed Pastor Rodney.

"Is it true he's also suing for the church to lose its tax-exempt status?" asked Darl.

"It's a frivolous lawsuit with many outlandish claims."

If that was the case, wondered Darl, why did Pastor Rodney look so flustered?

"We are a church of God," said the pastor, "but he's saying we're a political organization, and because of that we're subject to tax laws."

"Why don't you call him out on *These Holy Times*?"

The pastor shook his head. "I would except that now of all times the show can't appear to be political."

He turned to Darl, forcing him to meet his eyes. "That's why you and your confederate need to act. In fact I'm surprised you haven't acted before this. Deketomis needs to be distracted. And the world needs to see him in a different light."

"I'll talk to my . . . confederate," Darl informed him. "We'll set something up soon."

"The sooner the better," Pastor Rodney responded. And then his face turned red. "Domestic terrorism my ass."

Darl sat there and nodded. At first Pastor Rodney didn't understand why the man was lingering, but then he remembered what was motivating him.

"Take the money and run," he said, pointing to the bag.

Pastor Rodney had used surgical gloves while filling the bag. He wanted to make sure nothing connected him to this action.

Darl picked up the bag. "It's a pleasure doing business with you."

Two days later it was Darl Dixon directing someone out of his car. "He'll be along any minute now," Darl said. "Get moving."

Ken Thorn exited Darl's nondescript rental. Because Ken still looked unsure, Darl said, "Deketomis will probably only hit you once or twice. That's a small enough price to pay when you consider what they do to child molesters in Raiford."

Raiford was one of Florida's state penitentiaries. "You know what they do to them?" asked Darl.

"I don't want to know," Ken replied.

"That's right," said Darl. "You really don't want to know."

The plan was for Ken to confront Deke on the street and say a few things to provoke him. Darl had worked with him on the lawyer's hot buttons. Family was his Achilles' heel. With his daughter still laid up in the hospital, any slur against her was likely to produce the desired result.

On most Fridays Deke ate at the Prime Barbecue Steakhouse. Darl had been able to confirm that Deke had a reservation for two people at noon.

"You know where the car will be parked," Darl said. "I'll be in the park across the street having a smoke."

All the offices and restaurants in Spanish Trace were smoke-free, so smokers used the park to do their puffing. It was always crowded. And it provided a perfect vantage point to watch Deketomis beating the hell out of Ken. Darl would have his cell phone out and ready, and was sure many others would also get some footage.

Ken did his waiting for Deketomis while pretending to be window shopping at Don Carson's Clothing Store. He tried to be casual and not look nervous, but he felt sick to his stomach. And what was worse was how much he was sweating. His sports coat was almost soaked through. A security guard eyed him suspiciously.

The thought of being a punching bag was almost enough to make Ken vomit. All his life he'd tried to avoid fights, although in middle school he'd been beaten up on a regular basis. Well, it was time to get beat up again. But Deketomis was a big guy, as in scary big. He was a head taller than Ken, and probably had seventy-five pounds on him.

And Ken was supposed to pick a fight with him.

It was then that Ken caught sight of his target. Shit. He was even bigger than he looked in the pictures. As Ken moved into position he tried to remember the lines that Darl had made him rehearse. It was something about his daughter.

Ken looked up at Deketomis. Their eyes met, and Ken found himself hyperventilating. The lawyer paused for long enough to ask, "Are you okay, bud?"

"Fine," said Ken, and Deketomis walked off.

Deke spotted Paul Moses waiting for him at the restaurant bar. Moses had flown in from New York for their business lunch. Tall and thin with a stylish goatee, he was a sophisticated New York PR and marketing executive who handled some of America's most high-profile clients, including politically active celebrities of all kinds. Moses regularly worked with Deke to help develop public relations strategies on large mass tort cases. He helped Deke with the firm's many political agendas and also knew how to rein Deke in when necessary. Even Deke knew he could go too far with his take-no-prisoners political routines. For that very reason, the PR whiz was well appreciated by the rest of the firm's attorneys.

Deke and Moses took a seat at the private booth the lawyers usually frequented.

"How is Cara?" Moses asked.

"Every day, thank God, she's getting better and better," Deke told him.

He knocked wood and smiled. When it came to the safety of his daughter he was willing to be superstitious. He was willing to do anything.

"She wants to get back to work," Deke explained, "and is trying to get me to agree. Because I've forbidden her to work on the Ranidol case, she wants to get aboard this other case."

The other case was why Moses was there. Deke had already sent him a confidential file with the particulars. "You're really going after big game this time," he told him.

Deke nodded. "And I'll need a big splash to go after that big game. That's where you come in. I'm going to need a multilayered PR attack against Kurt and Anton Swanson. I need a big build up leading into my bringing a multibillion-dollar environment case against them in South Texas."

"You didn't provide me much in the way of details about that case," said Moses.

"It's a story about the Swanson brothers raping the land, pillaging the environment, and murdering the citizenry."

"Is that all?"

Over lunch, Deke filled in Moses on all the details about S.I. Oil.

"It's pretty much a repeat of what happened in 2000 with all the indictments against that West Plant refinery in South Texas," Deke said. "You remember any of the details of that?"

Moses nodded. "That's the company owned by Koch Industries, isn't it?"

"It is indeed. A division called Koch Refining Company owned the refinery near Corpus Christi, Texas. There was enormous pollution from emissions of benzene in their plant and in their company pipelines that transported natural gas liquids and chemicals across eight states. Federal and state regulators from six states cited them for spilling benzene and other toxins.

"In 2001 they agreed to a thirty-five million dollar settlement with the Department of Justice, the State of Texas and five other states. Even though it was the largest fine that had ever been imposed for violating the Clean Water Act, it was basically a slap on the wrist for the criminal pollution of our ground and air—a small payoff for three hundred oil spills in Texas and five other states occurring over a ten-year period. The same year that fine was paid, the company generated many billions of dollars in profit."

"I wish I could say I was surprised," Moses said. "So you're saying history is repeating itself?"

"This time it's even worse," Deke replied. "The Swanson brothers have oil pipelines in Texas that spill benzene along with a cesspool of other toxins into the earth. This witch's brew is polluting aquifers across three Texas counties, and moving into neighboring states. We'll be trying to show these spills have caused everything from cancer to Parkinson's disease."

"How is it those brothers aren't behind bars?"

"Because we've got a DOJ that lets white-collar criminals off with fines that are the equivalent of their lunch money," Deke said. "That's why."

"If you don't have the DOJ backing you," Moses asked him, "how do you hope to succeed in this case?"

"We're gathering cases and we're going to bring an action, but that won't be enough. If the case is tried in Texas, we'll be overturned on appeal, even if we win, so we need to go about this in another way. What we'll need from you is to low-launch the story in the media."

"So you'll want us to bring out the trumpets," said Moses, "and make some noise. And our storyline is the Swanson brothers and what they're up to."

Deke nodded. "And then you can move on to getting the word out through progressive blogs."

"And you'll certainly want media coverage when the Corporate Response Group stages a rally at the Swanson refinery plants."

"Great minds think alike," said Deke. "The Swanson brothers have thrown so much money at the media that they'll be reluctant to take on this story unless we provide them with a show. So first we'll prime the media pump with information, and then follow up with noise, and finally give them theater."

"It will be hard for the media to ignore Corporate Response," said Moses.

"That's what I'm counting on," Deke responded. Corporate Response was a professionally organized group that was akin in many ways to the Occupy movement. They counted on theatrics to get their message across. Twenty-five to fifty protestors loudly shouted out news that would otherwise usually go unreported. Corporate Response targeted bad corporate citizens and their actions. The organization generated media attention with press conferences, sit-ins, boycotts, and demonstrations in venues ranging from posh country clubs to corporate shareholder meetings.

"Cockroaches hate light more than anything," Deke said. "I'll need all the light on the Swanson brothers I can get."

16
SHOWTIME

"It's not over until the fat lady sings," Deke told his team as they prepared for trial.

It was an apt expression. A big jury trial is like the grand opera. The language used might be foreign to most listeners, but the audience can still understand what's going on. In operas and trials lots of characters have parts in the proceedings. Each show has props they need to get ready, all designed for a grand stage. And during the production there is a lot of loud wailing, and counter-wailing; there is the beating of the breasts, and the cries of the aggrieved.

The choreography of a trial is as important as that of an opera, and it never seems as if there are enough hours in the day to adequately prepare. Deke and his team meticulously reviewed and edited trial depositions, turning them into effective attacks of about an hour each. Strategies were discussed for direct examinations, cross-examination attacks, and motion arguments. In trying to prepare for the trial, there were rehearsals, rehearsals, and more rehearsals.

The pretrial was an exhausting marathon. Young lawyers working the case found themselves dragging, and they couldn't help but marvel at Deke's energy. They were half Deke's age, but couldn't keep up with him. He didn't tell them the source of his motivation, and what was so fiercely driving him, but some probably guessed. The thought of Annica Phillips and his daughter Cara pushed him to keep going.

The Ranidol trial was scheduled to take place in state court in Spanish Trace, not far from the Bergman Deketomis offices. It was nice for Deke and his staff that they weren't the out-of-town team for once. They didn't quite have home field advantage, but the good news was that they wouldn't be facing Judge Beedles, as he was now out of the judiciary rotation. Judge James J. Conte had been assigned to the case. Conte was a rare middle-of-the-road judge who had a reputation for fairness. He also didn't suffer fools, and had made it known to both camps that no shenanigans would be tolerated in his court.

Angus and Threepio joined Deke in his office. All of them were taking a rare break. "I hear the media circus has hit town," Angus said. "All the networks will be covering the case."

"I wonder if Bekmeyer gave the reporters fruit baskets," Deke remarked.

"Maybe their chef is cooking for them," said Threepio.

That drew a few derisive laughs. Bekmeyer's defense team had set up shop at the Crowne Plaza Hotel in downtown Spanish Trace, taking over its top three floors to house their lawyers, expert witnesses, corporate staff, and PR spin doctors. They had even brought in a renowned chef and received special permission from the hotel management to allow him to cook for their team out of the main hotel kitchen.

"Wharton was looking a little chunky the last time I saw him," Deke noted. "It must be from eating all that rich food."

Wharton Garrison had brought a half dozen lawyers from Benton, Craighill & Wasserman's Manhattan offices to assist him. He also had eight personal paralegals.

"But all the jury will ever see is Garrison and three other lawyers," Angus said. "No one will see he's backed up by the Fifth Infantry."

"And two of those lawyers at his table are mostly for show," Threepio offered.

They were lawyers from the local firm of Long & Burton; it was Bekmeyer's way of showing the corporation had roots in the community.

"I heard one of my kids singing the Bekmeyer jingle the other day," Angus said.

"So much for the gag order," added Deke.

Weeks before, Judge Conte had forbidden counsel from discussing the case with the media. That had only encouraged Bekmeyer's saturation of the Spanish Trace market with both direct and subtle advertising. They had purchased TV and radio spots, billboards, and newspaper ads. Everywhere you turned some Bekmeyer product was saving lives and making the world a better place.

"The bigger they are," said Threepio, "the harder they fall."

"I resemble that remark," noted Angus.

"Maybe we should point out all the Bekmeyer employees in the courtroom," Threepio suggested. "In addition to their shadow jury, we know they'll have at least three jury analysts."

One of the analysts would be handling strategy; the second analyst would be observing body language, and the third would be supervising the shadow jury. Bekmeyer's shadow jury closely resembled the jury that had been picked. They consisted of local citizens paid to sit in the courtroom and imagine they were members of the Ranidol jury. Every day the reactions of this shadow jury would be relayed to Wharton Garrison and his team as a guide to what was working, and what wasn't.

"Bekmeyer might have its army, but we have Deke," Angus said."

The Ranidol trial was called to order on a Wednesday, the first day of April, by Judge Conte. The judge was a tall, heavyset man in his fifties with a full beard that somehow contributed to the aura he projected of intelligence and authority.

Before the jury was brought in for opening statements, Wharton Garrison requested to be heard. "Judge Conte," said Bekmeyer's lead counsel, "I would like to be reheard on the admissibility of three depositions Mr. Deketomis intends to show this jury. As I said when I raised this issue earlier, there was no mention in the deposition notice that these depos were being taken for use at trial or that Mr. Deketomis himself would be taking one of them."

Judge Conte was clearly displeased by this request. "We've been through this already, Mr. Garrison," he said dismissively.

"Yes, Your Honor. However, we would like to present our argument in more detail for your consideration—"

"I'm not going to grant the motion," the judge said. "These were depositions that in the State of Florida can be used for any purpose. That includes use at trial, Mr. Garrison. For reasons that are not clear to me, your attorneys chose not to ask any questions in regard to most of the documents discussed in those depositions. I can only assume that was a tactical decision on the part of your firm, but I'm not here to second-guess an esteemed lawyer such as yourself. Motion denied."

Deke knew better than to show his satisfaction at the ruling as the jurors were being ushered in. The jury looked surprised at how crowded the courtroom was. Bekmeyer's undercover staff and all the shadow jurors had left little space. The judge read a few preliminary instructions and then directed Deke to proceed with his opening statement.

Rising to his feet, Deke smiled at the jury. "Good morning, ladies and gentlemen. I will start out by telling you that my client, Ms. Tricia Baker, is very fortunate. I say that because the injuries caused by the drug that was manufactured by this defendant have so far been less severe compared to what the defendant company *foresaw* and *expected to occur* with thousands of other women throughout this country. But you will hear from medical experts about what the future risks are for Tricia. She has serious physical challenges still ahead.

"Ms. Baker is one of the luckier victims in this sad story, because as you will see in this trial, Bekmeyer clearly knew that the product they were selling increased the chances of a woman dying from physical complications by a rate of six times higher when compared to other similar birth control drugs. This case will be about physical problems that Ms. Baker endured and still suffers from. It will also provide you with a firsthand look at what happens when a drug company phonies up clinical data, *knowing* all the while their data is a lie *and also knowing* that this drug has the capacity to kill and cripple patients who take it."

Pausing, Deke silently counted to seven before continuing. Looking directly at the jury, he saw he had their full attention. "This company's own paper trail will show that not only did they lie to the FDA, but they also lied to doctors. And these doctors unknowingly passed along Bekmeyer's lies to their patients—people like Ms. Baker. Bekmeyer actually had scientific and medical information showing exactly how dangerous Ranidol really is. Nothing on their part was a mistake. Lies are not mistakes.

"In fact, you will see in this trial that three managers who were decision makers at the top of the company's food chain understood every aspect of how incredibly dangerous this drug could be. But I think what you will be most interested in are the documents showing that this product they referred to as their 'cash cow' was rushed to market, no matter what the risk was to human life."

Deke delved into further details of the drug before summing up. "I won't ask you to make any leaps of faith in this trial and simply believe what I'm telling you. My request is a simple one. Just read the documents as closely as we've read them, and understand that as you're reading them, *every one of them* came directly out of the defendant's most secretive and confidential files. In these documents you will see the level of corruption that resulted in Ms. Baker sitting in this courtroom today."

It was Garrison's turn. A good speaker, he seemed sincere as he described Ranidol's four million satisfied users. He sounded convincing when he talked about its development, the testing that went into it, and the FDA approval process.

Because Garrison knew that Deke had him boxed in with the videotaped depositions, he attempted to diffuse the situation with the jury ahead of time.

"Mr. Deketomis is going to show you a lot of depositions of field agents and salespeople—individuals who don't have access to the real studies. These people, who are good, regular working

Americans, didn't know how to interpret these documents Mr. Deketomis threw at them. You will see he ambushed these individuals in a way that wasn't fair to them. None of those deposed have ever been to the corporate headquarters. They are not familiar with the science and research that went into Ranidol, nor are they familiar with the FDA approval process. They simply didn't know the company's history, or its intricacies and inner workings, or the methods used in the production of Ranidol.

"You will also see how so many of the documents shown in those video depositions were used totally out of context. That is why I will introduce you to several experts, including Dr. Lydia Southland. Dr. Southland is the scientist who knows the most about Bekmeyer's history and pharmaceutical products. I think you will like her and believe her."

Deke assumed Southland would walk the jury through a well-choreographed presentation of a drug company, with its mission statement focused on healing the sick and improving the lives of people. She would portray Bekmeyer in the best possible light, saying that at every turn the company tried to make honest and reliable decisions that benefitted the American public as a whole. Deke had seen videos of Southland giving speeches to business organizations, doctors, and hospitals—basically sales pitches for Bekmeyer and what she categorized as "the honest, decent people" who had sustained and grown the "remarkable" company for five generations. In one talk he'd heard, Southland had emphasized that Bekmeyer was one of the oldest drug companies in Germany and had built their reputation by always employing management leadership devoted to making people's lives better.

Garrison concluded by explaining how proud he was to be representing such a humane company, which for years had been contributing to the world's welfare by saving "one life at a time."

On the third day of trial, Bekmeyer sales representative Bill Persons took center stage in the courtroom with his deposition shown on a giant video screen. As it became clear to Garrison and his team, the jury was absorbed by what they were watching. Deke hoped the jury's complete focus would ultimately turn to fury at Bekmeyer's thuggish behavior.

The edited footage began with Persons reading a document about Bekmeyer expanding its marketing for the use of weight loss and acne control, despite the fact that the drug had not been approved by the FDA for any other purpose than simple birth control. The document made it clear the company fully under-stood they were breaking the law by selling their product for other uses, but the most powerful and most damning moment was yet to come. Persons then read aloud from an in-house email stating that Bekmeyer had calculated profits against the potential number of consumers who would be injured; this most damaging email concluded that the company could pay for thousands of low-end injuries and still make a monstrous profit. The subject line on this email string read: *"Considerations for an exit strategy."*

Next, Deke called Tricia Baker to the stand.

Walking up to the witness stand, the young woman appeared unsure, but once she took her seat and Deke began to gently ask her questions she grew more confident. The recent college gradu-ate explained that she had been attracted to Ranidol because of its weight loss promises, which set it apart from the other birth control pills. Tricia came off as sweet and sincere—but even more important, she was believable.

"After about four months on Ranidol, I started having bad chest pains and the paramedics took me to the hospital," she said. "I almost didn't go because I couldn't imagine it was really a heart problem at my age. My family was terrified. They thought they would be saying goodbye to me. Luckily I recovered, or at least partially recovered. I've been prescribed heart disease medicine that doctors tell me I'll have to take for the rest of my life. And I have my liver function monitored monthly." She paused in her recounting, and looked at the defense attorneys. "The doctors hope for the best. I hope for the best. But I'm not sure I'll actually live long enough to marry and raise a family."

Deke had taken a chance picking Tricia as lead plaintiff. Her residual medical problems were less severe than many other women who had been permanently crippled by Ranidol. In fact her situation was potentially less severe than Cara's. But the longer she stayed on the stand the more credible she seemed to get. What Deke had feared would be the weakest part of their case appeared to be passing muster.

Garrison's cross-examination was short and focused almost exclusively on the fact that Tricia had been free of life-threatening physical problems since the time of her first moderate heart abnormalities. He further emphasized that her liver problems were stabilized by medications and treatments. Clearly, the defense's goal was simple: Their lead attorney could not expect to win, but he was aiming to hold damages down to as little as possible. To that end, Garrison's cross-examination may have been effective.

"Thank you so much for your help today," he said, giving Tricia his best smile.

It was an old trick, and Deke inwardly groaned when he saw Tricia smile back. Body language often conveyed more to jurors than words. But Deke knew how to refocus the jury's attention.

He immediately followed up on Tricia's testimony with another damning deposition. After that he brought to the stand an even stronger witness, an expert who addressed Bekmeyer's failure to be honest about its own in-house clinical data. He followed that with another deposition.

By day's end, Deke thought he noticed some of the jurors looking at Bekmeyer's defense attorneys with ill-disguised contempt.

The final day of the plaintiffs' case was taken up with testimony by Tricia's treating doctors and Deke's expert witness Dr. James Cooper. As a former head of the FDA, Cooper's credentials and authoritative testimony appeared to impress the jury. He gave chapter and verse on the FDA approval process, the clinical details about the drug, and its marketing. He established that Ranidol was the only oral contraceptive that contained the chemical ethodoxtrilinal, and that the drug had been approved in May 2001 to prevent pregnancy but not for other uses.

In one pointed answer that caught the jury's attention, Cooper testified that "after Ranidol was approved for common birth control, Bekmeyer immediately began marketing it with the claim that it had the benefit of helping women to lose weight and clear up acne. They did this with the full knowledge that it would take the FDA five years to sort through the studies and determine if the drug was truly aiding weight loss in a medically sound way."

"Did the FDA aggressively try to test and monitor Ranidol," asked Deke, "once it was on the market?"

Cooper shook his head and said, "That's not really the FDA's job. We don't do testing, nor do we do independent monitoring." After a pause he added, "The way it works is that each drug company primarily takes responsibility for determining the safety of its own products. For some reason, the public believes that the FDA does in-house testing on drugs. We never have. The agency would need a massively greater budget to do that."

"How big a budget?" asked Deke.

Cooper raised his hands and shook his head. "I have no idea, but I would guess in the tens of billions of dollars, which is many times greater than what Congress now provides. So what it boils down to is that it's very much an honor system that is dependent on the drug companies giving us true and accurate information about their clinical trials."

Whispers whipped around the courtroom as the shocking implications of what Dr. Cooper was saying were digested. It was a highly effective way to end the morning's testimony.

When the trial resumed, Garrison began his cross-examination by asking the former FDA head, "How can you be so critical of Bekmeyer Pharmaceuticals when on two separate occasions you applied for a job as a research director there?"

"I don't see that I'm being critical," said Cooper. "I'm just trying to answer the questions."

"You applied for a job at our client's company because you recognized that Bekmeyer is one of the premier pharmaceutical companies in the business, didn't you, Dr. Cooper?"

"I don't deny applying for the position as research director," said Cooper. "But as you must be aware, there has always been a revolving door of employees leaving the FDA and going to work for pharmaceutical companies."

"And you see nothing wrong with that?"

"If I go to work for a pharmaceutical company, I can provide them with an understanding of how the FDA works. I can tell them what the agency is looking for, and what the company can do that will be okay with the agency, and what will get them in trouble."

"You make it all sound very noble," the attorney said sarcastically.

Dr. Cooper responded with a snide remark of his own: "As to your earlier question, I think at one time Bekmeyer was truly a superb company. I'm not certain I could say that today."

After that *ouch* moment, Garrison shifted to another attack: "Can you tell us, Dr. Cooper, if this product was such a public danger, why you didn't pull it from the market?"

"Despite severe understaffing, the FDA handles a heavy load," Cooper said, giving the standard answer. "It's simply not possible for the agency to accomplish everything we would like to do for every product on the market."

"So what you're saying is that the FDA made no effort to pull Ranidol from the market. And you want this jury to simply believe you were too busy. Do I have that right?"

Deke knew that often moments like this played themselves out differently in the jury room than they did in the media or in the court of public opinion. A tired jury might not see this as a ploy by the defense to distract them from the most obvious questions: Why was the drug placed on the market to begin with? And why did Bekmeyer leave it on the market once they saw so many women dying?

He hoped that wasn't the case as Garrison ended his cross-examination.

Late on Friday, Deke rested his case. However, before he could even sit down, Garrison was back on his feet, moving for a directed verdict requesting that the case be dismissed. He argued that Deke had not presented a case that established any wrongdoing on behalf of Bekmeyer and that the judge was required to dismiss the case because of this. Even Garrison knew he was making an empty argument; what he was really doing was preparing the record for appeal.

It was 4:50 p.m., the witching hour for court proceedings. Judge Conte declared he would take up the motion for directed verdict first thing Monday morning and excused the jury for the weekend.

17

BLOOD ON THE WATER

At half past six that night, Deke left the office and headed for the stadium.

He was tired, and knew he shouldn't be doing anything but going home. If he hadn't committed to the event long ago, he wouldn't be doing it. All he wanted to do was spend an evening on the terrace with Teri unwinding. But that wasn't to be.

At least it was a benefit for a cause near and dear to Deke's heart. After working to restore the Hudson River, Robert Kennedy, Jr. had created the Waterkeeper Alliance, a grassroots environmental organization designed to stop the polluting of America's water-ways. It was Kennedy who had challenged Deke to put together what was now called the Spanish Trace Riverkeeper. The group had already successfully put an end to longstanding corporate pol-luting of the bay. Every time Deke went windsurfing in the Span-ish Trace Bay he took pride in that fact, and was glad Kennedy had made him think globally, but act locally.

That's why he was going to be a good sport and show up for a good cause. After all, with the Ranidol case making headlines, Deke found himself being a featured guest.

Deke arrived at the top of the third inning. One of the River-keeper members had an interest in the Blue Mantas baseball team, and was holding the fundraiser in the Hancock Bank Club. The game being waged on the field was clearly more of an afterthought than anything to all those attending.

Mark Prescott, President of Bergman Deketomis, was the first to spot Deke. He came at him with a bottle of cold beer, which Deke accepted. "And here I thought the belle of the ball wasn't even going to make an appearance," Mark said.

"You know there's always a spot on my dance card for you, Mark," Deke replied.

Prescott was the steadying hand of the firm. While Deke and Martin Bergman got most of the press, it was Prescott who saw to the day-to-day operations. Besides, it was Deke who had twisted his arm to make a generous donation to Spanish Trace Riverkeeper.

"That's good to hear," Mark said. "But I think you should know that just about everyone here is expecting to two-step with you."

"I hope you'll be willing to cut in frequently then," Deke told him. "I really am exhausted."

"I will be your knight in shining armor," promised Mark.

"You usually are," said Deke.

Mark was more political than Deke could ever be. He was the one who smoothed ruffled members in the community. Mark even managed to get along with the "chamber of commerce types and country club set," as Martin Bergman referred to them. It was that same country club set that had once blackballed Martin from joining their clubs because he was Jewish.

Ted Stuber, the Blue Mantas owner, joined Mark and Deke. Ted was footing the bill for the evening's gala. He was a great corporate citizen, and it was not the first time Deke thought how lucky Spanish Trace was having people like him looking out for the city's best interests.

"Ready to glad-hand?" asked Ted.

Deke took a big swallow of his beer. "Getting ready," he replied.

Trying to forget how tired he was, Deke began making his way through the room, and did his best to be a good representative of Riverkeeper. Deke doubted that he could ever be a very good politician, though. There were some people he couldn't muster up any fake enthusiasm for. Maggie Lee was one of those people.

Maggie was there as a representative of the press, although Deke suspected that she was probably there for all the free drinks and fancy food. She was a petite strawberry blonde who worked as a columnist for the *Spanish Trace News Journal*. Deke sometimes referred to her as "Little Bo Peep" because of the bows she invariably wore on top of her well-coiffed hairdo. That night's bow was green. Maggie was consistently unkind to Deke in print, so much so that he never felt overly compelled to make nice with her.

Maggie's first words to him were, "You owe me an apology, Nick Deketomis."

"What did I do now?"

"As if you don't know," she answered. "On camera you told that New York correspondent that Spanish Trace was a, and I quote, 'News reporting dead zone.' And then you insinuated there was no difference between me and Paula Deen."

What Deke had actually said was, "The lead columnist of our local newspaper doesn't see the difference between actual news and a recipe from a Paula Deen cookbook." But Deke decided not to make this distinction to Maggie.

"I am sorry if you took offense, Maggie," he said. "But I don't like it that my hometown newspaper seems to be writing copy worthy only of Fox News."

"It must be a blow to your ego that I don't gush over you, Deke."

"I think my ego will survive."

"I don't think it's heroic that you've gotten filthy rich terrorizing corporations that house and feed our citizenry."

"You've made that abundantly clear in your column," Deke replied.

"And I'll continue to make that clear."

"Edward R. Murrow, Seymour Hersh, Maureen Dowd, Gloria Borger, and Maggie 'Bo Peep' Lee," he recounted. "What's wrong with that picture?"

"You must think I'm incredibly stupid," she said.

"I guess you're right," he said, excusing himself.

As he walked away Deke was struck by the contradiction of his life inside and outside of a courtroom. In front of a judge or jury, Deke was always able to control his emotions. Yet outside the courtroom he was all too susceptible to losing that cool.

*　*　*

In the seventh inning stretch, after two beers and two sausage sandwiches, Deke told Mark he was leaving. He had managed to circulate through the entire room and have a word with everyone there.

"Get some sleep," Mark suggested, "and on Monday go slay the Bekmeyer dragon."

The parking lot was nearly empty of people. There was a good reason for that. The game was tied at two apiece. At any other time Deke would have loved to watch the finish of the game.

Ken Thorn had gotten thoroughly chewed out after his last failed encounter with Nick Deketomis. Darl Dixon had told him, in very graphic terms, what would happen if he didn't get Deketomis to take a few swings at him.

Ken didn't know that making Deketomis look like an out of control hothead was important to Pastor Rodney as well as to Dixon. He'd been purposely kept in the dark. The only thing he knew was that right now Dixon was the only thing standing between him and prison.

For weeks they'd been hoping to have another go at Deketomis, but he'd been so wrapped up in his big trial that they hadn't been able to get to him. Tonight was their big chance. Deketomis had been linked to some environmental fundraiser going on at the game. This was their opportunity.

"Don't blow it this time," Darl had warned him. "If you do, I don't think I can help you out of your situation."

As motivational speeches go, that had been the best possible one. Ken now wished Darl was at his side, though. While he was in great shape from all those trips to the gym, he was small in stature and Darl could help if things got rough. "You don't want anyone to be able to link us," Darl had explained. "If they do, I won't be able to help you. That's why all this has to be hush-hush."

Ken had kept it hush-hush. He hadn't even mentioned anything to his wife, other than to promise her that Pastor Rodney was keeping him on the "straight and narrow."

He took a few deep breaths, then drank from a plastic water bottle. The liquid burned his throat a little. It was a vodka and orange mixture. Liquid courage, thought Ken.

"Damn hot, isn't it?" he said.

The kid who was with him nodded. He was a teenager from Ken's neighborhood that he'd paid a Benjamin (well, Darl had given him the money) to do some filming with his camera phone. Ken had explained that he wanted him there to record him confronting a bully.

Ken took another fortifying gulp. The thought occurred to him that it was a camera phone that had gotten him into trouble, and now it would be one getting him out of trouble, provided he could get Deketomis to hit him.

The sound of footsteps alerted him to someone approaching. Ken stuck his head outside the bus he and the kid were hiding behind and couldn't believe what he saw. Nick Deketomis had left the game early and was walking their way.

Ken signaled the kid. The filming started. Stepping out from behind the bus Ken put himself in the lawyer's path.

"Hey chickenshit," Ken yelled. "Aren't you that hotshot asshole lawyer?"

Ken mentally prepared for his next provocation. But before he could even open his mouth Deke turned around and walked quickly away.

"What do we do now?" asked the kid with the camera phone.

Darl Dixon had coached Ken through all kinds of scenarios, but no one had ever imagined the lawyer would turn tail and run. Ken felt rather proud of himself and stood there clenching and unclenching his fists. Before staking out this spot, Ken and his photographer had identified the lawyer's car in VIP parking. The showoff drove a Bentley, making it easy to pick out.

"He ran in the opposite direction of where his car is parked," said Ken. "I say we go and wait for him there."

As Deke made his way through the parking lot, even he was surprised by how he'd reacted to the loudmouth who had accosted him. His response probably had something to do with the way he'd reacted to "Bo Peep." It just made sense to walk away from trouble.

A few minutes passed before Deke encountered a security guard. He was a young Hispanic man, wearing a very large shirt. "I'm glad to see you," said Deke.

"Yes, sir," said the guard in heavily accented English.

"You speak English?" asked Deke.

"Yes," the young man said, but not very confidently.

Deke's Spanish, unfortunately, was about on par with the guard's English. For a moment he considered trying to tell him what had happened, but instead decided all he wanted to do was get out of Dodge, and the faster the better.

"Can you tell me how to get to the parking lot for VIP parking?" Deke asked.

The guard didn't immediately react. Deke tried to think of the word for parking. When he blanked he pointed to the parking lot and asked, "*Persona importante* parking?"

The security guard seemed to suddenly understand and smiled. He made some odd gestures to indicate the correct area, and Deke thanked him. Luckily there was signage pointing the way. He walked along quickly, almost at a trot. All he wanted to do was get in his car and get home. When he spotted his car he let out pent-up air and rapidly ran over to unlock the door.

That's when his antagonist showed himself again, running right at Deke.

"I hear your slut daughter almost died from taking birth control pills," Ken shouted. "That would have served her right for sleeping around with every Tom, Dick, and Harry."

Deke reacted with primal rage. With his left hand he grabbed the man's shirt and lifted him off the ground. Then he brought back his right hand and delivered a vicious punch to the man's ribcage.

His assailant doubled over and his windbreaker opened. Deke saw him reach inside his jacket. Old habits came to the fore. In Deke's rough and tumble youth he'd had knives and guns pulled on him, and knew hesitation could result in death. Deke grabbed the only weapon available to him, his ballpoint pen, and clenched it in his fist like he would a knife. That's when Deke's attacker lunged at him, trying to hit him with a head-butt.

The impact plunged the pen deep into the smaller man's neck, a direct hit to his carotid artery.

Instinctively, Deke pulled the pen out of the man's neck and jumped back. Removing the pen caused an arc of blood to shoot high into the air.

As the man slumped to the ground Deke fell to his knees and applied pressure to the wound. The pulsing stream of blood slowed but didn't stop.

"Security!" yelled Deke. "Security!"

From the shadows, the kid that Ken had hired continued to film. He was too shocked to know what else to do.

18
A FAMILY UNITED

Adversity had brought the Deketomis family together. Almost losing Cara had made everyone in the family that much more grateful for what they had. Deke's emotional breakdown had brought Andy closer to him. Since that terrible night in the hospital Andy had come to realize how much his father loved both Cara and him. Since that time their longtime verbal sparring had stopped and not resurfaced.

But now the family was faced with another crisis.

Law firm president Mark Prescott had arrived at the Deketomis house while the media news vans were setting up outside. Although it was a gated community, the media had somehow bypassed those gates.

With camera lights silhouetting him, the door opened and Mark came inside. Teri hugged him. Then she stepped back and said, "Thank you for coming, Mark." She allowed herself no tears. Since hearing of the incident, she had expressed no doubts that Deke was innocent of any crime but bad luck. Andy was doing his best to follow her example.

"On TV they're saying Dad killed a man," said Andy. "Is that true, Uncle Mark?"

Because Mark Prescott was such an old family friend, Andy had grown up calling him "Uncle Mark."

"I am afraid it is true," Mark said. "But I don't know much besides that except your father says this man attacked him. He didn't have time to tell me anything else but 'go help my family.' He was insistent on that even though I didn't want to leave his side."

Andy saw that his mom managed to stay dry-eyed. He wished he could deny his own tears, but they began falling.

"The truth will come out," Mark told Andy. "That's what your father is always saying. I would take comfort in that. I believe in your father as I do in few other people, and I don't need to tell you he wouldn't hurt anyone unless it was an accident or he felt his life was in danger."

Both Teri and Andy nodded.

"Right now the media is setting up outside," Mark told them. "I've called the police. In a short time they should be moving the media to the entrance of the community's gates. Of course I imagine they will continue to try and sneak in, so I am arranging for additional security to man the gates. I will also have someone outside your home to keep away any other gawkers."

Mark's phone buzzed. He quickly read the text, and nodded.

"My handyman's outside."

"Is that supposed to be reassuring?" asked Teri.

"Jorge can figure out everything from electrical, to carpentry, to pipe fitting, to plumbing. Right now he's figuring out your plumbing."

"Why is he doing that?"

"I am sure in a minute that will become clear."

"When can we see Dad, Uncle Mark?"

"Gina Romano is already at the station. She is working to arrange his release as soon as humanly possible."

Teri found herself sighing with relief. Regina "Gina" Romano was not only a top criminal defense lawyer, but a friend of the family. In fact she was Cara's godmother, and lately had been a frequent visitor to her daughter's bedside at the hospital.

"Gina said that for now Deke will be placed in a holding cell at the county jail," said Mark. "She wants me to bring him a change of clothes, soap, toothbrush, a washcloth, and a towel."

"I'll pack a bag right now," said Teri.

"Why does Dad need those things?" asked Andy.

"He needs to clean up from what happened," Mark explained gently. "Appearances are important in situations like this."

The Deketomis house suddenly became awash in lights. News cameras were shining in windows and at the front door. The invasion of privacy was not only illegal, but annoying.

"I guess it's time," said Mark.

"Time for what?" Teri asked him.

Mark clicked out a quick text, and moments later they heard shrieks and excited shouting.

"What's going on?" asked Andy.

"Jorge just turned on every sprinkler you have, and at this moment I'm guessing every news camera and reporter has run for the safety of the street."

Deke paced around the holding cell. He was wearing an orange jumpsuit, his bloodied clothes seized as evidence. Even now he could see traces of blood on his hands. There had been a time when those who knew Deke wouldn't have been surprised to see him end up in jail. There had been a time when even Deke wouldn't have been surprised. After his mom had skipped out for good, and after Deke ended up in foster care, there had been spells when he'd lived on the street. A boy living on the streets doesn't survive without fighting. His juvenile record was a testament to that. But all of that had occurred long ago. Deke had wanted to believe he put that behind him. He'd even managed to channel that anger into his chosen occupation. The righteous indignation he displayed in court wasn't some act, but a memory of youthful wrongs he wanted to redress.

But now he had killed a man. He had taken a life and could not understand why. Deke put his head in his hands and wept.

Early the next morning, low-flying TV station helicopters that were circling the house woke up Andy. It was a stark reminder of the previous day.

Andy went and joined his mother. As soon as he appeared in the kitchen Teri turned off the television set. "You might as well leave it on, Mom. There's no way I'm not going to hear about what happened."

Teri looked at her son. Her baby was growing up right in front of her eyes. "We'll turn on the news later," she said. "But I want you to be prepared. It's not pretty. And a lot of people are saying unkind things about your father."

"Then they must not know him," Andy told her.

"That's right, they don't know him. They just want to think the worst. But that doesn't make it any less hurtful."

"Who did Dad"—Andy couldn't quite bring himself to say the word *kill*—"hurt."

"His name is Ken Thorn," said Teri. "I'm quite sure your father doesn't know him. I know I've never heard him say his name."

Teri's cell phone buzzed. She hadn't turned the phone off because she was hoping to hear from Deke or Gina. As Teri read the text she looked puzzled.

She read the message out loud: "Open the front door."

The strange thing was who had sent the text. Suddenly Teri ran to the door and threw it open. Sitting in a wheelchair was Cara. Mother and daughter hugged, and then it became a group hug when Andy joined in.

"Hey," said Cara, "let's get inside before those helicopters figure out what's happening on our front porch."

When Cara was wheeled into the kitchen Teri immediately tried to drape a blanket around her. "I am not an invalid, Mom," Cara said.

"You should still be in the hospital," Teri told her.

"I was supposed to be home the day after tomorrow, but the doctor gave me his blessings to leaving early."

Teri opened her mouth to argue, but then she couldn't help but smile. "Oh, sweetie," she said, "it's so good to have you home."

Later, it was Cara who turned on the TV. She even insisted they watch Fox 10, saying, "If anyone has bad things to say about Dad, it will be Fox 10."

The young, blonde anchor—Fox seemed to hire only young blonde female anchors—was showing footage taken the night before. "Police sources are telling Fox 10 that officers arriving at the scene found attorney Nike Deketomis atop the victim Ken Thorn. Even though Deketomis was covered in blood, he is said to have sustained no injuries. The altercation apparently occurred in the vicinity of where Deketomis had parked his car. We go now to Mindy Marin outside the Deketomis estate in Sea Breeze . . ."

Judging by the coverage being shown on all the local television stations, the only news in the entire world seemed to be the story of what had happened between Nick Deketomis and Ken Thorn. A favorite spot for live reports was the Holiness Southern Pentecostal Church where protests were taking place. Based on the signs and the shouting, it was clear that the parishioners had judged Deke as being guilty, and wanted to see him pay for his crime. At the same time they were portraying Ken Thorn as a martyr. In some pictures he was shown ascending to heaven where he was greeted by Jesus.

"This is Dave Shrigley reporting from the Holiness Southern Pentecostal Church," said the field reporter. "At my side is Pastor Rodney Morgan."

The poster-carrying crowd continued to walk by. Many were chanting, "Jesus wept, Jesus wept."

Shouting to be heard, the reporter yelled, "Ken Thorn was one of your parishioners, was he not, Pastor Rodney?"

"He was, Dave," said a somber looking Pastor Morgan. "He even coached our championship softball team."

From the studio a picture was shown of a number of girls in uniforms kneeling. When they returned to the live shot, the pastor appeared to be wiping a tear from his eye.

"What else can you tell us about Ken Thorn?" asked the reporter. "Do you have any special memories?"

"He was a family man," answered the pastor. "I know his wife Angela. She has taught Sunday school for many years. I knew him to be a devoted father, and a caring coach. I think he was happiest out on the playing field."

The reporter had to shout even louder to be heard over the chanting of the protesters. They were saying, over and over, "Lawyers lie, innocents die."

"Do you know if Mr. Thorn had a temper or ever got into any other fight or altercation?"

Pastor Rodney shook his perfectly styled hair. "That is not the Ken Thorn I knew."

The protestors continued to chant, "Lawyers lie, innocents die."

From the perspective of the Deketomis family, matters went from bad to worse as the day went on. Somehow footage turned up that was reportedly shot in the midst of the fight. Deke, covered in blood, appeared to be manhandling Ken Thorn. The physical disparity between the two men could clearly be seen, but that didn't stop commentators from pointing out, "As you can see, Deketomis is some eight inches taller and sixty pounds heavier than the victim."

Fox put together a montage of Deke railing against organized religion, and in particular the Holiness Southern Pentecostal Church. The film footage was clearly put together to leave the viewers wondering if the conflict between Deke and Thorn might have somehow been related to Thorn's church and religious beliefs. And when Fox 10 referenced Deketomis, they usually used his booking photo, which made Deke look psychotic.

Not to be outdone, the *Spanish Trace News Journal* put out a special edition with the banner headline: **DEKE SNAPS?** The trailing dots under the question mark were made to look like blood splatter.

In their time of need the Deketomis family was being helped by another family—that of Bergman Deketomis. Gina Romano called with frequent updates, and Carol Morris telephoned them to say that she and her team of investigators were working to find out what had really happened.

Martin Bergman stopped by the house to offer hugs and his personal support. The venerable lawyer was a legend in Florida and had mentored Deke in the practice of law. "Even though it's a Saturday," Martin said, "we're doing everything we can to have an emergency bond hearing today. Everyone at the firm is trying to make it happen."

Teri had done her best not to cry through all that was going on, but Martin's words brought tears to her eyes.

Still, even with the firm's support system fully in place, in the face of all the bad news the family felt as if they were under siege. The rallies at the Holiness Southern Pentecostal Church had expanded beyond their grounds; their parishioners were now protesting near the Deketomis house, and at the law firm.

"Phone call for you, Mom," Andy said.

He had designated himself as official phone screener, and had saved his mom from having to listen to the rants of some of the crazies who'd somehow gotten their number.

"Who is it?" asked Teri.

"Matthew Weissing," Andy replied. "He says you know him."

Teri grabbed the phone. "Matthew," she said, trying not to sound as down as she was.

"Hey, doll," he said, the same greeting he'd been using for more than thirty years. Matthew and Deke had been roommates in law school. Both of them had gone on to be tort lawyers, with Matt specializing in union actions.

"I'm seeing a bunch of crazies on the tube," he told her. "They're yelling all sorts of things I know are a bunch of crap. I think it's time to turn up the noise, but this time in support of Nick Deketomis. How's that sound?"

"It sounds like the trumpets of the cavalry, Matt. And they're arriving none too soon."

19
THE KNIVES COMING OUT

When the Deketomis family arrived at the courthouse for the bond hearing, there were at least fifty protestors, many holding up signs calling for the execution of Deke. The rush to judgment seemed not only hasty, but vicious. There were pictures of frying pans accompanied by the words, TIME TO FRY, and graphic representations of Old Sparky awaiting another victim.

There were almost as many reporters as there were protestors, which seemed to further incite those who were demonstrating. Teri saw the shock in Andy's face and put a protective arm around him. The situation felt volatile and out of control, especially without the reassuring presence of Deke. It was Deke who had always made them feel safe, but now he wasn't there, and there was the possibility he wouldn't be there for some time. The protestors were certainly clamoring for his pound of flesh, and more.

With two of the firm's security team beside him, Mark Prescott was waiting for them in a blocked-off area free of protestors and media. Cara had tried to convince her mother that she should be allowed to go with them, but that was one argument the future attorney hadn't won.

Mark opened Teri's door and gave her a hug. Then he shook Andy's hand. "It's going to be all right, kid," he promised.

His Uncle Mark almost sounded as reassuring as his dad, but not quite.

"Say nothing, do nothing, respond to nothing when you go into the courtroom," Gina Romano stressed to Deke. "You are not the lawyer here today. You are not in charge here. You are a humble supplicant appearing before a judge. Can you be a humble supplicant, Deke?"

He nodded his head.

"You might hear people shouting things. Some crazy might even try and spit on you. No matter what happens, you are not to react."

"Yeah, yeah," Deke snapped. "I'm a humble supplicant."

With a hard look Gina replied, "You better remember that, Nick Deketomis."

"I will," he said, and then added, "I'm sorry."

Deke hadn't slept since his fight in the stadium. In his mind he'd replayed what had happened over and over. The horror of what had occurred sickened him, and he still couldn't understand how or why it had happened.

"Keep your head up," Gina advised him. "There will be lots of cameras. The media wants a spectacle, but we won't be contributing to it."

Deke nodded. Earlier Gina had personally applied makeup to his dark circles in preparation for those cameras.

"Ready?" she asked.

"Ready," he said.

When they made it to courtroom, Deke saw it was packed, mostly with media. It was no surprise to him that Sunrise County Prosecutor Darl Dixon himself sat in the prosecutor's chair with sidekick Orville Sizemore next to him. Darl was dressed in what appeared to be a leisure suit with a solid red vest. He wanted to look like a good ol' boy, which he certainly did. This was his long-awaited chance to bring down Deke, and have the spotlight on him. Deke's downfall couldn't come at a better time for him in his state senate race against Lumon Maygard.

Judge Farley Wheeler took the bench. With short blonde hair, clear blue eyes, and a *Glamour* magazine face, she wasn't the picture that most associated with a judge. But it wasn't only her looks that had earned Judge Wheeler her position. She was smart, and had considerable legal chops. Judge Wheeler had attended Deke's alma mater, Cumberland Law School, and worked as a federal prosecutor in Miami for ten years before becoming a judge. As an assistant DA she'd unflinchingly taken on the drug cartel.

She called the court to order. A murmur of whispers continued. Judge Wheeler slammed the gavel down hard enough to hammer a nail. "The first person to speak when not spoken to by this court will be held in contempt and removed by the bailiffs to a holding cell, where they will spend the rest of the weekend," she said.

The courtroom promptly fell silent.

Judge Wheeler spoke to Dixon, "Are you prepared to charge this defendant?"

Everyone who actually knew Deke had to be wondering the same thing: Without a special grand jury reviewing the facts, was Dixon actually ready to charge him with a crime?

Dixon jumped to his feet. He looked like a kid being called for ice cream. "Your Honor, the state is charging Nicholas Deketomis with manslaughter. We are reviewing the evidence, but it appears that the defendant Nicholas Deketomis and the deceased, Mr. Kenneth Thorn, argued in at least one location fifteen minutes prior to Mr. Thorn dying at the hands of Mr. Deketomis." Dixon paused for effect, no easy task because he was clearly so excited. "As there may have been premeditation, the state will be considering changing the charge of manslaughter to murder in the first degree."

Deke saw behind the calm gaze of his counsel the firm directive for him to do nothing. He wanted to react. He wanted to respond to Darl's ill-concealed smile. But he did the hardest thing—nothing. For someone used to being in control, this was torture. Behind him, Deke knew his family was watching. He hated thinking how helpless he must appear to them.

Darl opened his mouth to continue, but Judge Wheeler had already had enough of his showboating and spoke before he could. "Mr. Dixon, as I expect you are aware, the only issue before you today is the nature of the charges you are prepared to file. This is not a media appearance, is that clear?"

Dixon responded with a "Yes, *ma'am,*" heavily emphasizing the "ma'am" in such a way that it was more demeaning than respectful. Then he began his argument that the court should not allow Deke to be freed on any amount of a bond. "Your Honor, the defendant has a yacht, and he has a jet that can be in Mexico in an hour. If we bond him, it will look like you have granted unjustified favoritism based on his wealth and high profile in the community. Furthermore, Judge, you need to know that in the State of Florida, the law states—"

She cut him off. "Having graduated from law school and served on the bench for a number of years, Mr. Dixon, I'm well aware of Florida law. And you should take note that I will not be lectured in my courtroom as to what I need to know. Now let's move on. From what I see here, the charge in front of me today is manslaughter. Is that correct?"

Dixon nodded. "Yes, *ma'am*," he said, again hitting hard on the last word.

The judge turned toward the defense table where Deke sat with Gina Romano, and acknowledged his counsel. Gina stood up to address the judge. She was wearing her customary Chanel pantsuit; this one was a dark navy. The cut was flattering, but Gina could wear rags and make them look good. Her dark, Mediterranean good looks came from a combination of Jewish and Sicilian ancestry. What was of more interest to Deke was Gina's courtroom acumen. She had tried and won scores of complex criminal cases.

Although Gina had been prepared to discuss the setting of bond, she made the on-the-spot decision to try not to potentially misstep as Darl Dixon had. Getting on a judge's bad side was not a good way to start court proceedings. With no posturing, with a minimum of words, Gina put forth an offer that she thought Judge Wheeler would likely find acceptable. "Your Honor, we request bond to be set at two million dollars, and we will surrender Mr. Deketomis's passport."

Prior to the hearing, Gina and Deke had already gone over the strategy: Propose an incredibly high bond to provide the judge cover.

Dixon began to rise, but before he could straighten his knees, Judge Wheeler pointed to him. He sat back down, looking sheepish.

"Bond is set at two million dollars," she ruled. "Court's adjourned."

Assistant Prosecutor Orville Sizemore sat next to Dixon throughout the proceeding. As was usual, Sizemore said nothing. As was also usual, Sizemore couldn't help but think what a buffoon his boss was. It was a daily struggle to stay on this jackass's good side. Sizemore was clearly the number one lawyer on his small team, with a stellar record of twenty-six convictions in twenty-eight major felony trials. Of course he had his sights set on becoming the next state attorney for the district once Dixon moved on to the state senate.

Sizemore's distaste for his boss was more personal than philosophical. But there may have been more character and personality similarities between Dixon and Sizemore than he'd ever want to admit. Sizemore had a reputation for being ambitious and willing to promote his career at any cost, which made him suspect among other prosecutors and defense lawyers. He was also aware of whispers behind his back that he was willing to withhold exculpatory evidence that on occasion might have freed a defendant from prosecution. The gossip was true: Sizemore did whatever it took to get a conviction, even if that meant massaging critical truths when explaining cases to judges. Sizemore's threats and heavy-handed treatment of prosecution witnesses often rendered it impossible to know whether their testimony was the truth or coerced fantasy.

He had graduated from Pepperdine in California, where law students were heavily steeped in conservative ideology. He thought it was unfair that what he saw as an excellent law school was most famously known as the base for faculty member Kenneth Starr, the special prosecutor in the Bill Clinton-Monica Lewinsky scandal and author of the salacious Starr Report complete with detailed descriptions of oral sex and Lewinsky's stained dress. Even in Sizemore's mind, Kenneth Starr was an embarrassment.

As a conservative, Sizemore's values were not so very different from his boss's, but he thought Dixon erred in the direction of being too steeped in a tea party quality of politics. Nevertheless, both were genuinely convinced that if unchecked, the ungodly liberals would bring a disastrous end to the American way of life.

It was the good fight, Sizemore thought, but it would be an even better fight if his boss wasn't such a showboating bumpkin.

Prosecutor Darl Dixon rushed out of the courtroom so fast that he was on the courthouse steps and in front of the cameras even before the Deketomis family left their seats. As the cameramen set up their shots, Dixon straightened his tie and composed himself.

Clearing his throat, he said, "My office strongly opposes Nick Deketomis being released on bail. We are outraged that a judge who attended the same law school as the defendant would be allowed to render bail judgment in this tragic case. There are early indicators that Deketomis could have walked away from this incident but instead he jammed a fountain pen into the neck of a decent, unarmed man."

Publicly attacking a judge was out of line for a state attorney, but Dixon was going for broke, fully confident that in a matter of months he would be a state senator—a position far superior to that of any low-level state court judge.

The assembled reporters began shouting questions. Though Dixon provided no meaningful information about Kenneth Thorn's death, he dragged out his answers, hoping to parlay his remarks into receiving the maximum amount of television time. He repeatedly stressed how "a rich lawyer" had killed "a model citizen" whose interactions with the youth in the community enriched young lives.

Well aware that the media and local culture had a tendency to believe the worst, Dixon's goal was nothing short of destroying

Deke before any trial ever took place. He knew that the TV cameras would turn full focus even on someone as saintly as Mother Teresa if they could dig up any hints of a sordid story from years earlier. Most news outlets cared little that lives could be unjustly ruined from stories hastily created and then promptly transmitted. Dixon intended to use the media's recklessness to his advantage.

He was miffed to hear one particularly annoying reporter question his prosecutorial acumen. She said, "You arraigned this man far more quickly than usual, so quickly that there hasn't been time for a meaningful investigation of the facts. It would be easy to look at this and think it sounds like you are a prosecutor out for revenge." The nasty wench laid it on even thicker: "After all, it's no secret you and Mr. Deketomis have a fractious history. Does all the grandstanding we just saw in court have anything to do with that?"

Too happy with himself and the latest turn of events to let her rain on his parade, Dixon refused to be ruffled and stayed on message as he spoke with assurance. "My goal is to approach this case with a strong measure of responsibility. Mr. Deketomis does not have the right to privileges that separate him from anyone else. Of course, there is always a presumption of innocence. But we have overwhelming evidence against him, as you'll see."

Dixon was well aware that he was turning the Florida Lawyers Ethics Code on its head and that Judge Wheeler was bound to come unglued, but at the moment reckless abandon seemed like the most beneficial political course for him. He would overcome all potential annoying sanctions once he grasped his new power as a state senator.

Teri stayed behind with Gina Romano while Mark Prescott escorted Andy to their car. The firm had prepared for a bond possibly as high as five million dollars. Deke would soon be home.

Prescott could see the young man looked troubled.

"Hey, kiddo," he said. "Everything went fine. Your dad will be home tonight."

Andy nodded, but then asked the question weighing heavily on his mind. "If my dad is sentenced to manslaughter, how long would he be in jail?"

"That's not going to happen," Mark replied.

"But if it did happen?"

Mark shrugged. "That could mean fifteen years or more."

Andy merely nodded.

Not far away from them the demonstrators began their shouting once more. The reason quickly became obvious: The news cameras had returned.

20

BEHIND CLOSED DOORS

As Gina Romano had promised Teri, Deke was returned to their Sea Breeze home in the late afternoon. The awkwardness that Deke had felt about finally returning home vanished when his welcoming family showered him with hugs.

"What are you doing here?" Deke asked Cara. "You should be healing."

"Now that you're home I am healing," she said. "You can't imagine how much better I'm feeling right now."

"That's two of us," he said. "That's two of us," he repeated.

Deke fought back tears, but not very successfully. "Everyone is going to start thinking I'm a softy," he commented.

"Don't worry about that, Dad," said Andy. "We all know better."

The family settled on some much needed laughter. But when the smiles melted away Deke tried to address the elephant in the room.

"I wish I could tell you what happened last night. I don't have any answers yet. I can only tell you how sorry I am. One moment I was walking toward my car, and the next moment this man I didn't know was in my face screaming like a crazy person. I thought he was reaching for a weapon, so I grabbed the only sharp object I had, a ballpoint pen. That's when he came at me, and somehow in the struggle my pen ended up in his throat."

Deke stopped talking. The memory of all the blood made him still feel queasy and weak.

"We love you, Dad," said Cara.

There, thought Deke. That was the anchor he needed to hold on to. He bit down on his lip in an effort to hide its trembling.

"Are you hungry?" asked Teri. "We got some special takeout for you."

Since the incident Deke hadn't even thought about food. "What?" he asked. "Sprouts and lentils?"

"Barbecued ribs, chicken, mashed potatoes, baked beans, and coleslaw," she said. "Tomorrow you'll get the sprouts and lentils."

Behind closed doors other important meetings were taking place in Spanish Trace, including at the offices of Bergman Deketomis where the partners were having an emergency meeting. Martin Bergman had been on the phone all day. The last call he'd made had been to Deketomis who was now safely at home. What Deke had told him wasn't surprising; it was Deke all over.

Mark lit a cigar, Cuban of course. It was a nonsmoking office, but it was also an office with his name over the front entryway and on the company letterhead.

Martin was aware that many people regarded both Deke and him as being too flamboyant. That might not be an advantage to Deke in his current situation. Martin owned two local restaurants, the town's only gay bar, and the 24-hour cable TV station

WSBD-TV. He had spent an entire career needling the establish-
ment. Recently he had donated ten million dollars to the University
of Florida. Because of his donation the new law school library was
being named after him. That would annoy the old guard, Martin
knew. Those same silk-stocking, corporate trial lawyer wannabes
would even protest putting the name of Clarence Darrow on the
law school building simply because Darrow had defended the rights
of corporate prey rather than corporate predators.

The Bergman Deketomis partnership worked because both
Martin and Deke—and every other lawyer in the firm for that
matter—could muster at will the same caliber of contempt for
those who were comfortable doing harm to other people.

Martin had recruited Deke to join the firm twenty-seven years
earlier. At the time, Deke was a prosecutor in Tallahassee, not
earning much of a living, but in love with what he did. Neither
of the men would ever forget the day Martin stopped Deke in a
hallway after a trial and asked if he had ever considered private
practice. He explained to Deke that his firm needed a matrimonial
lawyer who could handle the big cases that regularly rolled in the
door. Soon after, Deke had signed on.

A year later, Deke abandoned matrimonial law for a huge lawsuit against beverage manufacturer Zest-O, a company that for
years had loaded their orange sports drinks with an unusual dye
known to be carcinogenic. Fitness enthusiasts had suffered and
died. Of course the lawsuit led to criticism by the U.S. Chamber of
Commerce that argued Deke and Martin's firm were ambulance-
chasing opportunists. Martin had been annoyed that Deke was
straying from his proscribed role as a divorce lawyer—that is, until
the tsunami of settlement fees flooded in.

He snubbed out his cigar, hoping his assistant wouldn't smell it
and castigate him for spreading putrid old man aromas throughout

the office. That was the downside to having a strong-willed staff, he thought.

Martin walked down the hallway to the firm's conference room. From inside he could hear all the partners talking among themselves. Martin walked inside, and the din in the room lessened. He took the empty seat at the head of the long table. All the other seats were taken except for the chair at the end of the table where Deke usually sat. Nineteen sets of eyes, every Bergman Deketomis partner, stared at him.

"The Ranidol case has been postponed until Wednesday," Martin said.

Everyone in the room already knew that, but nodded anyway.

"And I just finished talking with Deke. He assured me his difficulties were not going to interfere with Ranidol, and that he had no intention of willingly stepping aside as lead counsel of the case."

"I am glad to hear that Deke feels he's well enough to proceed," said Mark Prescott, "but in this instance that might not be the most prudent course. I think I would be remiss in my fiduciary duties to not point out that Deke's personal situation could impact Ranidol. And that's not all he's got on his plate. He's got the Swanson brothers and the S.I. Oil lawsuit that he committed to."

"What are our clients saying?" asked Angus.

"Our clients love Deke," Bergman countered. "They are not going to want him off any of their cases."

"In good conscience we're going to need to warn those clients," said Prescott. "Deke's situation is going to bring out negative media coverage, and potential jury poisoning. That might not sit well with other law firms and their Ranidol clients. If things don't go well, we might be potentially liable."

"Or we could just be looking for problems that aren't really there," Martin said.

When you get a roomful of lawyers, you have to expect a lot of talking. After fifteen minutes of discussions, it was clear the room was divided. Martin Bergman spoke over the others until his was the only voice in the room.

"There would be no Ranidol cases without Deke," he told them. "There wouldn't even be a mass torts division at this firm. He's the difference between us grossing forty million a year, and the hundred million gross last year. If Deke says he can finish the trial, I say we should let him finish the trial."

"What worries me," responded Prescott, "is that Deke might win the battle and lose the war. Yes, I'm sure he'll do a great job closing out Ranidol. But is the media going to take notice of that, or are they going to focus on his victim? Are they going to paint him as Nero busily fiddling while Rome burns? I spoke to Gina and she advised Deke not to go forward with the Ranidol trial for fear it will impact his criminal defense. How will his conducting a civil trial look just days after he's accused of murdering an innocent man? Gina says that he can't help but come across as callous and uncaring."

"I'm afraid she's right," Angus said. "The downside of his proceeding with Ranidol far exceeds the upside. That's why I'd like to take over the Ranidol trial. I can promise you we won't miss a step."

Heads around the table began nodding. Angus was known as being levelheaded and a clear thinker. His arguments were usually so well-reasoned that most people trusted whatever he had to say.

"And there's one other important factor to consider," added Angus. "An hour ago Pastor Rodney Morgan announced that he would be conducting Ken Thorn's funeral service this Wednesday morning at nine o'clock. That's no coincidence. Pastor Rodney apparently knows that's the same time as the Ranidol trial. Can you imagine how that's going to look? The media will make it look like our firm is complicit not only in a murder, but in a robbery. They'll portray Deke as trying to shake down Bekmeyer at the same time his victim is being buried. How can Deke not look ruthless and insensitive?"

"Your points are well-taken, Angus," said Martin. "In fact when Deke and I talked a short time ago he made most of the same points. At the same time, though, he said that he was convinced that nothing would make him appear more guilty to the general public than his backing out of the Ranidol trial. Deke contends that an innocent man wouldn't be deterred in his duty, and because he is an innocent man, he feels compelled to proceed."

"It's going to be a circus," mused Mark.

"If Deke wants to be the ringleader to that circus," Martin said, "then it is the position of this firm that he will be."

The patriarch had spoken, and though it was doubtful most of the partners agreed with him, all would be unwavering in their support of Deke, and of Martin.

Martin looked around the table. "No, it's not business as usual," he told them, "but let's try to make it appear to be business as usual. Now let's get to work."

21
TWIN TRIALS

As much as Deke tried to focus only on the upcoming Ranidol trial, he couldn't ignore his own trials and tribulations. All his life he'd been able to compartmentalize, but never had he been caught up in such a shit storm. His sleep, such as it was, had become troubled. Deke didn't tell anyone, but he was afraid he was suffering from a form of PTSD. Under very different circumstances two people had died in his arms. He wasn't the cause of Annica Phillips's death, but he'd never forget the way she'd looked at him while struggling to breathe.

Ken Thorn had also looked at him with bewildered eyes. It was as if he wasn't sure himself what had brought him to his untimely end. Everything had happened so quickly. Self-preservation had compelled Deke to grab his pen and brandish it. At the same instant Thorn had propelled himself at Deke.

No weapon had been found on Thorn. That made it look as if Deke had been the aggressor. He tried not to think about that. He did his best to avoid distractions. But there was no getting around his personal trials, or the impending Thorn trial.

On Monday, Judge Wheeler ordered everyone back into the courtroom, Deke included. That caused the media to be out in force again along with the protestors. As it turned out, it was Darl Dixon that Deke had to thank for taking him away from his Ranidol preparations. Darl had a habit of causing collateral damage wherever he went.

Judge Wheeler, like everyone else, had seen Dixon's comments to the press after the bond hearing.

"A gag order is now in effect," the judge informed them, eyeing all the principles of the case. "Anyone violating this order does so at his or her peril."

She singled out Dixon for her most threatening stare. "Is that clear, Mr. Dixon?"

Darl looked singularly unconcerned, "Crystal, *ma'am*," he replied, his mock-respectful answer managing to sound both petulant and insolent.

"I am putting you on notice now, Mr. Dixon, that at the conclusion of this case I will be holding a sanctions hearing on your conduct."

Darl stifled a yawn. The only thing people would remember at the conclusion of the case was that he'd put Nick Deketomis's ass in jail. Besides, it didn't matter that he couldn't speak in public. He'd already had his say, and it had gotten huge airplay. And there were other ways to be heard anyway, ways that he was already working on.

Dixon had put into motion a back-channel effort to leak selective information through right-wing social media backed by letter-writing campaigns from Pastor Rodney's church networking. It was a win-win for Dixon. Attacking Deketomis was hugely satisfying, and the media coverage was an even bigger plus that was already paying dividends for his electoral campaign.

While the pretty judge upbraided him some more, Darl sat there thinking it was time he bought himself a few new suits.

As the Wednesday Ranidol court date approached, Deke began second-guessing himself. Was his being lead counsel the right thing to do, or was it his ego speaking? Deke knew Martin Bergman had stuck his neck out for him. And there were plenty of others who had stuck their necks out, but in different ways.

The day before the trial Deke took a call from Texas attorney Tim Crum. "If you're not able to talk now I understand," Tim said. "I know this must be a terrible time for you."

As tempted as Deke was to say he'd call him back after the trial, he heard something in the man's voice that prompted him to say, "Now's fine for talking, Tim. What's up?"

"I'm sort of calling to find out how things are going with the Ranidol trial," Tim said, "especially after what's happened to you."

"Putting my personal problems aside," answered Deke, "I'm happy with how things are going with Ranidol, and I'm hoping tomorrow is going to be a very good day for us."

"How hopeful are you?" asked Tim.

"I'd say we definitely have the wind at our backs. In jury trials you never know, but my gut says things are going our way."

"I'm glad to hear that, Deke. I know this must seem like old hat to you, working all the big cases you have. I am more used to being in the trenches myself. Maybe that's why all this feels scary as hell."

"Everybody in mass torts started in the trenches, Tim. Me included."

"Yeah," Tim said, his voice trailing off. "But there's a difference between being involved and being committed. It's like the chicken and the pig talking about ham and eggs. The chicken is involved, but that pig is committed."

"What are you saying, Tim?"

"I'm committed to this Ranidol case. I've rounded up a lot of clients for you. A *lot* of 'em. Do you know what TV advertising costs?"

Deke could hear the fear in Tim's voice, and tried to reassure him with his own controlled tone. "I do. And I have a good understanding about the risks you have taken based on my word. I'm sorry that what happened to me has contributed to your unease. You think it scares you? I'd be lying if I didn't admit that it scares me too. But you heard it here first . . . I'm going to pull through every bit of this. And I'm going to pull you through with me."

"If it were only me, I wouldn't be as scared," Crum said. "I don't have an entire law firm behind me like you do. I've got eight people on staff that I won't be able to pay in a matter of weeks. All the costs have mounted up from the TV ads, and vetting prospective clients that have been on Ranidol and getting medical records and paying doctors to evaluate those claims. I guess when I signed on with you I thought we'd have settled by now. With the cash only going out, I'm desperate. I refinanced my house and took a big loan from the bank. All that's gone, invested in this case."

"What can I do to help?" Deke asked him.

"I hate to ask you at a time like this," Crum answered, "but I need a loan. I'm not asking for a gift, just a loan. If our Ranidol ship comes in, that's great. I'll pay you right back. But if it doesn't, I'm going to need money to keep my firm afloat. You'll get it back, I promise."

"I know I will, Tim. I'm not worried about that. How much do you need?"

"Can you loan me a hundred and fifty thousand? That will be enough for me to not have to lay anyone off. And I'll be glad to pay interest on it if you want . . ."

"That won't be necessary. I'll wire it to your bank right now if you have your account number and the ABA number."

Choking up, Tim said, "God bless you, Nick Deketomis."

Deke hoped God was listening.

Deke, Angus, and Mark drove to court in the same car on Wednesday morning. While the other two lawyers might have disagreed with Deke's continuing as lead counsel, they wanted to show him they had his back.

The area surrounding the courthouse was mobbed with camera trucks, protestors, and what appeared to be an entire church congregation wearing black clothes, presumably mourning Ken Thorn. Among their numbers was a group of children kneeling in prayer and holding small black crosses up toward the sky. Using their cell phones, other protestors gleefully took the little martyrs' pictures. Deke thought it was a scene that could have been directed by Wes Anderson, or maybe Cecil B. DeMille. Pastor Rodney's group had become well organized.

Union counter-protestors organized by Deke's friend Matthew Weissing held up signs supporting Deke. The union signs were straightforward and simple. Most read something to the effect, INNOCENT UNTIL PROVEN OTHERWISE. A few took aim at the religious protestors by quoting from Christ with such signs as: JUDGE NOT LEST YE BE JUDGED.

Flanked by two huge security guards, Deke, Angus, and Mark made their way toward the front entrance of the court. The other men had wanted to go in the back way, but Deke hadn't wanted to make it look as if he was hiding. He was there for his accusers, who roared their disapproval of him.

Police officers lined the steps and made sure the crowd was kept back. At the security checkpoint, the officer on duty took his time running his wand up and down Deke's body, even though he'd already walked through the metal detector. The photographers loved the display, snapping shots of Deke with his arms raised.

The attorneys started the morning in Judge James J. Conte's chambers to argue the motion for a directed verdict that Wharton Garrison had asked for on Friday. Most directed verdicts were rarely granted. All the plaintiff had to prove was that they had established valid questions about key facts raised in the trial that the defense didn't or couldn't answer. As far as Deke was concerned, Bekmeyer was still on the hook for having created a dangerous product that harmed the claimant, as well as having clearly marketed the drug beyond its approved purpose. Still, it was up to the judge to determine whether Deke had presented a sufficient amount of evidence to enable a jury to answer yes or no to those key questions.

When Deke and Mark arrived in Judge Conte's chambers, Wharton Garrison and his team were already there. The defense lawyers didn't even try to hide their glee. They were clearly enjoying Deke's misery.

"How was your weekend?" Garrison asked.

Deke let out a genuine laugh. He could appreciate gallows humor, even at his own expense. "Your concern is touching, Wharton," said Deke. "Just as I am sure you would have asked Mrs. Lincoln how she enjoyed the play."

Mark Prescott wasn't as charitable, and offered up a rare profanity. "Fuck off, Garrison."

"Touchy, touchy," replied Garrison. "You guys sure you're up to working today?"

At that moment Judge Conte entered the chamber and made it clear that he'd overhead the entire exchange. "Mr. Garrison, based on what I heard last week, you might have other issues to worry about instead of what kind of weekend Mr. Deketomis had. Now let's start, shall we?"

The judge briefly heard from both sides on the motion for a directed verdict and then promptly denied the motion. The case against Bekmeyer would continue. Judge Conte invited the lawyers to return to his courtroom.

As soon Deke entered the courtroom, the chatter picked up considerably. Catcalls rang out from the rear of the room. "Murderer!" one woman yelled. That was enough for the bailiff to make his way to her seat to remove her. When the bailiff grabbed her arm, the woman began slapping at him.

While this skirmish raged, Judge Conte took the bench. "Order!" he yelled. "I will not allow outbursts in my courtroom. In fact if I hear even a peep out of anyone else I will clear this courtroom except for the parties involved in this trial. Is that clear?"

The silence showed that it was. Judge Conte glowered at those in the courtroom while order was restored. He instructed court security to charge the woman and have her detained twenty-four hours until she could be arraigned. When the jury returned to the courtroom, Garrison's consultants had a laser-like focus on its reaction to Deke's presence in the courtroom. Even the shadow jury was watching for their reaction. Interestingly, there was none. The judge had clearly given them instructions, and they were admirably behaving like poker-faced soldiers.

Garrison rose to present his first witness. He needed to establish that Deke's depo document blast was irrelevant because the salespersons were not experts. He called Dr. Lydia Southland to the stand.

Southland was nicely, if conservatively, dressed. She had on a print jacket, a button blouse, and a skirt that extended below her knees. The makeup she was wearing looked professionally applied. Deke suspected it had been put on to try and temper her somewhat severe looks.

In preliminary questioning, Garrison reiterated her many qualifications. Dr. Southland held doctorate degrees from Yale and Cornell and was a Bekmeyer in-house scientist with an office wall covered with honors she had received during her twenty-four years with the company.

Garrison needed Southland to resonate with the jury. It was her job to wash away the previous week's damage. The attorney proceeded with a series of softball questions that allowed her to extol the safeguards used by Bekmeyer in developing and producing its products. She explained the process in detail and looked toward the jurors in a matter-of-fact manner, as if assuring them of her rectitude, and Bekmeyer's. "The hardworking salespersons you heard from last week would not have been included in the information loop about the nuances of product research and testing. Nor would those individuals have played any part in the FDA approval process. But I can answer the questions they couldn't, the questions that they frankly weren't qualified to answer."

She testified about how Bekmeyer went through an exhaustive process to provide safe medicine and accurate research. Her testimony centered on how the company conducted endless studies and counted on the FDA to give them guidance about their products.

"There have been a lot of powerful accusations leveled by both sides against the FDA during this trial," she said. "The simple fact is that every drug company relies on the FDA for guidance. After all, shouldn't we be able to do that? Where else would we be expected to turn?"

It was clear Southland had been coached to sell the defense line that shifted blame to the FDA. "We have a reputation to uphold," she said, "and we did our part. Being a longtime and proud employee of Bekmeyer, I know the history of the company. And I know the history of this drug. Both are sound."

Garrison decided to expound on Southland's last statement. Deke's face showed nothing as he listened to the opposing counsel's line of questioning, but inwardly he exulted. Garrison asked her to tell him about some of Bekmeyer's glorious accomplishments, which Southland was more than happy to do.

As far as Deke was concerned, Southland could have saved everyone time and just inserted Bekmeyer's name into Boy Scout law and said, "Bekmeyer is trustworthy, loyal, helpful, friendly, courteous, and kind." He listened as she extolled the company as a bastion of ethics, honesty, compassion, and decency. Without flinching or making any objections, Deke sat silently as Garrison opened a door to a line of questioning that he should have avoided.

In considerable detail, Dr. Southland explained to the jury that the reason Bekmeyer was such a remarkable company could be traced to its stellar leadership that went back almost a century. Deke saw that the jury appeared impressed with her testimony. Some of the jurors nodded when Dr. Southland testified, "Bekmeyer has developed a marble reputation for honesty and integrity because of the superb reputation of the people who built it."

To Deke's delight, Garrison had chosen to overreach, ignoring a fundamental rule when it comes to trial testimony about the overall character of the defendant company. Character—good or bad—is never an issue that can be broadly attacked on cross-examination by a lawyer unless the other side introduces that specific topic during direct examination. Once the issue of a company's "good character" is introduced by a defendant, the door is blown wide open for the opposing counsel to cross-examine and fully explore the witness's actual knowledge of the company's "bad character."

Deke could only assume that the publicity surrounding his arrest had made Garrison overconfident. His questioning of Dr. Southland opened the door for Deke to thoroughly and aggressively cross-examine her.

After another highly rehearsed thirty minutes, Garrison finally thanked Dr. Southland for her clarity and wisdom.

Deke slowly stood to begin his cross-examination. "Dr. Southland, you said in your testimony that you know the history of your company in part because you have worked there for the last twenty-four years. Is that correct?"

"That is so, yes," she replied, her tone pushing back. "Isn't it also true, Dr. Southland, that you've given speeches all over the country and spoken at length about what a responsible and wonderful company Bekmeyer has been since its inception? Isn't that right?"

"Yes, I have, and it is."

Deke pressed on. "Just a few minutes ago, you told this jury in effect that we should judge the honesty, decency, character, and level of compassion of Bekmeyer favorably in large part because of the fine people who have built the company all the way back to the 1930s. And I think you described those people as honest, decent, and compassionate. Is that right?"

Southland remained self-satisfied. "I am glad you were apparently listening so carefully to everything that I said, Mr. Deketomis."

"Oh, I was listening very carefully, Ms. Southland. And I just want to clarify that you said 'Yes' to my last question."

"That's *Doctor* Southland," she said, emphasizing her professional title. "And, yes, I did agree to the moral character that has been associated with Bekmeyer since its beginning."

Deke saw that a few of the jurors had taken notice of how testy Southland sounded. In short order he hoped she'd sound a lot testier.

"Dr. Southland, are you aware that the company of which you are so proud created a product called Blood Bond Five that resulted in the death of thousands of hemophiliacs?"

Garrison objected, citing the lack of relevancy to the Ranidol case, but Judge Conte overruled the objection. During pretrial hearings, it was an argument Garrison had already raised and lost.

"And let me ask you this, Doctor," Deke said. "In that testimony you just gave you didn't mention one time that your 'honest, decent, compassionate company' pleaded guilty to three felony counts involving the sale of the tainted product Blood Bond Five to hemophiliacs, did you?"

Lydia Southland muttered something.

"I apologize, Dr. Southland, but you will need to speak up," Deke said. "I didn't catch your answer to my last question."

Southland took the only direction she could. "I wasn't involved in that project at all. You're just trying to distract everyone."

"No," said Deke, "what I'm doing is refuting a number of your statements. For example, do you think Bekmeyer displayed a sense of honesty when it continued selling a blood product it knew was contaminated with HIV? Just a minute ago you talked about how proud you were of the character of your company. That surprised me because I'm sure you must be aware of the three separate felony convictions Bekmeyer incurred through their selling of this product."

Garrison objected again.

Judge Conte instructed Deke to move on, but he never actually sustained Garrison's objection. That was a good sign. Another good sign was how intently the jurors were listening.

Dr. Southland looked anything but shaken, though, and stared him down with what looked like bravado. She assumed Deke had hit her with his best shot, and that he had now gotten all the yard-age he was going to get out of the hemophiliac drug story.

"I agree with you that Bekmeyer's history is fascinating," said Deke, "but in that long history lesson about what you call your decent, honest, and compassionate company, you failed to mention that a man named Hermann Spiegelman served as CEO of your company for eight years, didn't you?"

Garrison jumped to his feet and shouted, "Objection, irrelevant!"

Deke oozed sincerity as he said, "Judge, the witness says she is fully knowledgeable about the history of this company, and Mr. Garrison chose to make the unimpeachable character and conduct of Bekmeyer a feature of his direct examination. That was his choice, and I believe I should have the opportunity to proceed with that line of questioning, Your Honor."

Judge Conte overruled Garrison's objection, which seemed to surprise the defense counsel. "The witness will answer," the judge declared.

"Well . . . I can't," Dr. Southland said. Her eyes signaled pure malice as she glared at Deke. Then she lamely concluded, "That was before my time."

"But surely you know *of* this famous man," Deke insisted.

"I have heard of him," Dr. Southland admitted.

"If it pleases the court," said Deke, "I have a picture of Her-mann Spiegelman."

In his wildest dreams Deke had never thought he'd be able to introduce Spiegelman's picture, but he had come prepared just in case. While Garrison objected, Deke queued up the shot. When Judge Conte allowed him to proceed, Spiegelman's picture appeared on the court screen. It was a most unflattering mug shot, a black and white photo of pure evil.

"For almost a decade Hermann Spiegelman was the chairman of Bekmeyer, wasn't he, Dr. Southland?" Deke asked.

It was obvious the witness did not want to talk about the man on the screen. She continued to look to Garrison for help in stopping what she knew was a train wreck in slow motion.

Deke raised his voice and quickened his cadence. With his body obstructing the witness's view of Garrison, Deke launched his attack. "Hermann Spiegelman was later a convicted Nazi war criminal. He performed biological experiments at Auschwitz, but you must have known that when you just testified on direct examination about Bekmeyer's character, am I right, Dr. Southland?"

"Objection!"

Deke continued talking over Garrison. "You knew that he was part of Bekmeyer's 'character' story even before you walked into this courtroom, didn't you, Dr. Southland?"

"Objection, Your Honor. Move to strike!" Garrison shouted.

Judge Conte's voice boomed out into the courtroom: "Sidebar!"

Southland was left sitting on the witness stand, stunned. It must have been her dazed state, or her shock, but it appeared she was sitting there smiling at Hermann Spiegelman's mug shot. It was a shame, thought Deke, that there were no cameras in court to catch that moment. But the jurors had caught everything.

As the lawyers conferred with the judge, Spiegelman's image faded and changed. Beneath the picture appeared a caption: "NUREMBERG #66521 7-30-1948." The jury was looking back and forth between the video screen and the judge, confused about what they were supposed to be doing.

At the sidebar, Garrison became unglued with rage. "Judge, I move for a mistrial. This pathetic show put on by Mr. Deketomis was so inflammatory that the prejudicial effects outweigh any possible probative value. Further, this is irrelevant to this case.

Hermann Spiegelman was with Bekmeyer during World War Two, and that was in Germany. This is the twenty-first century, and we are in the United States. I insist it be stricken from the record, and I want a motion on mistrial to be heard."

Instead of responding to any of Garrison's comments, an undaunted Deke kept up his attack. "What I find even more disgusting, Your Honor, is that in Berlin, to this day, the Bekmeyer Scholarship Foundation gives out two annual graduate school scholarships in honor of this mass murderer. And Bekmeyer's corporate executives make an annual pilgrimage to Hermann Spiegelman's gravesite to celebrate his achievements. And here is what really gets me, Judge. This witness has attended at least three of those war criminal pilgrimages. That is the plain truth, Your Honor, and this is the company that both Dr. Southland and Mr. Garrison tried to lead this jury into believing was built on the good character, the decency, and the compassion of its leaders. They chose to take that approach in this case, and now they're asking the court to not allow me to explore it further."

"I'm going to allow it," the judge said. "Mr. Garrison, two things you should take away from here. First, you should have prepared this witness for this line of questioning. And second, I will never understand why you chose to open this case of character so wide. I may have an appellate court tell me I'm wrong, but I'm going to allow this line of questioning to proceed."

Judge Conte denied Garrison's motion for mistrial and told Deke to continue.

Then Deke simply walked back to his counsel table and told the witness he had no further questions. By that time, he knew the case was either won or lost.

Judge Conte told Dr. Southland that she was free to step down.

Her heels echoed in the courtroom as she hurried down the aisle, no doubt wondering how much money her wonderful and decent company would need to spend to pay their way out of this one.

A recess was granted, giving everyone time to ponder that same question. Deke felt the exchange with Dr. Lydia Southland about Hermann Spiegelman was enough to do Bekmeyer in. The focus had shifted almost exclusively to questions about the credibility and honesty of the company and by extension the believability of Garrison and Southland.

Fifteen minutes later, Garrison texted to request a meeting in an adjacent conference room. Several things were immediately apparent to Deke. An appeal strategy was not Garrison's best call. If Bekmeyer didn't settle now, the jury could potentially hit them with a massive judgment. And even if Garrison did win on appeal, the serious damage would have already been done. From the publicity alone, a multimillion-dollar verdict would create a tsunami of new claims.

When Deke took a seat in the small conference room, this time Garrison didn't ask him how his weekend was.

"I can settle for fifteen million dollars," he said. "That's the upper limit, and all the authority I have."

Deke shook his head, not believing a word of what Garrison was telling him. On a notepad, he wrote down a figure: $24,191,023. "That's our number," said Deke. "I'm not taking a penny less."

Garrison studied the figure. "It's excessive," he told him, "but I'll take it to Bekmeyer." Then he asked the question he was dying to know.

"How did you come by this number?"

"My daughter is 24 years old," Deke said. "Your product almost killed her. Annica Phillips was 19. Your product did kill her. Annica was born on October 23rd. There you have it: 24191023."

Garrison frowned and then left the conference room to call his bosses.

He returned five minutes later.

"We will settle for $24,250,000," he said, "providing there is no publicity surrounding how you figured damages."

"And you'll pull Ranidol immediately?" asked Deke.

Garrison nodded.

Then it was Deke's turn to ask another question. "In all my years litigating, I've never seen damages rounded up. How did that come about?"

Garrison offered an evil grin. "It's a gift to you from upper management at Bekmeyer. They are pretty sure you're going to need extra cash to fund what they expect will be your murder trial."

Deke wished he had a comeback. And he hoped Garrison was wrong. But he had to give it to opposing counsel and to Bekmeyer: they'd taken his feeling of victory away.

22

FIRST, LET'S KILL THIS LAWYER

Senator Roger Dove sat in the back of the conference room. He was listening closely to the speaker, a former congressman who, like himself, had been bounced from office. In politics it is said you don't want to be caught in bed with a dead girl or a live boy. Before being voted out of office, Representative Scott Cornwall had been accused of both. Dove almost felt righteous when he was in his company.

The conference was sponsored by the Foundation for Civil Justice Reform (FCJR), a division of the U.S. Chamber of Commerce. It was an invitation only event with the self-avowed purpose of promoting the interests of American business, as well as the conservative agenda. There were few empty seats to hear Congressman Cornwall's presentation on, "Ways to Reform Tort Litigation." Funding this reform were drug companies and insurance conglomerates.

"We need to get our story out," the congressman said. "As one, we need to talk about the lawsuit crisis. The more we say there is a lawsuit crisis, the more it will resonate with the American people. No matter what the situation, if the news is bad, we as a group need to reference the lawsuit crisis. Our united narrative needs to be that the threat of lawsuits is what is crippling American business. Why have jobs gone overseas? Answer: the lawsuit crisis. Why have wages been stagnant or gone down? Answer: the lawsuit crisis. Why is China's manufacturing growing, and America's declining? Answer: the lawsuit crisis."

The former congressman held out his microphone. "I want to hear it from you," he said. "What ails America?"

Most yelled back, "The lawsuit crisis."

It was an effective presentation, thought Dove. It was also a call to misinformation. The so-called "litigation epidemic" was a fiction created by the drug and insurance companies. They hated pesky litigants who dared to sue them when their loved ones were killed or crippled by their products or their failure to act. It didn't matter that every shred of empirical data concluded there was no lawsuit crisis, and there was nothing to show that litigation drove up the costs of health care, medications, and insurance premiums. But screaming "lawsuit crisis" was a much better alternative than trying to explain the truth of corporate greed.

The U.S. Chamber of Commerce was the biggest spending lobby in the country. In the last election it had doled out more than $100 million on its congressional lobbying efforts alone. The organization's connections to the FDA and other oversight committees ran deep. With deeper pockets than Exxon Mobil, they had tentacles everywhere. Though they liked the public to believe that their support came from local mom-and-pop businesses, the chamber was financed almost exclusively by twenty of the world's biggest megacorporations.

"But now we have a very special opportunity," said Cornwall. "As important as it is to keep hammering at the lawsuit crisis, now we have a chance to cut off the head of the snake."

Everyone in the room leaned a little closer. Everyone wanted to hear about the snake.

"I am sure all of you know about the Mass Torts Made Perfect convention," the congressman said. "Every year our enemies gather in Las Vegas. It's like a modern day Sodom and Gomorrah, I understand."

Dove thought the congressman almost sounded wistful, and remembered that during his last term in office many had referred to Cornwall as "Congressman Cornhole." But the congressman quickly got back on topic. "These ticks, these bloodsuckers, gather together in Las Vegas to confer and strategize. They come together for the sole purpose of trying to better scheme how they can suck at the teat of business and industry, and extort windfalls of money.

"I am sure all of you have heard the name of the founder and president of Mass Torts Made Perfect. For many years there has been no bigger blight on industry than Nick Deketomis."

At the mention of Deke's name, hissing and catcalls filled the room.

"I see you know his name," said the congressman. "You'll be happy to know that FCJR has barf bags available at the end of each aisle."

Cornwall clearly enjoyed the laughter, letting it build throughout the room. When it was quiet again he spoke. "Now I don't know if Old Nick will be giving his usual opening speech at the gathering of Tart Lawyers this year," he said, pausing while the audience laughed at his play on words. "Mr. Deketomis, as you've no doubt heard, has gotten himself into quite a pickle. And because of that, it is time that we made his misfortune our fortune. We cannot let this snake slither away."

Cornwall gestured to his assistant, and the lights in the room dimmed. In the front of the room a PowerPoint presentation appeared on the big screen.

"As you can see," explained the congressman, "this is a picture of Deketomis and his poisonous ilk."

At the top of the chart was Deke's name and picture. Beneath him were lines that connected the top mass tort attorneys and plaintiff lawyers in the country—firms like Givens and Givens, Perry Weitz, Howard Nations, and half a dozen more.

The screen graphic changed, showing the past mass tort cases that Deke had been involved with including Blood Bond Five, Fen-Phen, Vioxx, Fosamax, YAZ, Pradaxa, and a dozen others. The schematics that followed identified each of the plaintiff's lawyers on the list.

"Is it enough to sit here and brag about our victories with tort reform in states like Texas and Alabama and Mississippi? Or do we really want to go on the offensive? Do we want to win the war?"

Deke's picture again appeared on the screen. "We are in a unique position now to do away with these pariahs, starting with the low-hanging fruit."

He used his laser pointer and began making circles around Deke's head. "Here's that low-hanging fruit. Here's our target."

The picture on the screen changed again. "Once we get Deketomis out of our way," said the congressman, "we'll target the others one by one. Our battle plan is to proceed with a three-pronged attack funded by your contributions. We've already hired a law firm, a cyber intelligence group, and a world-class ad agency. In the days to come you will see a sustained and well-financed attack on Deketomis and his firm. And this, I promise you, will be only the beginning."

Most of the listeners rose to their feet and started applauding. They knew there was more to the story, things the congressman dared not say aloud. The cyber experts would turn over every detail of Deketomis's life. Any dirt they found would be shared with the world, and the First Amendment be damned. The smear campaign would be conducted by the ad agency, and their hired gun law firm would take on Bergman Deketomis. After all, they had to fight fire with fire.

"I am glad I am not Nick Deketomis," said the congressman. "He thinks things are already bad now that he's been charged with murder and the man prosecuting him is his enemy. But what Deketomis doesn't know is a whole world of trouble is coming his way." Using air quotes, Cornwall said, "Let me show you the murder 'reenactment' video we are working on."

The room went dark except for the screen. And then, though the image was grainy, they watched as a man raised his right arm and plunged a sharp looking object into the throat of a man lying on the ground. As a maniacal looking face turned toward the camera, a man who resembled Deketomis smiled as geysers of blood shot up into his face. The text that followed read: "Don't let this man get away with murder! Call the North Florida State Attorney's Office and share your outrage!"

"Goodbye, Mr. Deketomis," said Congressman Cornwall with a cute little wave as the video faded to black. "This is where we begin, ladies and gentlemen. If you are serious about ridding our land of these vermin, we start with Deketomis."

Those in the room stood and cheered. Seated in the back, Roger Dove didn't join them. What he'd seen on the screen made him feel queasy. He knew better than almost anyone that politics was a blood sport, but guessed he didn't know just how bloody. Of course a momentary pang of conscience from watching a slasher film wasn't enough to stop Dove. Directly after the conference he would be meeting with Nick Deketomis's nemesis, the prosecutor Darl Dixon. He would give Darl his marching orders, advising him on the best way to bring down Deketomis. And then he would give Darl the funds to help him do this.

Shakespeare was famous for his offering up the line in *Henry VI*: "The first thing we do, let's kill all the lawyers."

The words had been spoken by Dick the Butcher, but it seemed no one had taken him seriously, at least until now. The FCJR wanted the head of one lawyer in particular. And it sounded as if they'd even be willing to put a bounty on him.

23

WELCOME TO THE BRAVE NEW WORLD

Deke knew he had a lot of enemies in the world. It came with the territory. He challenged wealthy interests, and they hated to have their toes stepped on. These were people who were used to having their way, and they very much blamed the messenger when they were stymied. Deke was that messenger. He had accepted being the lightning rod. It was all right with Deke that the right wing vilified him, because for as many enemies as Deke had, he was convinced he had a lot more friends. David Packman was one of these good friends. Normally Deke wouldn't have taken a call so late at night, but when he saw Packman's name come up on his cell he didn't even hesitate.

"Working late, David?" he asked.

"Guilty as charged," Packman said. "And I called the one person who I also knew would be burning the midnight oil."

Deke had to laugh. Spread across his desk were the S.I. Oil documents. "The Swanson brothers are keeping me up," he revealed. "What about you?"

"I was working on my blog," Packman said, "and hearing from a few of my sources. You'd be surprised at how tongues loosen late at night after a few drinks. My best information always comes after 10:00 p.m."

Packman might not have been a credentialed journalist, but he took his blog very seriously. Others did as well. His stories had been picked up by the *New York Times* and the *Washington Post*, and had been featured in magazines like *Time* and the *U.S. News and World Report*. Even though Packman was a progressive, his sources were of all political stripes. Some of his whistleblowers were even disgruntled conservatives, many of whom couldn't abide the Republican Party truckling to teabaggers and the religious right. Of course he had to check and double-check his information to make sure he wasn't being used to promote misinformation.

Deke looked at his own glass of single barrel whiskey. He had justified the pour because of his having to spend a late night with the Swanson brothers. They would make anyone want to drink.

"That wouldn't surprise me at all," Deke said.

"Anyway, with all that's going on in your life, Deke, I wouldn't be calling you if I didn't think it was important, but recently I heard the mutterings of an attendee of the FCJR get-together in Washington. I followed-up on what I heard and got the same report from another attendee."

His friend sounded worried, thought Deke. And that made him worried. "Don't worry about what's on my plate, David. Just tell me what you heard."

"The FCJR has declared that you are Public Enemy Number One," he said.

"That's nothing new," remarked Deke.

"What's new is that they're acting on it, and putting their resources behind it. And in case you didn't know it, the FCJR takes in three hundred million in corporate donations every year."

"That much?" asked Deke.

"That much," he said. "And they see your being down as the opportunity to get you out. That's why they've vowed to discredit you personally and professionally. They're financing a campaign against you that's employing a law firm, an ad firm, and a cyber security firm. It's the last I'd worry about the most."

"Why is that?"

"Because they're going to be dredging through everything, and I don't think they'll worry much about legal niceties. If they can, they'll hack your computer or your company's computers. They'll use drones and surveillance equipment. Given an opportunity, they'll listen in to your personal calls."

Deke gave a low whistle. With all that was going on in his personal life he already felt as if he was being put through the spin cycle; this would roil up matters even more.

"You got any good news?" Deke thought he'd just ask.

"How about forewarned is forearmed?"

"I'm already walking around on an ice mountain," said Deke, "but I'll pass on your information at work, and to friends and family."

"It couldn't hurt," responded Packman.

"They want me to run scared," said Deke, "but I'm not going to do that. I need to go to Texas. It's important for our media campaign against the Swanson brothers."

"Just don't become part of *their* media campaign," said Packman.

"And I'm also scheduled to make the opening address at the MTMP, something I've done for the last twenty years."

"That's reason enough for you to consider bowing out. They've put a bull's-eye on your back, Deke. You don't want to make yourself an easy target."

"I'll think about it," Deke said.

"You'd better. This time these guys aren't kidding."

"Thanks for keeping an ear to the ground for me. I hope you'll even consider doing a story on what you heard. McCarthyism was scary, but these guys are making him look like an amateur."

"I hear you," Packman said. "And I promise I'll start working on that story tonight."

24
BEWARE THE GREEN NARCOTIC

Deke refused to run scared. Besides, it was better if he remained busy. That saved him from having to think about Ken Thorn; that saved him from ruminating about the blood on his hands. The FBO terminal in Houston was a dreary brown brick structure that a rusty sign proclaimed had been built in the 1970s. At the front of the building was a semicircular diner with floor-to-ceiling windows. Offices and a pilots lounge were in the rear. But for the oil companies that had long done business in the area, this airport wouldn't exist.

At the front doors, Deke and Angus Moore were greeted by Carol Morris. "Nice flight?" she asked them, knowing very well it couldn't have been. Bergman Deketomis's lead investigator had landed at the terminal enough times to know the ride was invariably bare bones and bumpy.

For Angus and his huge body, the puddle-jumper flights were always torture. He groaned while stretching out. "Next time let's not schedule anything in this neck of the woods unless we know the citation is free. How does that sound?"

Martin Bergman had reserved the corporate jet for other company business, but Carol wasn't sympathetic to Angus's plight, especially because most of the time she had to take commercial flights.

"Poor baby," she chided him. "Wait until you see what passes for food around here."

Carol led the two men to her four-wheel drive SUV rental. In Spanish Trace people drove similar huge SUVs, which were often jokingly referred to as urban assault vehicles. In Florida such vehicles were usually fashion statements, but in this part of Texas it was just how people got around.

"Everything set for the rally?" asked Deke.

Later that day a protest was scheduled to be held at S.I. Oil. It would be one of the initial salvos in Deke's "hearts and minds" campaign against the Swanson brothers.

"The protestors are being transported to the staging area," Carol answered, "but they're still a few hours out."

"We don't want to be late for the party," said Deke.

Before going to the rally, though, Deke and Angus were scheduled to interview two potential claimants in the S.I. Oil case. Clem Walters, the attorney who had first alerted Deke to S.I. Oil, was still actively working the case, but the health of his client had deteriorated. Although she promised to "keep kicking" until S.I. Oil "got the hurt it deserved," her health wouldn't allow her to be lead plaintiff. Deke didn't think he could stand going through what had happened to Annica Phillips.

Carol drove, filling in the two lawyers about the couple they were about to meet. "John and Joan Puckett are the salt of the earth," she said, "or at least they were until they were poisoned. If you were to guess their age it's likely you'd gauge them as being in their sixties. The reality is that they're both in their mid-forties.

In the last five years John has gone from two hundred pounds, to one hundred and thirty. Because he always wears a baseball cap, you might not notice that he's lost almost all his hair in those five years as well. Doctors diagnosed John with prostate cancer. As bad as that is, Joan's condition is worse. She's had all sorts of ailments, and doctors now tell her she has leukemia. Her chemotherapy has caused her to lose all her hair, but she covers up with a blonde wig.

"'I always wanted to be a blonde,' she told me. Somehow she's managed to keep her sense of humor."

The Puckett's farm was a thirty-minute drive from the terminal.

They drove down a long, dirt driveway, and parked in front of a yellow farmhouse. The property looked well-kept, and two dogs came out to greet them. Cats and chickens could also be seen. Parked in the driveway was a pickup truck with a wheelchair in the back.

John and Joan Puckett were sitting on wicker chairs on the porch. John stood to greet the trio while Joan remained seated. Deke couldn't believe he was older than the couple—their ailments had caused them to waste away.

The three visitors pulled up chairs. Deke took the lead, asking questions about their lives. He even offered a few confessions of his own that surprised Carol and Angus, for Deke rarely talked about his experiences growing up.

"When I was fifteen or so I lived with a family that had a chicken farm," Deke said. "That was quite an experience for me. I had no idea how much work it took. I was always having to haul feed, and always cleaning up. I remember it was a long time before I was able to eat chicken again."

The Pucketts offered up some of their own farming stories, and then began talking about their health and difficulties.

"When one of us was sick it was bad enough," said Joan, "but when both of us went down everything went to hell in a hand-basket. We were always driving to Houston for chemotherapy and blood platelet transfusions. That left both of us weak and sick, and when you're a farmer there is no time to be weak and sick. To keep this place going, we'd always worked twelve-hour days, and we're talking seven days a week. Getting sick was a double whammy. Getting treated ate up our savings, and being sick meant a huge decline in production. That's when we started falling behind on our mortgage payments."

Joan stopped talking. It was too painful for her. John took up her narrative. "I went to Houston and met with the bankers. It didn't seem to matter to them that we'd been sick, or that for fifteen years we'd always made our payments. What mattered to them was that we were six months behind on payments. Their idea of a reprieve was to give us thirty days to make good on what we owed. If we couldn't do that, they said they'd have to sell the property.

"About that time things got real strange. A week after I met the bankers I was sent a letter from the bank thanking me for paying off the mortgage. I wasn't sure what I should do. I didn't want to look a gift horse in the mouth, but I also didn't want to be played for a fool. So I phoned the bank and talked with a woman in their mortgage department, and she confirmed we no longer had a mortgage. Somehow our prayers had been answered, and our mortgage had been paid off. I asked this woman who our benefactor was, and she said that the payment had come from a community fund for those in need of mortgage assistance, an outfit called WE CARE."

It was Joan's turn to talk now. "At first the two of us thought we should leave well enough alone, but I couldn't help being curious about this WE CARE. Since my brother is mighty handy with a computer, I asked him to find out what he could about them. About a week later he told me that WE CARE is a political PAC. I didn't even know what that was until he explained. Then my brother said some muckraker had written an article about WE CARE that explained it was nothing but a shell organization funded by Swanson Industries."

John and Joan exchanged a glance, and John hung his head a little. "We knew about the Swanson brothers. It was kind of hard not knowing about them. But their paying off our mortgage put us in a funny position."

"It's called the Green Narcotic," said Deke. "The Swanson brothers, and those like them, have found if they throw money at a problem it usually goes away. Of course the money they distribute is only a pittance of what they've taken in. It's not like they're Robin Hood. They're more like the Sheriff of Nottingham, returning just a little of what's been stolen."

"We stewed about what to do," Joan told him. "Deep down, though, we knew what we'd gotten was blood money. In the last three years there have been seven deaths from kinds of cancers most people have never even heard of—*seven people*—all within five square miles from this house. Most everything that walks around on this land—from roosters to mules—has been afflicted with disease and death. Dr. Bob, the local vet, says he never in all his days has seen the likes of it."

"That's why we decided we couldn't stay quiet," John said. "This land was good once. But now all it's good for is a cemetery."

John choked up, stopping him from saying more. Even though she was in obvious pain, Joan extended a hand, which he accepted. The team sat in silence, embarrassed to be intruding on such a private moment.

"When Carol came around," said Joan, "we agreed to help her. That's when she brought in all these scientific sorts who drilled and took samples, and went from one end of the property to another."

Carol nodded as she said, "There's no sugarcoating it. Your farm sits on top of a poisonous chemical sludge. It's no wonder the two of you got sick. The chemical analyses show that the invasive sludge contains carcinogens galore. And all that poison originated from the S.I. Oil refinery wells."

There was a long thoughtful silence before Joan asked, "What do you need us to do?"

"We need you to tell your story," Angus said. "Our law firm's medical expert has reviewed both of your medical records, going all the way back to the time you were teenagers. It would be critically important in our civil action against Swanson Industries to have a lead case where injuries could be linked to chemicals originating from S.I. Oil. In your case, Joan, even your own oncologist—a highly qualified doctor—concluded there was a relationship between the chemicals used at S.I. Oil and the types of cancer you and your husband are suffering from."

"Your doctor's testimony will really help us," Deke told them, knowing how much he was asking of the doctor, as well. "His aunts and uncles are living around this same area, so he's taken a special interest in what's going on. Most doctors don't want to be involved in any kind of potential litigation and refuse to help."

"That all sounds good," said John.

"It is good," agreed Deke. "But I don't want to mislead you. I have no doubt that this case is going to get ugly and that the two of you will be likely recipients of that ugliness."

"You can expect the Swanson brothers will be expending a lot of their Green Narcotic throughout the area," Angus told them. "It's their MO. By the end of the month they'll have a perky army of cheerleader sorts going door-to-door spreading goodwill in the form of money. These gifts will be their way of buying off people who might otherwise be considering joining this lawsuit."

"They'll try to turn your neighbors against you," Deke said, "and they'll do their best to delay decisions. I don't know how to say this is any other way, but their hope will be that the two of you will die before this case goes to trial. They did not pay off your mortgage out of a sense of decency. They thought by doing that we'd never hear your story. They also hoped that you'd be focused on healing, and not want to participate in a lawsuit. If I were faced with your health problems, I might very well choose to spend all my energy trying to get well. Certainly we couldn't fault you for doing that."

"They can't undo what they did with the payment of our mortgage, can they?" asked John.

"No, they can't," Deke replied.

"So about all they can do is wait for us to die?"

"That's about the size of it."

John and Joan exchanged a glance, and then each of them nodded. "Then let's make them wait a long time. And in the meantime, Joan and I would be pleased if you put our John and Joan Hancocks all over your lawsuit."

25

AND THE ROCKETS' RED GLARE

The lawyers headed southeast through a Texas countryside that was brown from drought and desperate for rain. There was little conversation in the car. Deke knew everyone was thinking of Joan and John Puckett. Their quiet dignity, their bravery in the face of their afflictions, brought the case home. It also put Deke's own problems in perspective. He was healthy, and so was his family. There was nothing more important than that.

"Per your instructions, Deke," Carol said, "last week I told Joan and John about the charges that have been brought up against you."

Deke nodded. Everyone involved in this case needed full disclosure.

"I was afraid this might give them cold feet, but they already knew about it," she said. "And instead of discouraging them, it might actually have brought them into our camp."

"That surprises me," Deke said.

"It surprised me as well," Carol replied. "But the Pucketts seemed to think you were being railroaded. And they also said that you were clearly a fighter."

"Even when I don't want to be," whispered Deke, "even when I don't want to be."

They continued their drive along a landscape that most would categorize as being in the "middle of nowhere." They went along the country road and encountered few people other than truckers. Every few minutes a truck came from the opposite direction and raised so much dry dust into the air that no one could see through the haze.

After twenty minutes, a large plant came into view. This was one of the Swansons' oldest oil refineries, and it showed its age. Appearance notwithstanding, for fifty years it had been providing local jobs all the while contributing to the cash flow of the Swanson family.

The crude oil being processed there originated in the Canadian oil sands in Southern Alberta where reserves were estimated at 175 billion barrels, an immense total that was second only to the available oil reserves in Saudi Arabia. A pipeline that was part of the first phase of the Keystone Pipeline carried the oil from Canada to North Dakota, and from there it was transported by rail to US refineries like this one.

The media had convinced the American public during the time of booming prices of oil and gas that allowing increased drilling both in Canada and on US soil would lower prices that Americans paid at the pump. But the truth was that those pipelines had not lowered the high price of fuel one penny for most Americans. As for all the hydraulic fracking that had taken place, only recently were the horrors of fracking coming to the fore. The truth was that the refined oil was pumped onto huge transport ships, which then were sent out to remain at sea until the price for oil went up somewhere in the world. When that occurred, the ships were ordered into the ports of countries where the price was highest. It was a shell game that the media was unwilling to report, fearing the loss of ad revenue from the oil and gas industry.

Just south of the plant, they turned onto a small, winding road that after a mile dead-ended at the Alamo River. The group climbed out and walked down to the water's edge. To the naked eye, the sight of the wide, slow-flowing river with little vegetation was unremarkable. However, scientific studies and analyses had shown it to be a lethal delivery system for dozens of toxins.

Carol had been accompanying scientists around the area for a week and briefed the lawyers on their findings. "The headline is that water samples drawn from test wells in areas within a fifty-mile radius from the plant put the benzene levels at some locations as high as twenty parts per billion," she said. "That's far above the federal standards that set the top limit at *five*."

She then offered a brief geography lesson on the water flow in this part of Texas. The Alamo River flowed south and eventually dumped into Galveston Bay near Houston. Along the way, streams flowing off the river ran into lakes, as well as smaller streams and tributaries that were partially responsible for refilling the drinking water aquifers all along the way.

"Even though there isn't a high density of population," she explained, "these aquifers impact the water supply of more than a quarter of a million people."

Deke nodded. The number was even larger than he'd thought.

"Our investigators tested the Alamo River water just north of the Swansons' plant," she said, "and found benzene levels only slightly above acceptable limits. But downstream is a whole other ballgame. From the plant the benzene flows directly into the many smaller waterways that have very little volume and slower movement. In those areas we routinely found benzene and a host of other toxic chemical contaminants at a minimum of five or six times their projected safe levels."

Deke and Angus surveyed a topography map prepared by Carol's team that showed these findings.

"I am sure the Swanson brothers will want to delay any actions while they tell us that the solution to pollution is dilution," Angus observed.

"And that will only result in a bigger disaster," Deke said.

Polluters wanted the public to believe their rhyme so that they could continue to dump their deadly chemicals, but every credible environmental scientist disagreed with that industry-generated theory. It was unfortunate that the EPA still seemed to buy into the dilution solution.

Historically the EPA had also been skittish about pinpointing the source of deadly toxins, even with plenty of smoking guns. This dragging of their feet frustrated environmentalists. What was even more frustrating was the "risk versus benefits" model the EPA frequently applied to criminal polluters, with money trumping human health. Often the only recourse to avert toxic disasters and take on entrenched and powerful forces like the Swanson brothers was a well thought out and financed lawsuit.

At the rally staging area just south of the S.I. Oil plant, Carol pulled the SUV in behind a row of busses parked along the street.

At the expense of Bergman Deketomis, more than five hundred protestors had been driven in those busses to an area directly in front of the plant. In addition to those protestors were at least a hundred people from nearby communities who had been harmed by the plant's toxic pollution.

The protestors were a combination of young and old and haves and have-nots. There was no common denominator in what could be called a motley crew except for their genuine outrage over the Swansons and S.I. Oil. Many had spent hours on a bus ride, coming from as far away as Louisiana. Along the way, they had studied reading material written by experts who had analyzed the Swanson plant operation for years.

Inside the fences of S.I. Oil, employees had parked a dozen huge transport trucks. Each time a protest speaker on the small makeshift stage attempted to communicate with the crowd, horns from the transport trucks blasted ear-piercing whistles in an effort to drown out the speaker's words and annoy the protest crowd.

With the PA system turned up to full volume, the speakers were barely audible over the horns. In spite of the war of noise, scientific experts explained to the crowd the level of reckless abandon the Swansons had shown in regard to human health. Many in the audience were holding signs taunting the Swanson brothers, now dubbed the "Benzene Brothers" by a group of locals.

Two news trucks from local media affiliates were on the scene covering the protest. A third truck with news broadcast capabilities was also on site and overseen by the firm's tech-savvy media staff. This ensured that the rally received live coverage by streaming it online to progressive bloggers. Deke's PR team knew they couldn't count on corporate media. Investigative journalism was rarely practiced on a national level. The news cycle often seemed to stop and start with the likes of Kim Kardashian, or the latest in beachwear.

The law firm had stocked the organizers' tent with doughnuts and coffee. That's where Deke's group went to refuel. Milling around the sugar and caffeine station were union leaders, two Democratic state representatives, three local mayors, and an array of environmental activists. Also there was Texas lawyer Howard Nations, regarded as the baddest trial dog in Texas.

Deke had his ear bent, and bent a few ears, while he drank a cup of coffee. Then he returned outside and tried to listen to the speaker. The truck horns didn't make that easy. When it was Deke's turn to go to the stage, he signaled everyone to move in closer.

Those in the refinery had apparently been waiting for his appearance and ratcheted up the noise. Even the deafening blare of truck horns wasn't going to stop Deke from speaking.

"Do you hear those horns?" yelled Deke. "That's the sound of censorship. That's the noise of those who would question our right to assemble, and our right of free speech! That's the noise of those who would deny us our First Amendment rights!"

The crowd screamed its approval.

"I am not surprised by the tactics of the opposition," said Deke. "But we aren't going to let their noise, and their lies, and their money, silence us. This case is going to be a brutal combat. We have declared war against two of the richest people on this planet, as well as the politicians who enable them and the media they own and operate. They have the money to spread around, but we have the truth on our side. And we are committed to having the truth come out, just as we are committed to this fight! Their noise won't stop us, and their money won't stop us!"

Deke's stentorian voice could not be silenced even by the din of the trucks, and the crowd roared its approval.

"But if we're to succeed," he continued, "we'll need your help. I am afraid that Texas has become one of the most polluted unregulated states in the Union, and that's because the entire court system has been packed with industry-friendly judges. This will be a long road to justice, and we must be ready for that pitched battle. We must remain firm in our united resolve, for by doing so we will make the Swanson brothers accountable for what they've done here."

The roar of applause changed to screams at the sound of gunfire. Shots were coming from the direction of the plant. Many protestors threw themselves to the ground. The rapid bursts of firecrackers made it sound as if automatic weapons were raining down on them. Many in the crowd panicked, running for cover.

It appeared that tracer bullets were targeting the protestors, which only increased the pandemonium. Red flares rained down on those assembled. Instead of running, Deke had remained on the platform, and now stared down those in the refinery plant.

As if on signal, their noise pollution came to a sudden end, and in that silence roars of laughter could be heard coming from the plant.

White-faced, Deke let the laughter continue. He waited for the protestors to get off the ground, and come out from behind the buses.

"They can laugh now," Deke called out to them, "but we will laugh last and the loudest. That I promise."

Howard Nations joined Deke up on the stage. "There used to be something called Texas hospitality," he said. "I look forward to its return. I look forward to a day when it's not the Swanson brothers calling the shots, but the people of Texas." Loud cheering greeted his words. The demonstrators weren't going to be deterred by false threats. As some semblance of order returned to the scene, two reporters with camera crews approached Howard and Deke for comments. A local Fox News reporter asked Deke if he understood that Swanson employees had acted the way they had since his lawsuit could threaten their jobs.

"After what we saw here today," Deke responded, "I really don't care whether that group of thugs has to make a living picking up trash along the highway. What the Swanson brothers are doing here in South Texas is murdering people for profit, and you can spin that any damn way you want."

A scorched-earth policy wasn't usually Deke's way, but he had already determined what his approach would be to winning this case. He also knew that he would not be getting help from corporate media or from the Texas federal court system. Part of his plan included focusing the attention of the Department of Justice criminal division on the criminal conduct that had allowed the Swanson brothers to kill at will via their refinery operations—but whether he could get the DOJ to act responsibly was a great unknown. After all, this was the same DOJ that had failed to criminally prosecute any of the key operators on Wall Street who had virtually stolen $13 trillion from the American public in the last mortgage meltdown.

26
FIGURES LIE, AND LIARS FIGURE

Carol drove Deke and Angus back to the airport. As much as she wanted to fly back to Spanish Trace, for now, with her investigation not yet completed, she had to remain in Texas.

"My husband is calling himself a widower," she said.

"I'll make sure to get you some time off," Deke promised.

"Maybe you ought to take some time off of your own, boss."

"I know some people are working hard to make sure I have lots of time off," Deke reminded her.

His gallows humor got brief smiles out of Angus and Carol, but no one was in the mood to laugh. What had happened at the demonstration was sobering stuff. The firecrackers had sounded like automatic weapons, and the flares had looked like rockets. Or maybe it was just the unexpectedness of the attack that had made everything seem so real.

There was also the feeling that next time it might not be a joke. Next time it might be real bullets being fired.

Deke's cell phone rang. He looked at the display and saw Gina Romano was calling. For a moment Deke thought about letting the call go to voice mail. He could blame it on the cell reception in the area, and could put off calling her back for hours. But it wasn't like him to duck calls.

"Hi Gina," he greeted her.

"I got the polling results in," she said.

Gina prepared for her high-profile cases by taking the pulse of the electorate. It always helped to know which way the wind was blowing, she said.

"Am I about to hear that I exist in a state of denial?" asked Deke.

"I don't think denial adequately states it," she said.

"That bad?" asked Deke.

"Of the one hundred and seven people interviewed," responded Gina, "ninety-five believe you are guilty at some level."

"By my math that means only twelve intelligent people were part of the polling."

"It's not funny, Deke. You got your way with the Ranidol trial. Over my advice, and, from what I understand, over that of most of the partnership, you still went to court. According to your reasoning that was what an innocent man would do."

"And I still think that."

"The public disagrees," said Gina. "The majority of those polled thought your being in court was wrong, especially as you'd just killed a man. They believe this showed arrogant indifference."

"I wonder what your polls would have shown had I gone into hiding."

"Your numbers might not have looked much better," Gina conceded, "but you know why that is?"

"I'm afraid to ask."

"Those polled wonder why it is that you haven't shown public remorse."

"I was the one attacked," explained Deke.

"With that attitude," she said, "you'll also be the one who is convicted."

"Anything else?" asked Deke.

"Those polled thought it would be better if you took a leave of absence from the firm. They think it puts you in a bad light—that your life seems to be business as usual."

"Would it be better if I went around in sackcloth and ashes?"

"It couldn't hurt. And if you're still considering going to Las Vegas, then you're crazy. That's your lawyer talking."

"Do the polling numbers tell you that?"

"My gut tells me that. Can't you see it would be a PR nightmare?"

"There are a lot of people counting on me to make that appearance."

"It's your funeral, Deke. I only hope I'm speaking figuratively."

Neither Angus nor Carol had been privy to both sides of the conversation, but they'd clearly filled in the blanks. They didn't comment further, although Deke was pretty sure they would have sided with Gina.

The rest of the ride was oppressively quiet.

Once they were inside the regional airport, matters didn't improve. It was one of Deke's pet peeves that when there were televisions in public spaces they always seemed to be tuned in to Fox News. Once again that was the case. What made the viewing even worse was that Deke was forced to watch coverage of the demonstration at the S.I. Oil refinery.

The footage taken during the demonstration was short, and there was no mention of what the Swanson goons did. It didn't surprise Deke that the crowd numbers were downsized, and the issues were trivialized. In fact, the entire protest was summed up in two lines delivered by one of the station's talking heads:

"Several hundred people showed up at the protest held at the S.I. Oil refinery. Protesters claimed that the plant has been spreading, and continues to spread, cancer-causing toxins into communities throughout this area."

Then the broadcast switched to the news desk's blonde anchorwoman who said, "Benzene is a chemical produced by natural events such as forest fires and cigarette smoke, but it is also a natural part of crude oil."

The anchor smiled for the camera. "At issue," she said, "is whether the S.I. Oil refinery is emitting dangerous amounts of benzene into the soil and water. To get answers our own Dan Devine went to the S.I. Oil refinery."

The broadcast cut back to a young reporter standing with a gray-bearded man.

"This is Dan Devine," said the reporter, "and I'm with Texas A&M Professor of Chemistry James Nicks."

Deke saw the professor was actually wearing a white lab coat. But he also had on cowboy boots, apparently showing he was no egghead.

"The two of us are at the rear of the S.I. Oil refinery plant where the alleged contaminants have supposedly been running into the groundwater for decades. Fox 25 News hired Professor Nicks to test the ground samples around the perimeter of the plant. Professor Nicks, what have you found?"

"Not much," said the professor, and both he and the reporter laughed. "The benzene levels present in this ground are, in fact, lower in concentration than the benzene found in secondhand cigarette smoke. The bottom line is that your drinking water is safe."

The report ended with the reporter looking into the camera. "This is Dan Devine," he said, and paused long enough to chug down a glass of water, "reporting from the S.I. Oil Refinery, the site of today's small demonstration."

The smiling anchor reappeared on screen telling her viewers, "We talked to officials at the S.I. Oil Refinery and were told that today's demonstration was the handiwork of tort lawyer Nick Deketomis, and was part of a nuisance suit he is bringing against them."

She gave an even bigger smile. "In other news . . ."

Deke turned away from the broadcast. He wanted to be outraged, but was too tired. "Gravity is pulling me down," he said to Angus.

"Tomorrow is another day," Angus replied brightly.

But what Angus really thought was that in all the years he'd known Deke, he'd never seen his friend look so beaten down.

27

HACKED

The day after returning from Texas Deke reluctantly agreed to meet with Gina in person. They sat down at Deke's kitchen table.

"Why is it that I feel like a kid going to the woodshed?" he asked.

"Maybe because your conscience knows you deserve a spanking."

"What do you want from me, Gina? I know you don't want me to work, but the only thing that's keeping me from going crazy *is* work."

"I don't mind you working. I mind your keeping a public profile while you work."

"For the sake of my clients, I need to keep a public profile."

"What might be good for your clients is not good for you. I am your lawyer, Deke. Don't make my job harder than it has to be."

"And I'm trying to leave you to your job, Gina. You know how hard that is for me. Maybe you should be thankful that my work is keeping me busy. If I was just sitting around I'd probably be trying to butt in with my own case."

"If you did that you'd have to get yourself a new lawyer," Gina reminded him. "And in case you get tempted, let me remind you of the old adage: 'The lawyer who represents himself has a fool for a client.'"

Deke raised his arms into the air. "I surrender. Now how can I help you?"

"You said you didn't know Kenneth Thorn, and never heard of him," she said. "But then you seemed to recollect that his face was familiar, and you might have run into him somewhere."

Deke nodded. "I'm good with faces, and it bothered me thinking that I'd seen this guy's face before. I kept racking my brain and just yesterday it came to me: I'm pretty sure I ran into this guy just before my lunch meeting with Paul Moses."

"When was this?"

Deke pulled out his cell phone, checked the calendar, and provided Gina with the date. "The reason I remembered him is that he was sweating and pale, and looked frantic. I stopped to ask him how he was doing because I was afraid he might be experiencing a stroke or heart attack."

"And where did this occur?"

Deke gave her the location, which wasn't far away from where he'd had his business lunch. Gina chewed on her pen a moment. "Where you and Moses dined is your usual Friday haunt, isn't it?"

When Deke nodded she said, "If I were looking to ambush you, it makes sense I'd stake out a spot near the restaurant. The park is right across the street from there, isn't it?"

"Yes, it is," he said, "but I wasn't ambushed that day."

"Thorn might have gotten cold feet."

"But why would he have wanted to stop me?"

"Why did he want to stop you on that day of the fight at the stadium? Your testimony is that he was trying to provoke you, correct?"

"He called Cara a slut," whispered Deke. "He pushed my buttons like I never imagined they could be pushed, especially after my beautiful daughter was almost taken from us."

"Someone wanted you to go off on Thorn," Gina declared. "He was the sacrificial lamb."

"What purpose would that serve?"

"We can only conjecture," she said. "Maybe it was payback. Maybe someone wanted to taint you. Maybe catching you in a violent act helped someone in some way."

"Why would Thorn put himself in that position?"

"I am sure he didn't do so willingly. I imagine he was coerced. Our investigators are looking into the background of Ken Thorn. We haven't uncovered anything definitive yet, but I can tell you that he is not the saintly man being portrayed in the news."

Deke digested that bit of good news. For the rest of his days he would always feel terrible about the death of Ken Thorn. But Deke also knew he had been baited by him. If Gina could bring Thorn down from his pedestal the rest of the world might begin to believe Deke's story.

"What about the stadium security surveillance tapes?" asked Deke. "All this time I've been sure they would vindicate me."

Gina shook her head. "The closed-circuit TV surveillance system they have is old, and has a lot of holes. Unfortunately, where the altercation occurred is one of those less than optimal spots for viewing. The clear film we wanted of your encounter apparently doesn't exist. The good news is that we can corroborate the fact that you tried to avoid a confrontation. I have the testimony of the security guard, and your roundabout route, showing you went out of your way to get to your vehicle."

"You told me Thorn wasn't alone," Deke recalled. "You told me he was accompanied by someone else."

"We're still trying to find that someone else," she said. "He was wearing a hat, though, and had on a baggy sweatshirt. We've pulled the best pictures possible from the footage, but even those aren't very good. He's around five foot ten, white, and a hundred and fifty pounds, with nothing distinguishing him physically. Thus far no one has been able to identify him, but we're still on it."

"I heard there was some terrible footage of the fight circulated on the Internet?"

"Our experts are checking on that. At this time the early consensus is that someone took a video—probably from a phone camera—of your fight with Thorn at the stadium, and the footage was doctored. That's still being reviewed, though. If the video is a fake, it's not the only video reenactment being circulated. Your political enemies have their knives out. They've put out their version of what they think happened. It's pretty vile, even by their standards. The video makes you look like Hannibal Lecter, complete with a bloodbath. And at the end of their gruesome little video they ask people to not let you get away with murder by calling the North Florida State Attorney's Office."

David Packman had warned Deke about that piece. And he had also warned him that his enemies were coming after him. "I guess you didn't know you were defending Jack the Ripper," he said.

"I know it seems bad, Deke, but you need to trust me. Right now we're playing rope-a-dope."

For a moment the phrase eluded Deke. He was that tired. "That doesn't sound like a legal strategy," he said.

"It's not. It's a boxing strategy. Muhammad Ali used it against George Foreman in their Rumble in the Jungle."

Deke smiled and remembered seeing the old boxing tapes. Ali had stayed on the ropes, his arms upraised to protect his torso and face. George Foreman had hit him time and time again, until he was finally punched out. That was when Ali came off the ropes and took control.

"I'm glad you're in my corner," he told Gina.

Despite all of Gina's entreaties, Deke decided to attend the MTMP conference. It was his baby, after all. And now, more than ever, he was convinced that America counted on lawyers like him to keep the corporate world honest. Democracy was based on checks and balances. Unfortunately, there was no longer much checking the power of the plutocracy. The corporate world had convinced Americans that lawyers were the enemies. *They* were only out for money. If there had ever been a better example of the pot calling the kettle black, Deke didn't know it.

"The corporate world says tort lawyers are villains," Deke often told audiences. "I say we are patriots."

On the flight over to Las Vegas, Deke worked on his opening address. There were generally about eight hundred attendees at his Thursday morning opening speech. This year he'd be talking about the S.I. Oil/benzene case. His address would be both an update, and a pitch, as he'd be encouraging other lawyers and firms to assist Bergman Deketomis both financially and with sweat equity. Tort campaigns were complex and expensive, and dragon slaying was never easy. If Deke was to prevail in Texas, if he was to put a stop to the spread of benzene and other environmental toxins, he'd need other law firms to advertise for clients that had been injured.

As Deke worked on honing his address, his satellite phone rang. His face brightened when he saw Cara was calling.

"Hey, honey," he said.

His daughter's words were mostly unintelligible through her sobs, and Deke was immediately fearful that she'd had a relapse. "Are you sick?" he asked. "Is it your heart?"

Cara responded to the sound of her father's panicked voice. "No, no, I'm okay Dad," she said. "It's not me. Well it is, but it's not my health. It's my phone. I think I was hacked. And Andy thinks he was hacked, too."

Deke almost said, "Is that all?" As soon as he heard his daughter was physically okay his relief was tangible.

"I'm sorry you were hacked," he said.

"I think they also got into the phones of my friends. They're circulating pictures, Dad, and they're making them look much worse than what really happened."

"What did happen?" asked Deke.

"Last year Wendy had a pool party. It was a reunion of my group from high school. It was miserably hot and we had a few drinks. Then we decided to do the same thing we'd always done in high school: We went skinny-dipping."

"And let me guess, some of you took pictures."

"And someone has taken those pictures and made it look like we were shooting a porn film."

Cara sounded as if she was about to start crying again. "I'm sorry," he said. "I know how upsetting this violation feels. But it's not your fault, sweetie."

Deke could hear her sniffing.

"Did you say Andy was also hacked?" he asked.

"He's afraid you're going to be really mad at him, Dad. His text message to Kurt was somehow intercepted."

"And what did it say?"

"Kurt wanted to know if Andy was up for some partying, and Andy wrote back something like, '*My old man is hearty partying in Vegas, so I'm ready to do some hearty partying myself.*'"

"That doesn't sound so bad," said Deke.

"It isn't," said Cara. "But Andy's words sure don't sound good when they're announced next to a picture of Ken Thorn. And a picture of your topless daughter doesn't help you either."

Rope-a-dope, thought Deke. He hoped his arms could take the beating. He hoped he could take the beating.

"You and Andy did nothing wrong," he told her. "I love you, and I love your brother. Tell him that for me. And no more crying, young lady. Your doctor said you need to concentrate on getting well, and that's what I want you to do."

28
PLACING YOUR BETS

Deke's bad luck streak didn't end when he landed in Las Vegas. "The flu seems to be going around," Angus told him. "There won't be a candidate's forum this year because there won't be any candidates."

"Then maybe they aren't the candidates we hoped they were," said Deke. "Were part of their flu symptoms a yellow streak down their backs?"

At every year's mass tort convention a handful of progressive politicians went around currying favor with the lawyers. Their forum was often called the "swimsuit" part of the beauty program.

"It's not exactly a big loss," remarked Angus. "It's just a few politicians."

"I guess they were afraid to be photographed with me," Deke suggested. "You sure you want to be seen with me?"

"That's not pity I'm hearing, is it, Deke?"

"I wouldn't call it pity. But now I know how lepers feel."

The guest relations manager walked Deke through the bustling lobby, around the edge of the casino, and past the meeting rooms to the villa elevators. When the manager opened the door to Deke's villa, the accommodations were almost enough to get him out of his funk. The massive suite was spectacular, decorated in tone-on-tone tans and whites. In the spacious living room was a fully stocked black marble bar that matched the color of the Steinway & Sons baby grand piano. Through double doors off the living room was a large terrace overlooking Steve Wynn's world-class golf course.

Deke dropped his briefcase in the master bedroom and kicked off his shoes. He walked out onto the terrace and soaked in the view. It felt as if he was in the midst of an ancient Japanese garden. The sun was setting but the golf course greens were shining under the light of the moon as well as the lights designed for night play. The greens were so perfectly manicured they looked like expensive carpet and the water hazards had active waterfalls. In the distance the Encore Hotel building, Wynn's sister property, began to glow as it picked up the orange tones from a setting sun.

Deke plopped down on a chaise lounge and breathed in deeply the desert breeze. Within ten minutes he was asleep.

The next morning, in front of a packed ballroom, Robert Kennedy, Jr. took the stage to introduce Deke. It was a sign of his friend's character that he hadn't come down with the flu as so many others apparently had.

Having spent his entire life as a committed warrior for the environment, Kennedy had joined the firm years ago as an outside counsel to its environmental practice. Renowned as a public speaker, Kennedy always drew a crowd.

"I want to talk for a minute about my law partner, Nick Deketomis," Kennedy began. "Most likely, everyone in this room has heard about what Deke is going through down in Florida. I am also assuming that no one in this room would be so naïve as to believe that there is any truth to the stories being spun about him right now. You see, this kind of thing can happen when someone is crazy enough to stand up to powerful interests. We all know that Deke has never been afraid to step on the toes of the high and mighty. When we stop doing that, the fragile democracy we take for granted is toast. So for our twentieth year at this conference, let me introduce your friend, and most certainly my friend, Nick Deketomis."

Deke couldn't help noticing that the applause was not all it could be. He'd always been greeted by a standing ovation in the past. On this occasion only half the room was standing, if that. Nevertheless, Deke began his speech as if he were a man without a worry in the world. He started by focusing on a need for tactical change in the way progressives wage their battle to preserve democracy. "Three decades ago, a small group of wealthy and politically influential billionaires set out to reconstruct the rules about how democracy should operate. They needed to gain control of the media so they purchased it. Today, there are basically four major corporations that control all forms of news media, from newspapers to cable TV. In 1995 that same gaggle of billionaires determined that they needed to dry up all of the money flowing to progressive politicians by going to war with unions and attorneys. When all that started, almost 30 percent of America's workforce was unionized. Today, that number is less than 10 percent. Again, they succeeded."

Deke took a sip of water. He also gave his audience time to digest those numbers. It was unions that had gotten livable working conditions. It was unions that ended child labor and instituted forty-hour workweeks. And now those unions, and the safety nets they provided, were gone.

"In 1997 less than 40 percent of the federal judiciary was controlled by what we would consider conservative ideologues. Today, that number has reached 75 percent. That means every time you go in a courtroom, the chances are three in four that you'll be speaking in front of a conservative judge. And in 2010, while Democrats were completely without leadership, that same gaggle of billionaire inheritance babies took control of twenty-three state governorships and state legislatures so that they could gerrymander Democratic Party politics out of existence in those states. Again, the rich plutocrats succeeded."

Deke continued providing facts and figures, none of which were encouraging. Then he asked, "Are you tired of taking it on the chin? I know I'm tired of fighting a rigged game. And unless we act together, the game is going to get even more rigged. Do you remember what Ben Franklin told the other signers of the Declaration of Independence? 'We must hang together,' he said, 'or we will hang separately.' And that's what I say to you right now. It's time for us to hang together. It's time for us to get up from the floor and fight."

His audience was leaning forward. They were listening a lot more closely now. Deke offered up his own hit list of what needed to be done.

"I'm working on a case in South Texas," he said. "I'm going up against two fellows you might have heard of. Kurt and Anton Swanson to a large degree financed this conservative revolution. They've worked hand in hand with big business to get what they want, a toothless opposition. It's time we found our teeth again. With the S.I. Oil case, Howard Nations down in Texas and my law firm intend to show those two brothers that the revolution ain't over. As this week progresses, we will be talking about one of the most important environmental disasters in this country. Over the next couple days I'd like you to let me know whether you want the opportunity to use your special set of skills in a way that will make you proud. There is room for everyone, and frankly we need your help."

Deke sat down to loud, but not thunderous, applause. Even though they were in Las Vegas, it seemed to him that most in the audience were hedging their bets.

Martin Bergman thought Deke had delivered a damned fine speech, and screw anyone who disagreed. The grumbling of some of the convention attendees pissed him off. Over the years, Deke had made some of these jackasses buckets of money. That they'd be so quick to abandon him now made Martin rue the state of humanity in general.

"Gentlemen, and gentlewoman, place your bets," said the croupier.

Martin was playing roulette with Gina Romano and Angus Moore. It was a high-stakes table. Martin didn't gamble very often, but when he played he often took the same high-risk and high-reward tactics that came with his cases.

Orlando lawyer Dick Bryan was also at the table. It was Bryan's very vocal opinion that under the circumstances Deke shouldn't be handling any complex litigation. The more Bryan drank, the louder his looney rants became. He also seemed to be taking great personal pleasure in Deke's misfortunes, which baffled Martin. Schadenfreude might be understandable in the case of a sworn enemy. That might justify, at least for a little while, deriving

pleasure from someone else's pain. But Deke had never been anything except accommodating to Bryan.

Not only that. Bryan and his firm had made lots of money
in the past by participating in Deke's tort cases. Deke had done
all the work, and Bryan had benefited tremendously. Bryan for
years had been typically referred to among his peers as The Fat
White Rat, not only because of his vermin-like physical features
but also because of his overwhelming number of defective personality traits. Those qualities were in full blossom at that moment.

As Bryan downed another bourbon he said, "I'm going to bet
on the Swanson brothers this time. Too bad the casino isn't spon-
soring that action. And that means I am not going to put out even
a dime in advertising on Mr. Dekes' insane new project."

Typically on a case like S.I. Oil, Bryan's firm might be counted
on to spend upwards of three million dollars in advertising. Martin
had little respect for Bryan, not simply because he was an obnox-
ious and sloppy drunk, but because he was a lawyer who hadn't
tried a case in more than thirty years. He rode the coattails of people like Deke, and typically only advertised and collected mass tort
cases which he then bundled up for small inadequate settlements.

Instead of taking on Bryan with words, Martin decided to
let his chips talk. However Bryan bet, he made the opposite play.
When Bryan put his chips down on red, Martin played black.
When he chose odd, Martin went even. What Martin was really
betting on was karma, which was biting Bryan in the butt. It wasn't
long before Martin's stack of chips was sky-high, while Bryan's had
dwindled down to almost nothing.

Finally, Martin opened his mouth. He'd had enough of Bryan's
rants against Deke and how everything was going to hell in a
handbasket. "Look, Dick, Deke's case is a gamble, just like every
other case he has ever brought to you. But don't worry about your

advertising money. We don't want it. In fact you've convinced me that our firm wants all the action. So we'll be putting up the money ourselves."

Martin waited for Bryan to make his bet. He hesitated, and then put all his remaining chips on red. That was good enough for Martin. Even though it was a high-stakes table, the house limit was a $20,000 bet. His pile was big enough to be able to cover three of those bets. He divided his stack into three piles and gestured to Gina and Angus.

"Both of you take a stack and put it on black," he told them.

When the bets were placed the croupier hesitated, signaling for approval of the pit boss.

"Spin the damn wheel," said Martin.

The croupier's boss approved the bet, and he let the wheel spin . . . the hard white ball bounced around . . . and around some more . . . before landing on black.

Gina and Angus broke into hysterical laughter and applause, and then tried to pass their earnings to Martin, but he waved them off. Martin gathered his winnings and stood up from the table.

Then he looked at Dick Bryan and said, "Next time, schmuck, bet with us."

29
RED-LETTER DAY

In the days following the conference, Deke did his best to maintain a low profile. Mostly he worked from home, seldom venturing out. Gina praised his restraint. Deke knew it made sense; when your enemies are trying to get you in their crosshairs it doesn't do to be visible—but every day he was getting more stir- crazy. So when Andy asked if he'd be attending the De Soto landing reenactment where Andy was going to be one of the conquistadors, Deke didn't even hesitate.

"I wouldn't miss it for the world," he said.

"Are you sure?" asked Teri.

"I don't think that's a good idea, Dad," Cara weighed in.

"I'm going," Deke said. "And I don't want either of you ratting to Gina."

"How about the two of us sit in a nice, quiet spot away from the crowds then?" Teri asked.

"I don't need a babysitter," Deke answered, "and I don't think you should be forced to sit in a nosebleed seat. It's not every year your son turns into a conquistador."

"Wait until you see what I'm wearing," Andy told him. "It's like the most garish outfit you've ever seen, but it's got this cool breastplate and I get to carry this big axe. The only problem is that the axe is made out of plastic."

"I am glad to hear that," Teri said.

"We'll take separate cars," Deke told them. "And don't worry, I promise I'll stay far from the madding crowd, at least if that's possible."

Every year the landing drew thousands of spectators.

"I must admit though, Andy, that when you told me you'd been selected to be a conquistador I was a bit disappointed."

His son looked surprised. "Why, Dad?"

"Because this year I was planning to sit with the demonstrators, but I don't think your mom is going to allow me to do that."

Every year there was a contingent of Native American demonstrators who took issue with the glorification of the beginning of what they termed a genocide. They also hated white people (many with a belly full of mimosas) dressing up as Native Americans in Indian costumes. Deke could understand their antipathy, and in the past he had threatened to throw his lot in with those demonstrators.

"I am most certainly not going to allow you," Teri said.

"You know what they say about the Pilgrims," Deke replied.

His wife bit. "What do they say?"

"That first they fell on their knees, and then they fell on the aborigines."

On Saturday morning Teri scrutinized Deke's outfit. At her behest he was trying to go incognito with a baseball cap, sunglasses, and sweats. Teri nodded at what she saw. It would be hard for anyone to pick out her husband.

"Since I've been banished to the cheap seats," Deke told Andy, "I'm bringing a spotting scope to watch your grand entrance."

Deke and Teri usually used the spotting scope to watch the hundreds of varieties of birds that came and lived in Spanish Trace.

"We'll bring some nice takeout home for lunch," Teri promised, kissing Deke on his nose. She then dropped Andy off at the staging area and went in search of a parking space. Andy joined the teenage boys, many of whom were his good friends—but not all. One of those boys was Delmar Reed, the star of the show. His full mane of brown locks would fly in the wind at the front of the old ship *Catalina* as he played the role of the Spanish explorer and conquistador Hernando de Soto. Andy knew Delmar was good buddies with Madison Dixon, Darl Dixon's son, but he tried not to hold that against him. What Andy couldn't help noticing, though, was that Delmar reeked of rum.

"Here comes the axe murderer," said Delmar. "Like father, like son."

Not all the boys laughed, but enough of them did that Andy could feel his face start to burn. Andy didn't get a chance to say anything back because there was a call for the boys to get into their uniforms. Everyone put on their Spanish conquistador outfits. To set Delmar apart, one of the organizers glued a beard to his chin. Then the boys headed to the pier and boarded a large-masted ship.

Catalina was outfitted to give the appearance of an ancient Spanish ship. But in Andy's opinion that was like trying to put lipstick on a pig. The same tired looking vessel had been used for five decades to reenact this event. Its bow was sloped up twenty feet from the deck, and three huge sails somehow managed to propel the old relic through the water.

Climbing onboard, the would-be conquistadors prepared for the reenactment of the landing of 1539. Andy took his position on the starboard side, next to the honorary De Soto. A professional crew dressed as Spaniards were on board to sail the boat.

When everyone was in place, the *Catalina* sailed toward the beach. As it came into view, cheers could be heard from the mostly liquored-up white people dressed like Native Americans. Sailing through the harbor, the Conquistadors Court members were supposed to maintain their regal poses.

Over a loudspeaker, an announcer offered a brief history lesson. "Under orders from King Philip II of Spain, more than 450 years ago the great conquistador Hernando de Soto sailed through the Gulf of Mexico's magical blue waters onto the shore of what is now Spanish Trace Beach. De Soto claimed the land he found for Spain, and Spanish Trace became the first European settlement in the United States."

As the *Catalina* neared the shore, more cheers erupted from the crowd. "Hernando de Soto is making his way ashore!" the announcer declared.

Most of the Spanish Trace aristocrats liked to claim that their ancestry went back to the conquistadors. Delmar was the fourth generation of Reeds to live in Spanish Trace, and his family owned a large stretch of the waterfront. As the ship headed closer towards shore, Delmar decided to continue his digs about Deke. "Hey, Andy, I hope you don't go berserker on us like your dad did. Maybe you should give me that axe of yours for safekeeping."

"You're hilarious," Andy responded, trying to ignore the drunken conquistador.

Delmar bowed. He was acting convinced that he was the commander in real life. "Maybe I'll give your old man a pardon for killing a pervert," he said. "But maybe I won't. I mean having one less lawyer in this world is a good thing, isn't it?"

From his vantage point Deke was watching Andy and the other conquistadors through his spotting scope. When he saw Andy throw down his axe, Deke wondered if he'd gone off-script. And then when Andy grabbed Delmar Reed by his breastplate, and began pounding him in the jaw, Deke was fairly sure the historical reenactment had gone off the tracks.

Then Andy tossed Delmar off the ship and into the water. Even though he was far away from the reenactment, Deke could hear all the Native Americans cheering. They were apparently enjoying this revisionist history.

Deke grabbed the spotting scope, and ran for his car.

"Want to tell me what happened?" asked Deke when he found Andy on the dock.

"No," said Andy.

"Then let's get this over with," Deke replied.

Tom and Laura Reed were fussing over Delmar. He looked more like a drowned rat than a conquering conquistador. His glued-on beard was holding on to his chin by what looked like a single hair, and there was the beginning of a shiner under his left eye.

"Andy has come over to apologize," Deke told them.

"Sorry," Andy said, almost spitting out the word.

"With all this armor Delmar could have drowned," said Laura.

"Your kid coldcocked mine, Deke," said Tom Reed. "That's not right."

"No, it's not right," said Deke. "But because neither boy seems to want to talk about what happened, I suspect there's a lot more to this story. I'm hoping the boys get past this. I remember a long time ago we had a run-in, Tom, but I'm glad to say we got past that."

That old history, stretching back thirty years, made Tom stop to think. Then he offered an almost imperceptible nod.

Deke took that as encouragement. "So I'll say again what Andy didn't do a very good job of saying: We are very sorry."

Deke extended his hand and Tom shook it. Laura didn't look as ready to make nice. She was still making a fuss over her son. But at least she didn't stop the peacemaking.

"I know you have a lot on your plate," Tom said, "and I don't want to add any more. Let's forget about this incident."

"I appreciate that very much," Deke said.

Deke gave Andy a stern look, and his son said, "Thank you."

With the uneasy truce arranged, Deke and Andy took their leave of the Reed family. It was only when they were out of sight that Deke put his arm around Andy's shoulder. Without asking, he knew Andy had reacted to something Delmar had said about him. He probably shouldn't be proud of his son, but he was.

"Another red-letter day for the Deketomis family," said Deke. "I'm sure your mom is on her way over here right now. You'd better call her and say everything is fine. And tell her you'll be going home with me."

"How about I text her?" asked Andy. He wanted to avoid his mother's wrath.

"Call her and take your medicine," said Deke.

Because of the Three Conquistadors Celebration, traffic was unusually thick on the Two Mile Bridge. As they slowly made their way across the bridge, Deke glanced in the rearview mirror. There it was. Ever since they'd left the beach a blue van seemed to have been following them. Deke didn't want to alarm Andy, but at the same time he was on the alert. Like the old saying went, just because he was being paranoid *didn't mean* that others weren't trying to get him.

"You've got better eyes than I do, Andy," Deke said. "Who's in that blue van that's a few cars behind us?"

Andy turned around and squinted. "It's some older dude in Ray-Bans. And it must be his wife with him. The two of them sort of look like Ma and Pa Kettle in that famous painting."

"*American Gothic?*" asked Deke.

"That's it," said Andy.

Deke decided he didn't have to be worried about Ma and Pa Kettle. After coming off the bridge into Sea Breeze he took a right turn into their neighborhood followed by a left turn onto the narrow street that wound its way towards the cul-de-sac where they lived. But just as he made the left, Deke was forced to abruptly brake. A wide dump truck was stopped just in front of two cars parked on either side of the street. There were only a few inches of clearance on either side of the dump truck, and it appeared its driver had stopped to avoid scraping the sides of the two parked cars.

Just as Deke was about to put his car in reverse, the blue van that had been following slammed into them from behind.

"Damn it!" Deke yelled.

At that moment, the dump truck's lift tipped up and its load of gravel, heavy rocks, and sand rained down on their car. Deke jammed the vehicle in reverse, but it was no use. The van had pinned them in. The airbags exploded into their chests and faces as the avalanche of rocks continued.

"Get out!" Deke shouted.

"I'm stuck!" Andy cried.

His son's airbag hadn't retracted. Deke grabbed a penknife and began slashing to free his son. This was no longer a joke. With all the gravel still being dropped, Deke feared for his son's life. It would be better to run from the car than get crushed inside. With a few slashes, and some hard tugging, he removed the obstruction. By that time, though, the gravel was piled up so high they wouldn't be able to get out through the front doors. Deke slammed his hand on the horn and held it down. Someone had to hear their plight.

He rolled down one of the back windows. The car filled with dust and debris and flying gravel, but Deke didn't care. There was still enough space for Andy to crawl out. "Go out the back window!" Deke screamed.

"What about you?"

"Go!" screamed Deke.

Andy began moving, but then stopped. The dump truck was lurching away. He looked behind them and through the dust and haze could see that the blue van was also retreating.

Once the storm of gravel stopped, a neighbor helped dig them out with a shovel, but the car wasn't going anywhere. Deke wondered if it was even salvageable.

As soon as they got home the police interviewed Deke and Andy in the Deketomis family room. Police Chief Larry Hackett had decided to show a personal interest, and was there with Deke's counsel Gina Romano.

Hackett was a third generation Spanish Trace police chief. A few years earlier Hackett had been hit with a grazing shot to his butt at three o'clock in the morning as he was climbing out the window of his neighbor's house. The shooter was Hackett's wife Priscilla, who claimed she had shot a 20-gauge shotgun full of birdshot at what she thought was an intruder. At the time Hackett said he was responding to "suspicious noises" in the house of their young, divorcee neighbor. The lawman suffered relatively minor injuries and the divorcee relocated across town within days.

Despite that youthful indiscretion, Deke knew that Hackett was a good and honest investigator, and would thoroughly look into what had happened to him.

It was a shame others weren't as scrupulous. Later that night he watched Fox's Mindy Marin's account of what had happened. There were a few seconds of footage of his damaged car, followed by footage of Ken Thorn coaching his softball team.

"Troubled Spanish Trace lawyer Nick Deketomis today claimed that he was ambushed by two other vehicles and that his very expensive car suffered damage," said Marin. "Skeptics are claiming this accident was staged in an attempt to have a change of venue in his upcoming trial for the murder of Kenneth Thorn."

Deke was glad the rest of the family wasn't around to see the report. He had tried not to show it, but the ambush had left him shaken. More than anything else, Deke cared about the safety of his family. First Cara had almost died, and then Andy had been forced to suffer through an attack meant for him.

I'm scared, Deke thought. I'm scared for my family, and frightened for myself. It was a difficult admission. And though he kept telling his family that everything was going to be fine, Deke had no idea if this was true.

30
GET OFF OF MY CLOUD

Deke hated being dependent upon others. He had always liked to imagine he was master of his universe, but now he knew better. It was a tough, humbling lesson to learn.

He knew there were people working tirelessly for him. They were trying to find out things on his behalf. They were trying to prove his innocence. The hardest thing for Deke was waiting. Usually he was the one out there making things happen. But now he was being treated like an invalid.

Deke just hoped his condition wasn't terminal.

Early one afternoon about a week before his trial, Deke's cell phone rang and the display on his phone said *Unknown Caller.* Deke had never seen those words before.

"Yes?" said Deke.

"This is Matt Ortel," said the voice on the other end. "I'm calling from a secure line. Gina told me that you'd want this call."

"Hey, Matt," Deke responded.

Ortel was a computer and electronics whiz. He had no pretensions about his talents, and merely called himself a "hacker." Deke had met him only once or twice, but knew he was a freelancer used by Carol Morris as a member of her investigative team. Ortel was only a few years older than Andy. "I've been studying those videos of you at the stadium that have been turning up on the Internet," he said. "It's obvious they were edited."

Deke tried to understand what Ortel was telling him. Apparently it was all about the camera angles, lighting, and time sequencing.

"Whoever doctored the videos had one goal. They wanted you to look like the aggressor. My guess is that the editing was done by pretty talented professionals," Ortel said.

"And you can prove this?" asked Deke.

"Easy peasy," answered the young man. "And I'm also getting closer to the shooter."

"The who?"

"That person who shot the footage of your struggle with Ken Thorn. He's no pro, that's for sure."

Then Ortel went into another explanation about camera "signatures," recognition signals, and video identification software. Deke didn't understand half of what he was saying, but pretended he did.

"Gina also wanted me to tell you about what I found on the cloud showing city surveillance video of the area on the day of your lunch with Moses. You were apparently being followed," Ortel said.

"What cloud?" asked Deke.

Deke heard another explanation about backups, and then heard Ortel say, "The camera surveillance footage from that date was still there in the cloud."

"Which date was that?" asked Deke.

"The important date of your lunch with Moses," said Ortel. "The date you stopped and talked with our guy before entering the restaurant."

"You mean Ken Thorn?"

"That's who I mean," Ortel confirmed. "I pulled down footage of the two of you talking on the street."

Deke found himself breathing a little easier. His defense team was telling him they could make the case that Thorn had been stalking him.

"And that's not all," said Ortel. "The city's surveillance camera footage gave us a look at about two dozen people in that downtown area. Gina and Carol Morris are looking at pictures now and checking out the scene."

"Explain," Deke said.

"They're looking for bad guys," Ortel told him. "But I guess Gina calls them 'interested parties.'"

Deke was able to get Gina and Carol on a conference call. "Talk with me," he said.

"We still don't have a positive ID of another person of interest in the area at that time," said Carol, "but we're working on it."

"And who haven't you been able to positively identify?"

No one immediately answered, and Deke knew both women were probably gesturing to each other as to what to say. Finally, it was Gina who spoke: "It looks like Darl Dixon is in the park."

"Darl Dixon," said an incredulous Deke.

"That hasn't been confirmed yet," Gina said. "I don't want you going off half-cocked."

"What is Darl's connection to Ken Thorn?" asked Deke.

"Darl is a deacon at Holiness Southern Pentecostal Church," Carol answered, "the same place where Thorn and his family were parishioners."

"Why do I get the feeling that Pastor Rodney Morgan is involved in this?"

"You're not alone in that feeling," Carol told him. "Right now I'm doing my best to connect the dots. Everyone already knows that Darl is the pastor's darling for office. Have you seen those commercials with the pastor's arm around him?"

"We need more than commercials linking the two," Gina said. "Our evidence has to be irrefutable, or else we'll come across like a bunch of tinfoil-hat conspiracy nuts."

"They're all in bed together," Deke said. The more he thought about it, the more sure he was.

"Even if that's true," said Gina, "I still say we should go ahead and ask for a change of venue."

"No," said Deke.

"The waters in Spanish Trace have been muddied," Gina said.

"They've been muddied everywhere."

"Have you given any more thought to a stand-your-ground defense?"

George Zimmerman had made Florida's stand-your-ground self-defense laws famous—or more accurately, infamous.

"If we can show the jury that you reasonably believed there was a threat to your personal safety, and convince the jury that you believed Kenneth Thorn had a gun, that might fly. But to do that we'd have to put you on the witness stand, and that's not something I want to do."

"Like I've told you," he said, "I'm fine with being on the witness stand."

"You know how doctors are supposed to be the worst patients?" said Gina. "Lawyers are definitely the worst witnesses."

Deke wanted to argue, but from his own experiences he knew Gina was right.

"Right now you've got to sit tight, Deke," said Carol. "We're working on another angle, and it could be a good one. Six weeks ago paramedics picked up Thorn from his home and rushed him to the emergency room. The family cover is that he had food poisoning, but a friend of a friend who works in the ER says they treated him for an overdose of drugs. I'm trying to reconstruct his hospital event without any formal kind of discovery requests because I'm pretty sure it's not on the prosecution's radar screen and I want to keep it that way. But if my preliminary information is correct, I'm wondering: What was it that drove Thorn to take those pills?"

"I'd like to know that myself," said Deke.

"We've already determined Thorn was no Boy Scout," Carol continued. "On Sunday he was a churchgoer, but the rest of the week he definitely wasn't. We're working on getting some interesting witnesses to testify to that."

"But we'll have to do that carefully," declared Gina. "People are inclined to be sympathetic to the dead."

"Why would he have tried to kill himself?" Deke asked aloud.

"I am not convinced he was the suicidal sort," Carol replied. "Lots of suicide attempts are cries for help. Some are just attention getters."

"What if Ken Thorn was trying to show his wife he was sorry for something?" said Deke.

"I've tried to get her to talk to me," Carol reminded him, "but she won't."

"Try again, Carol," said Deke. "Something's there. I quit believing in coincidences long ago."

31
PRETRIAL JITTERS

Angela had felt sick to her stomach ever since hearing Darl Dixon's voice on the kitchen phone. Sweet as pie, he'd asked if she would meet him for coffee the next morning. After hanging up, she'd had to sit at the kitchen table for an hour just to calm down.

Even from the grave, her late husband continued to torment her. Angela could hardly bear the thought of the upcoming trial. She knew about Ken's double life. In fact, she supposed she had always known. That was terrible enough, but the trial was making everything worse. Angela knew that Ken had met with Pastor Rodney. Ken had also told her about his meeting with Darl Dixon. He hadn't told her about his discussions with those men, but had said he was doing "important" work for them.

Angela had told the pastor about those awful pictures of Ken and that girl. And she had a feeling that the prosecutor Darl Dixon had also been privy to that secret. She wondered if Ken had ended up in that stadium doing the bidding of those other men. Just the thought of that made her feel afraid. Even from the grave Ken could still make her feel ashamed and unclean.

Angela had tried to beg off participating in the trial. She'd told Darl's assistant Orville Sizemore that she was doing poorly and couldn't testify as a character witness. Orville hadn't been happy about that. He'd tried to convince her that for the sake of her husband's memory she needed to take the stand. Angela wanted to tell him that for the sake of her husband's memory she couldn't take the stand, but she'd ended the conversation saying that she would think about it. Her reluctance to testify had prompted a number of fake friendly calls from Prosecutor Dixon. During his last call he'd all but insisted that she meet with him at Makin' Bacon Restaurant on Thursday morning.

It took fifteen minutes of sitting in the parking lot before Angela found the courage to go inside the restaurant. She found Darl Dixon waiting for her in a back corner booth. He rose and smiled ear to ear as she approached the booth.

"Don't you look pretty this morning," he said.

Angela knew she didn't look pretty. She looked tired and beaten down, which she was. People thought she was a grieving widow. She wasn't. Most of Angela's mourning had been done while Ken was alive.

The waitress approached. "You want coffee, dear?" she asked. At Angela's nod of the head, her cup was filled. Before the waitress left the table she paused to say, "I'm so sorry for your loss, dear."

In a voice barely more than a whisper Angela said, "Thank you."

Darl nodded in approval. When the waitress was out of earshot he said, "You see that? All over Spanish Trace, all over this country, people who don't know you feel sorry for you. And that's why I need you on the stand."

Angela shook her head. "I don't want to be in a courtroom. I don't want everyone judging me."

"All you'll be is a character witness, Mrs. Thorn," Darl said. "I'll ask you a few gentle questions about your husband, things like where you met and how long you were married. And then you can go on your merry way."

My merry way, thought Angela. It had been a long time since she'd had her merry way.

"If you don't go up on the stand," Darl continued, "it won't look good for our side. Everyone will wonder why you weren't there."

He looked at her, trying to bend her to his will, but Angela looked away.

"The thing is, Mr. Dixon," she said, "I know things about my husband, and they're not nice things."

Darl didn't directly respond, but Angela sensed he was well aware of these "not nice things."

"Mr. Dixon," she said, "I believe in the power of Jesus to save people, but Ken, he was caught in the devil's grip. He wasn't right in his head or his soul."

"Call me Darl," he said, reaching out to her and putting his hand over hers. "We're old friends, you and me. Known each other a long time, haven't we?"

Angela nodded in agreement even though she knew the two of them hadn't spoken ten words together before the incident. At church Darl Dixon, his snooty wife, and his out-of-control kids had never paid much attention to any of the Thorns, but now Darl Dixon was pretending deep concern for her. He continued rubbing her hand.

"Now, Angela," he said, and then asked, "Is it okay if I call you Angela?"

She nodded, and he continued: "Angela, if you trust me everything will work out just fine."

Angela didn't reply, but she couldn't help but wonder if Darl Dixon had said those same words to Ken when he was alive.

"I don't want you to worry your pretty little head. All you have to do is bear a little witness about poor Ken."

Darl must have seen she still wasn't convinced. "This isn't only about you," he said. "Think about your daughter. After the trial is over the two of you need to get on with your lives, and doing that will be a lot easier if people around here remembered your husband fondly. The jury needs to see the widow Ken left behind. Do you understand that?"

Angela reluctantly nodded. That's when Darl decided to press his advantage. He'd shown her the carrot, but now he wanted her to see the stick.

"You'll need to paint a nice picture of Ken," he said. "I don't want you speaking any ill of the dead, you understand? If you do right by me, I'll do right by you. And I can assure you it helps to have friends who can protect you."

If Angela had any doubts about this man knowing things about Ken's death, they were now long gone. He stared her down in a most threatening way. "People sometimes underestimate me, Angela," he said, "and I don't want you making that same mistake. I want us to understand each other perfectly. Do you understand me?"

Slowly, painfully, she nodded.

"That's good," he said, "because I have some pictures in my possession that don't show your husband in the best of lights. I think you told our good mutual friend about finding some similar pictures of your husband, isn't that so?"

Angela struggled for air. The prosecutor knew about her conversation with Pastor Rodney.

"I want to do my best to make sure no one else ever sees these pictures," said Darl. "It would be terrible for your daughter to have to remember her father in such a way, wouldn't it?"

"Yes," she whispered.

"I'm glad we understand one another then," he said. "I know you're going to do just fine in the courtroom."

Darl began the slow process of disengaging himself from the booth. After standing he looked her up and down from head to toe and pursed his lips in disapproval.

"I'm going to want you looking better for court, girl. You'll need to comb your hair and gussy up some. You got a modest looking black dress? You're going to need one of those."

Then he offered her an imaginary tip of the hat. "You have yourself a good day now, you hear?"

He winked and then ambled off.

Angela continued to sit mutely. Only when she was convinced that he was long gone did she get up to leave.

32
WORLD ENOUGH AND TIME

It was strange, thought Deke, how he always slept well when he was preparing for a trial. It didn't matter that he was working sixteen-hour days, or that the judgments involved big issues and big money. In these cases Deke felt as if he was *all in*. He could sleep knowing that he was completely invested physically and mentally.

But when it came to his own trial, he felt almost disembodied. He felt out of sorts because he wasn't in control. And because of that his sleep had suffered. Insomnia only made everything worse. He had to refrain from calling Carol and Gina in the middle of the night. Deke knew the two of them were working a lot of angles on his behalf, but it was maddening not to know up to the second details.

In a week matters would finally begin to reach a resolution. That's when the trial would commence.

The door to the master bedroom opened and Teri surprised him by appearing with a tray of food. "Breakfast in bed," she announced.

Deke fought off tears. That was another thing that was bothering him—this trial had him behaving more emotionally than he could ever remember.

Without breaking down he managed to ask, "What's the special occasion?"

"Every day is a special occasion," said Teri. "Lately I've been reminded of that a lot."

"Amen," said Deke. "You are going to join me, aren't you?"

By way of answer she got into bed with him. Teri had made him an egg white omelet filled with spinach. By the looks of it, she'd even picked oranges fresh from their garden to make him a glass of OJ.

"I'd give anything to not have to put you and the kids through this," he said.

"I wish you'd stop beating yourself up," said Teri, "and think about all the wonderful things you've given us instead."

"It's been quite a journey, hasn't it?"

She nodded. "It seems like just yesterday this brash upstart with his funny Greek name came into my life."

"Would you do it differently if you had the chance?" he asked.

"Never," she said. "I was sure then, and I'm sure now. I didn't play games with you. There was no coyness. I *knew*. I didn't want to wait to get married and for us to start our life together."

Then Teri surprised Deke by reciting, "'Had we but world enough and time, this coyness, lady, were no crime.'"

"What's that?" asked Deke.

"It's a few lines from an old poem I learned in college," Teri said. "With you, I always felt there was world enough and time."

"My trial is in a week," he said. "It doesn't feel as if there is world enough and time."

"I'll be there before and after the trial," she said.

"I feel trapped. I'm innocent, but I still killed a man, and that makes me feel guilty. And maybe because I'm the defendant, I don't see a clear path to acquittal. Usually I know exactly how a trial is going to unfold. Even the curveballs don't surprise me. I'm expecting them. But now I'm not sure what to expect. I've even reluctantly come to accept that I could be found guilty. What will the family do then?"

"We'll continue to love you," said Teri. "And of course we'll appeal."

Deke couldn't help but laugh, but then he grew serious again. "I don't want to relive Ken Thorn's death," he said. "It was terrible enough the first time around. And there are going to be a lot of ugly pictures—that's why I don't want you and the kids in the courtroom."

"For once, would you worry about yourself and not us?" Teri actually sounded annoyed. "We will be there. And together we'll get through this. Is that clear?"

"Yes, ma'am," he said.

"Good," said Teri. "Let's eat."

The next day Deke went into the office to meet with Gina. He kept hoping that they'd get a lucky break. There were plenty of smoking guns, but they needed evidence. Thorn had provoked Deke, egging him on to hit him. Now they needed to collect evidence showing this. Everyone knew the answers were out there. Deke hoped those answers would surface before the trial, but knew he couldn't count on that.

When he arrived at his office, Deke was reminded that he wasn't alone. A box of his favorite glazed donuts had been left on his desk with the note: *We Believe in You!* All the assistants and paralegals in the law firm had signed it.

"Thank heavens for comfort food," Deke remarked to his loyal executive assistant Donna as she gave him a hug.

"I think I've gotten more hugs in the last month than I have in my lifetime," said Deke.

"Then one more won't hurt," said Donna, squeezing him hard.

If he was hoping to get any comfort from Gina Romano, it never developed. She was more the tough-love type. Their latest disagreement was on character witnesses.

"I don't want you parading in and out a bunch of people all saying what a great guy I am," said Deke. "I am not going to look like a sad sack."

"Would you rather look like a murderer?"

Deke faced her glare and said, "Maybe."

"It's come to my attention that the prosecution now has in their hands an account of you assaulting another man."

"I was seventeen," Deke said. "All of that should be sealed."

"Darl is trying to unseal it, Deke. Why didn't you tell me?"

Deke sighed. "I just never imagined that might surface to bite me in the butt."

"I need to know things like this, Deke. I can't be blindsided in court."

"What do you want to know?" he said, his voice tired.

"Who, what, when, where, and why, for starters."

"Like I said, I was seventeen. At the time I was, as the foster care system says, 'between families.' That meant I was pretty much living on the street. Anyway, the guy I ended up attacking was the son of a former foster family I had lived with."

Gina looked confused. "How did that come about?"

"There was a family named Pfeiffer that took me in for a year when I was fifteen. They were okay to me, but they made it clear that I was a short-term solution to replenishing their familial coffers. There were two kids in the Pfeiffer family, a boy named Vince who was a year older than I was, and a girl named Audrey who was a year younger. Audrey was by far the most welcoming member of the family. We were just friends. There was nothing romantic between us. But we really connected. In fact when I was given my notice, she gave me a going away present.

"Anyway, long story short, I ran across Audrey a year later. I was surprised at how glad she was to see me. I guess she needed to unload on someone. That's when she confessed to me that she'd just had an abortion. Back in those days it wasn't impossible for an underage girl to get an abortion. And then she swore me to secrecy and told me who the father was. It was all I could do not to throw up. Her own brother Vince had impregnated her. According to Audrey, he'd been abusing her since she was thirteen.

"After saying good night to Audrey, I went on the hunt. I had run across Vince a few times since leaving the family, and I knew where he liked to hang out. When I caught up to him, I never said anything, but he knew. And I proceeded to beat the shit out of him. I did it so thoroughly someone must have been afraid I'd kill him, and the cops were called. I was arrested, but Vince refused to press charges. I guess he knew what charges could be pressed against him."

"That it?" asked Gina.

"The whole sordid tale," Deke promised.

"You have anything else you need to tell me?"

"Yeah," said Deke. "I enjoyed beating the shit out of him."

It wasn't exactly what his lawyer wanted to hear.

33

FULL SPEED AHEAD

When Deke decided he'd disappointed Gina enough for the day, he went back to his own office. But even the prospect of raised glazed doughnuts didn't make him feel any better. He felt his cell phone vibrate and saw Howard Nations was calling.

"You got a minute to talk, Deke?" Howard asked.

"I'd feel better if you called on the office line," Deke said. "I know that's secure. For the last few weeks we've had security teams sweeping the offices."

"Will do," said Howard.

Deke went out and signaled Donna to put the call through to him. When he picked up, Howard began talking as if they hadn't been interrupted.

"I know you got a million things on your plate, Deke, so I thought I'd make this short and sweet."

"You're not saying you actually have good news?" asked Deke.

"I do. You okay with that?"

"It's been so long since I've heard good news that I might not know what to do."

"Maybe you'll allow yourself to smile," Howard said. "Anyway, I recently saw *our friend*."

Even though they were both on secure lines, Howard didn't want to advertise the fact that he'd visited the Collector.

"Was it a fruitful visit?" asked Deke.

"It was," Howard proclaimed. "And it was also a very expensive visit. But I'm hoping it will be a much more expensive lesson for the opposition. We can now show they had their hand in the cookie jar, and a lot more."

S.I. Oil was being defended by Backerman & Sharp, a firm Deke was sure was the dirtiest corporate defense in the land. Of course that made sense in that their clients were the Swanson brothers. In the past Backerman & Sharp had been caught destroying documents, and compounding that sin by claiming those documents had never existed.

Even in a regressive Texas federal court, destroying documents and directing witnesses to deny those destroyed documents ever existed was seldom tolerated.

Their past misdeeds had resulted in million-dollar fines and sanctions against the firm. Three of their lawyers had been disbarred after shredding documents the court had ordered them to produce. Backerman & Sharp considered it perfectly acceptable to lie and cheat in presenting a case for their high roller corporate clients. That's why more than a dozen of their lawyers had been suspended from the practice of law.

Both men continued to talk cryptically. It was ironic, thought Deke, when good guys had to act like wise guys.

"You sound happy," said Deke.

"I'm very happy. Our friend came through with four important pieces of news."

Four documents, thought Deke.

Howard decided to stop using doublespeak. "Back in 2009, S.I. Oil paid for some environmental studies near their Texas refinery. The results were worse than anything they could have expected, so they decided to bury the study.

"That's when I decided to do a formal discovery with our friends at Backerman & Sharp. I even specified the year 2009."

What that meant was that Howard Nations had served Swanson Industries with numerous tightly drafted, very specific interrogatories and requests to admit evidence to the court centered on the four documents he already had in hand.

"And what was opposing counsel's response?" asked Deke.

"They claimed no such documents showing results of environmental studies have ever existed. Those pricks just couldn't help themselves."

"I am smiling, Howard," Deke said. "I really am. And fifteen minutes ago I would have thought that was impossible."

"Are things that bad?"

"Let's just say they're not good," Deke responded. "But maybe your good luck will be contagious."

34
OUR TOWN

Two days before Deke's trial date, Gina Romano came to him to ask, "What do you think about me petitioning the court for a later trial date?"

"It sounds like desperation on our part," remarked Deke.

"We have a lot of balls in the air. Carol says her team is close, really close, to breaking the case open. It doesn't make sense to go to trial before we can present our best case."

"So you'd like to ask for more time to prepare?" asked Deke.

"Among other things," Gina divulged.

"What other things?"

"It wouldn't hurt if a shrink saw you, Deke. He could speak to state of mind. We've got Thorn on video pursuing you. We can introduce your upbringing. The jury would be sympathetic if they heard about the difficult time you had growing up."

"No," said Deke. "I am not going to sing poor, poor pitiful me; not now, not ever."

"That could be your get out of jail card."

"It's not something I'll play."

"You are one of the most intransigent clients that I have ever had the misfortune of representing."

"I love you too, Gina."

"I can also ask for an extension because of personal emergencies. I know Cara's doing physical therapy and needs to take a handful of pills every day."

"You're a great godmother to Cara, Gina. But I am not going to use my daughter as a shield."

"You're not giving me many options, Deke."

"Then I guess that's your answer. Let's go forward with this thing."

On the first day of his trial Deke wished he felt as sure and brave as when he last spoke with Gina. The truth was, he was neither. He'd been in courtrooms for most of his adult life, but this was different.

Welcome to hell, he thought.

Luckily Deke's presiding judge was Robert Heath, an experienced criminal trial judge. Prior to Judge Heath being asked to serve at Deke's trial, six judges had recused themselves. Four of those judges knew Deke personally, and felt there could be an appearance of impropriety. The other two recused themselves because Deke had been instrumental in having them appointed to the bench. This necessitated bringing in a trial judge from another district to hear the case.

Judge Heath was from West Palm Beach and had served as a trial judge for more than twenty years. Having presided over more than two hundred major criminal cases, he was well-equipped to handle high-profile criminal trials. He had a reputation for being hard-nosed, especially with lawyers who deviated from the script of court decorum. As a stickler for the law, he came down hard on lawyers that transgressed. Deke was betting that Darl Dixon would soon be out of favor with this judge.

His trial was getting some serious national attention, but locally it wouldn't have surprised Deke to see the news about it reported only in the entertainment section of *The Spanish Trace News Journal*. The prevailing attitude was that attending the trial was like getting a ticket to some hot show. There was even a story about "how to best score a seat."

Deke had agreed to let Gina drive him to trial; she didn't want her client out of her sight. A block from the court they got their first inkling of the freak show that awaited them. Protestors were out in force. Most could be easily identified as people from Holiness Southern Pentecostal Church. What Deke had faced in the Ranidol trial was only a small taste of what he was now seeing in his hometown. There were lots of posters with hellfire. In one of them Satan was smiling. The caption read, "I'm waiting for you, Deke!"

"Are you still glad you didn't want a change of venue?" asked Gina.

"I've spent pretty much my entire life in Spanish Trace," said Deke. "No way I am going to be run out of town now."

"At least you're consistent, Nick Deketomis."

"What we're seeing isn't our town," said Deke. "It's just a group of crazies trying to take it over."

But sometimes, Deke had to concede, it seemed like the crazies had taken over the country if not the world.

Deke thought of Thornton Wilder's *Our Town*. He wasn't much of a playgoer, but every few years he liked seeing productions of this particular play.

"'Whenever you come near the human race there's layers and layers of nonsense,'" Deke quoted.

Gina looked at him with surprise.

"That's from the play *Our Town*," said Deke. And then he wistfully remembered another line: "'Oh, earth, you're too wonderful for anybody to realize you.'"

"I didn't know you were a philosopher, Deke."

"I'm not. I guess I'm just taking a moment to look back, like everyone in that graveyard was."

"Don't stop now," Gina pleaded. "This reflective Deke is someone I want sitting next to me as we go to trial."

"The other day Teri was talking about world enough and time," explained Deke. "I'm going to try and remember that, and appreciate all that I've had."

Then he summed up with what Thornton Wilder had written in his play. "'Choose the least important day in your life. It will be important enough.'"

When they got past the Holiness Southern gauntlet, Deke actually began seeing some friendly faces. Perhaps a hundred union members were showing their support, along with an almost equal number of members from the Spanish Trace African Methodist Episcopal Church. A decade earlier Deke had been outraged when an arsonist had tried to burn down the AMEC. It was Deke who had given a private donation to help them rebuild, and now, unexpectedly, the membership was remembering what he had done. His throat tightened, and he didn't dare speak to Gina. One sign in particular caught his eye: *Remember Deke's Civil Rights!*

The zoo-like atmosphere was confined well away from where the trial was taking place, and it was clear the heavy hand of Judge Heath was at work. Much to the media's displeasure, Judge Heath wasn't going to allow a disruptive atmosphere anywhere near his courtroom. A number of media reports derided the judge's draconian ways. Judge Heath appeared to take no notice of the slings. It was clear he wasn't going to make Lance Ito's mistake and allow the media to make a circus of his court proceedings as had occurred during the O. J. Simpson trial. He had barred cameras not only in the courtroom, but anywhere near the courtroom, prompting a number of editorial cartoons of Judge Heath with his bushy gray eyebrows running wildly rampant like a weed.

Deke was all for the judge's take-control orders. Judge Heath had even made available a side entrance for those involved with the court proceedings. Deke didn't have to worry about being put on display, as he had during the Ranidol trial. Since the judge had also ordered a roped-off perimeter around his courtroom's entrance, only essential personnel were allowed admittance and those not cleared by security were turned away. People entering the courthouse were surprised by how well-ordered everything seemed. All of the judge's precautions had set the correct tone for jury selection to proceed.

With a minimum of fuss, Deke and Gina were seated, and it wasn't long before the courtroom filled with people. After assuming his august position at the bench in the expansive courtroom, Judge Heath introduced himself to those who had managed to get a seat.

"Ladies and gentlemen," he began, "we are not yet fully acquainted, but I believe it is of paramount importance that you understand what I will and will not tolerate.

"First of all, this is not some reality TV show, and I would ask anyone suffering from that misapprehension to vacate these proceedings at once. This is a courtroom trial where a man has been charged with a crime that carries severe penalties if he is found guilty. Right now, sitting here in this courtroom, he is an innocent man. He is no more guilty, at this point in time, than any of you. If even for a moment I hear any of you say a solitary word that might be deemed prejudicial, and I have very good ears mind you, then you will be forcibly removed from this courtroom. I can't stress enough that there will be zero tolerance for any conduct that in any way might prejudice this gentleman on trial, or prejudice the state's case against him. If you engage in such behavior there will be serious legal consequences brought against you. You've chosen to sit in this courtroom and observe this trial. That is your right, but with that right comes responsibility."

The judge's stern words and strong persona left little doubt that he meant what he said. His gaze extended across the courtroom, making sure that everyone understood, as well as perhaps daring anyone to challenge him. No one did.

"Very well, then," he said, and turned to the bailiff. With a nod of his head Judge Heath gave the bailiff leave to begin bringing out the potential jurors. *Voir dire* was about to start, the proceeding that examined the jurors' qualifications to serve. Even more importantly, it was a chance for the lawyers to try and figure out which jurors they wanted and which they didn't.

Deke knew how complicated and contentious voir dire could be, but for him the stakes had never felt higher. Twelve people were going to hold his fate in their hands.

Gina Romano had a simple and clear goal in the process: to elicit from potential jurors the most painfully ugly truths of what each thought about her client Nick Deketomis. It wouldn't do to hear half-truths, or have simmering unspoken biases and prejudices. Having those negatives surface sooner rather than later was critical. Gina needed to hear the worst of the worst in open court. If she didn't, those prejudices would surface at the worst time—in the jury deliberation room.

Deke knew it was his job to not react when a terrible thing was said about him. He put on his best poker face, listening but not responding. During the course of the voir dire he observed Gina skillfully drawing out what people really thought about him. Anyone that is in need of humbling should be the subject of a voir dire proceeding, Deke thought. Deke got to hear that he looked "shifty," and had the kind of face you'd expect from a "used car salesman." People didn't hesitate to say what they knew about him, and what they didn't like about him. According to one woman he was "godless," and she didn't trust godless people. One man said he heard that Deke was a card-carrying ACLU member, and when Gina asked him what he thought about the ACLU he said the organization was leading to "the ruination" of America. It had been years since Deke had heard anyone use the word "pinko," but that's how one man categorized him. Then there was the seventysomething self-described "patriot" wearing a bow tie who was particularly incensed over Deke's regularly referring to tea party members as "teabaggers."

Upon hearing that, it was all Deke could do to keep a straight face.

Deke's attacks over the years against conservatives hadn't gone unnoticed. A number of potential jurors questioned Deke's "pernicious" attacks on the Grand Old Party. Instead of getting a break from Democrats, potential jurors also found fault with Deke's attack on the sitting president, who happened to be a Democrat.

During a break from voir dire, Gina commented on the irony of Deke being attacked from both sides of the political spectrum. "How is it," she whispered to Deke, "that you've managed to piss off people of both political stripes? But I think that understates it. How have you managed to piss off virtually everyone, and how does Teri put up with you?"

It was a rare moment when both lawyer and client could relax. "Teri's ability to put up with me would qualify her for sainthood, but I have, no doubt, also pissed off the Catholic Church. And just in case you were wondering, she does tell me to 'hush' on a regular basis."

"Apparently you haven't been very good about taking her advice."

"Apparently not," agreed Deke.

More than one potential juror expressed resentment that Deke had grown wealthy by taking advantage of honest corporations. It was beyond Deke's understanding that so many people could be sympathetic for what charitably could be called robber barons.

One of the most consistent dings against Deke was how he had alienated so many by his behavior after Ken Thorn's death. Many of the potential jurors perceived Deke as calculating and heartless, and were incredulous that he'd conducted a trial just days after Thorn died.

Gina had warned him about that, thought Deke. She had warned him about lots of things. Even now he was resisting her advice. Gina had expressed her desire to bring Cara to the stand so that she could talk about Ranidol. Gina was sure Cara's testimony would put a different spin on Deke's character. Everyone would understand that Deke's decision to proceed with the Bekmeyer and Ranidol case was just his way of protecting his daughter and redressing her physical injuries. That would make Deke look more like a good dad than a heartless killer. But even though both Cara and Gina pressed Deke to allow this, he had refused. He didn't want his daughter put on the stand. Gina would have to find a way of making him look sympathetic without involving his family.

The long vetting process continued. Deke was actually more heartened than discouraged by what he heard. More than half of those being interviewed didn't seem ill-disposed towards Deke. In fact, some people even had nice things to say about him. Quite a few said Deke had the reputation of being a good father and husband, and some panelists remembered Deke serving as a sports coach for many years. There were even a few who remembered Deke's charitable contributions to the community. While Deke's occupation drew more than its share of cynical comments, there were a few who appreciated his going up against powerful interests and holding their feet to the fire for the wrongs they had committed. Oddly enough, some of those who were politically opposed to Deke revealed their grudging respect for his willingness to stand firm on his political beliefs in a community where most adamantly disagreed with him.

At the end of what felt like a very long day, Gina believed that they had selected the best possible jurors from the panel. The two jury analysts that Bergman Deketomis had hired agreed with her choices. Even though Gina had wanted a change of venue, Deke hoped he was right in his belief in the overall decency of the people in Spanish Trace. After all, his life was going to be in their hands.

By day two, the perimeter around the courthouse was even more active with protesters and rubberneckers.

There were also plenty of vendors catering to the crowds, with food trucks selling favorites like waffle fries and Pronto Pups. Anyone unaware of the proceedings might have assumed the county fair was going on.

As much as Deke didn't want his family there, Teri and Cara had insisted on attending. Andy had tried to be there as well, but Deke had insisted his son go to school. As Deke navigated the courthouse hallways with his lawyer and family, the eyes of the curious trailed after them. Although that was something Deke could have done without, others were busy enjoying their notoriety, especially Darl Dixon who was all but posing at the entrance to Judge Heath's courtroom. Although he knew Gina wouldn't approve, Deke couldn't resist putting the spurs to his longtime adversary as they passed by him.

"Hey, Darl," he said. "You've been looking real good on TV. Any truth to the rumors that you've been seen hanging out with Senator Roger Dove? Maybe if your election plans fall through Roger can get you a job on Fox News. I think it would be a mistake not to have a Plan B!"

Gina gave Deke a glare that would have felled a weaker man. "Really, Deke?" she said. "I mean, really?"

"I promise to behave the rest of the day," he declared.

"You better," said Gina.

They entered Judge Heath's hushed courtroom. Gina and Deke sat at the defense table, while Teri and Cara took seats next to one another in the front row.

Deke looked over to the prosecutor's table and the front row behind them. Sitting there was an uncomfortable looking Angela Thorn. She was dressed in a black dress. Deke noticed her daughter wasn't with her. Angela's support system consisted solely of a severe looking woman who held her hand. The woman's plain frock was like the ones worn by most of the Holiness Southern female protestors.

It didn't take long for the 105 court observers to seat themselves—the maximum number allowed by Judge Heath.

As day two of the trial convened, Judge Heath explained to the jury that they were now part of the civil justice process in Florida, and they had been chosen to sit as deciders of facts in a criminal case.

"Nicholas Deketomis has been charged with manslaughter," he said. "It will be your solemn responsibility to determine if the state is able to prove its accusations against the defendant in this case beyond a reasonable doubt. Your verdict must be based solely on the presented evidence. As Mr. Deketomis sits in front of you today, he is presumed innocent. And this court also makes presumptions about you. Those presumptions are that you will set aside any bias or prejudice that you might have towards either Mr. Deketomis or the prosecutor's office that has brought these charges. To speak more simply, I ask you to pay attention to the facts presented and to keep an open mind."

Judge Heath then explained how the presentation of evidence would take place and how, at the end of trial, the jurors would be instructed on all the specifics of the law surrounding the charge of manslaughter.

The judge instructed Assistant Prosecutor Orville Sizemore to begin. Sizemore was to do all the real lawyering in the trial while Dixon worked the media.

As Sizemore went through his opening presentation, Deke was reluctantly impressed. Sizemore was good at acting the role of the everyman, from the Dockers he wore to his folksy demeanor. Deke knew Sizemore was a more than competent lawyer; his impressive conviction rate spoke for itself. It would not do for them to underestimate him.

Sizemore began by describing what witnesses had observed about Deke on the night of the "tragic death" of Ken Thorn at the stadium. Deke was described as being "noticeably angry and agitated." Sizemore went on to explain that a forensic expert would testify there was no sign of a serious struggle between Kenneth Thorn and Nick Deketomis before the moment that he stabbed the victim in the throat with a ballpoint pen. In addition to those important elements of his case, the prosecutor made clear he thought it was a key fact that Deke had been standing next to his vehicle with the car door opened. Sizemore asked, "Why didn't Mr. Deketomis simply get in his car, lock the doors, and drive away?"

After fifteen minutes more of explaining what the forensic experts found and the reasons the prosecution was convinced Ken Thorn was not a serious threat to Deke, Sizemore said, "Some of the bloody pictures showing the slaughter of poor Mr. Thorn may seem too graphic for some of you, but it is your duty to consider all the evidence."

Deke hoped that the jury would indeed consider all the evidence, especially since a few of the jurors had shot him venomous looks. The sharp glances hadn't gone unnoticed by his counsel.

"Nothing like a hometown jury, big guy," she whispered to Deke.

35
BLOOD EVIDENCE

As Deke continued to witness Sizemore's opening presentation, he became more and more convinced that the prosecutor sounded too confident at such an early time in the trial. When Deke heard Sizemore tell the jury that Ken Thorn was "well-adjusted, healthy, and happy," he knew at least one of Gina's prayers had been answered. As if that wasn't enough, the prosecutor told the jury that, "Mr. Thorn suffered no maladies" and "had no conditions" that required medication. Sizemore concluded that "there was nothing chemical or medical that could have set him off."

It was clear that the prosecution had no idea the defense knew about Thorn's drug overdose or his suicide attempt. On those points alone, Gina's "rope-a-dope" defense would win some points.

Sizemore continued to extol Thorn's virtues. Deke had reason to hope that even if Sizemore won the battle he'd ultimately lose the war. Carol Morris and her investigators had given plenty of information to Gina to demonstrate he was no Vestal Virgin.

"Ken was a good man," Sizemore crooned, "a softball coach, a church deacon, and devoted husband, as you can see by his devastated widow here today. To the first officer on the scene, Nick Deketomis described poor Ken as 'crazed and angry,' but this is inconsistent with everything you will soon learn about this well-adjusted, churchgoing man."

After the prosecutor sat down, Gina stood. "Your Honor," she said, addressing Judge Heath, "the defense would like to reserve its right to give an opening statement after the prosecution presents its case."

"That is acceptable to the court," said the judge. "Is the prosecution ready to proceed?"

Sizemore got to his feet. Although he tried to hide his apparent pleasure, it was obvious to all. "The prosecution is ready to proceed, Your Honor."

Orville thinks he hit a home run, thought Deke. And now he thinks he can put the game out of reach. Although it wasn't usual to defer an opening statement, Deke knew that Gina recognized an advantage in waiting.

Deke was sure she was still hoping for more damning information on Thorn. She was probably also hoping the prosecution would further tip their hand.

Sizemore began his case by calling several less important witnesses to testify. He started with the arresting officer, and then brought to the stand the security guard who'd witnessed the first contact between Deke and Ken Thorn. Then he brought up *Spanish Trace News Journal* columnist Maggie Lee for questioning. As usual, she had a signature bow in her hair. Today's was blood red. Deke wondered if she'd picked the color as a rebuke to him.

As Orville Sizemore gently questioned her, Maggie Lee at first played the role like a dramatic lead.

"Ms. Lee," said Sizemore, "you were one of the last people to talk to Mr. Deketomis at the fundraiser. Shortly after your conversation he departed the gathering, and half an hour later Mr. Thorn was dead."

Maggie slapped her hand on her chest, as if just hearing the dreadful news.

"Can you tell me, Ms. Lee, if Mr. Deketomis seemed agitated during the time the two of you talked?"

The question resulted in Maggie's emphatically nodding. "It seemed to me he was spitting mad," she said.

"That sounds to me as if he was angrier than normal," said Sizemore.

"I have always found him to be a very angry man," said Maggie. "It's always seemed to me that he's been angry at the world, and for no good reason."

Every word Maggie Lee uttered was good reason to be angry, thought Deke, but he kept his feelings to himself. The more she nattered, though, the tougher it was not to react.

When it was Gina's turn to question Maggie, she chose to give her enough rope to hang herself. "My client has a radio show, as you know," said Gina, "and it's my understanding that you were pretty unhappy with something he said on the air about your journalistic standards, or about one of your columns. Is that right?"

"That's one way to put it, I suppose." Maggie frowned and expelled air out of her nose. "I believe Nick Deketomis is purposefully and hopelessly provocative. He absolutely relishes stirring the pot." Clearly confident in her opinion, Maggie Lee didn't understand that the more she talked, the more she came off sounding bitter, vindictive, and unlikeable.

"You may be right," said Gina, surprising everyone by ceding the point. "So you heard Deke say something about you on the radio sometime not long before you encountered him at the stadium fundraiser. It sounds like you were already upset with

Mr. Deketomis before you encountered him that evening. Is that correct?"

"He was being provocative, like he always is. You ask me, he's always been a pain in the you-know-what."

"I'm curious as to what he said about you on the radio?" asked Gina.

Maggie reddened and said, "I don't remember."

If she hadn't already destroyed her credibility before, Maggie had done so now.

"As it happens," said Gina, "I think I have a transcript of what Mr. Deketomis said. Yes, here it is. Without referencing you by name he said, 'The lead columnist of our local newspaper doesn't see the difference between actual news and a recipe from a Paula Deen cookbook.' Is that correct?"

By that time Maggie's face was as red as her blood-red bow. And that was before everyone in the courtroom began laughing.

"I have no more questions, Your Honor," Gina told the judge.

Judge Heath didn't seem to mind the laughter as much as Deke expected he would. Maybe it had something to do with the witness, he thought. But Orville Sizemore knew how to regain control of the courtroom and impress upon them the gravity of the situation, and he immediately moved to call to the stand Geri Grimester, a forensic reconstruction specialist.

"Mr. Deketomis would have us believe he acted in self-defense," said Sizemore. "I wonder how you'd go about determining this, and whether your findings are consistent with his assertion."

Grimester was better than most forensic specialists in explaining what she believed the evidence showed. With pictures, diagrams of the stadium parking lot, and her own personal choreographing, she explained her findings.

"In most self-defense cases where the combatants are in close proximity of one another," she said, "it is usual for both individuals to show signs of significant physical contact—which is to say we usually see a lot of scratching and bruising."

"And was that found here?" asked Sizemore.

Grimester shook her head. "We did find some slight bruising on Mr. Thorn's chest which looks consistent with his having been struck with a fist. In addition, there were what police forensics described as 'grip bruises' around Mr. Thorn's right forearm."

"What do you mean by 'grip bruises'?" asked Sizemore.

"The evidence suggests that Mr. Thorn was grabbed by the forearm and yanked forward."

Sizemore nodded and then asked, "And it's your contention that it was this action that killed Mr. Thorn, is that correct?"

"It is," said Grimester. "The pen that killed Thorn struck him in an exquisitely precise place."

"I guess it was a terrible accident then," suggested Sizemore. "Is that right?"

"An accident is not out of the realm of possibility," she answered, "but it would be very difficult to randomly hit such a spot in the neck."

"I wonder if you could demonstrate to us," said Sizemore, "the inherent difficulties of hitting such a specific location."

Grimester stood in front of the jury box. Using a forensic mannequin that was often brought out for homicide trials, Grimester demonstrated the precise nature of how the pen had killed Thorn. "As you can see," said Grimester, demonstrating on the mannequin, "death was delivered in a specific location. If the pen had been directed almost anywhere else, it wouldn't have resulted in a fatal injury."

After Grimester concluded her well-rehearsed show, Sizemore asked to approach the bench, and Gina joined him in the sidebar. She knew what Sizemore would be asking of the judge, and desperately hoped he wouldn't agree. In pretrial motions, both sides had argued for more than an hour over the admissibility of including into evidence the police car dash-cam video taken when the police arrived at the scene. The video showed images of Deke kneeling on the ground. According to him, he was trying to hold back the geyser of blood shooting out of Thorn's carotid artery. The prosecution, of course, saw it differently. It was their contention that the video showed Deke applying the coup de grâce to Ken Thorn.

Regardless of how the jury might interpret what they saw, Gina knew how damaging this video was. The scene was particularly gruesome because of the eerie light flooding the parking lot, a result of the squad cars' flashing lights and strobes. An enlarged full screen presentation captured what might charitably be described as a maniacal expression on Deke's face. But worse than that were the images of Thorn's last gasps for air as his body appeared to jump and shake while it struggled to stay alive.

It was perfect material for a horror movie, especially because Deke was covered with blood.

Sizemore began his argument: "Judge, I recognize that you have not yet ruled on Ms. Romano's motion to exclude the police car camera roll, but I would like to admit it now through this witness."

Gina responded: "Your Honor, for the very reasons already stated in my motion, and relying on the case law cited in that motion, it is abundantly clear that this particular film is not probative of anything in regard to whether or not this is a case of self-defense. Furthermore, the unnecessary showing of this film to the jury is incredibly prejudicial, as well as having zero probative value in regard to how this entire incident developed."

Gina understood that Sizemore would play and replay the ghoulish scene for the jurors in slow motion and in as drawn-out of a manner as possible—both with this witness and again in his closing argument. Deke would be portrayed as the blood-drenched freak who had menacingly knelt beside Thorn's body as it struggled to stay alive.

Knowing the value of what he had, Sizemore pressed on. "Judge, this film is being offered to assist the state's expert witness in further pinpointing the angle of the stab wound. The trajectory of the blood from Mr. Thorn's neck is crucial to understanding that this murder did not take place in the way the defendant reported it to the police. The state has the burden of proof in this case, and we have a victim who cannot tell his side of the story. We should be given very wide latitude here."

The judge had heard enough. "Mr. Sizemore, I am going to allow you to use this film, but that permission comes with very specific limits. If you try to exceed those limits, and if by doing so you push my ruling towards reversible error, I promise you will regret that."

Gina spoke quickly and forcefully, doing her best to make the judge reconsider while trying to float new arguments. After listening to her entreaty, Judge Heath shook his head and said solemnly, "My decision stands." When Gina opened her mouth, he held up his hand, and she knew better than to say anything else.

Then the judge turned to the prosecutor and announced his ground rules for showing the video. "Mr. Sizemore, I must again stress there are to be no games here. You may use the big screen, but you better limit this to relevant and necessary use."

He then turned to Gina and said, "Ms. Romano, while the film is being set up I'd like you to take a few minutes to state your entire argument on the record before we proceed."

Gina thanked him. She had known the admissibility of the video could have gone either way, and while Judge Heath's ruling was unlikely to be deemed unreasonable by an appellate court, she would have the means of taking up that issue with them.

It took Sizemore less than half an hour to get ready. The prosecutor didn't overstep his boundaries, but then he didn't have to. As the brutal scene played out for all to see on a six by eight foot viewing screen, Gina knew that the blood and gore spoke more powerfully than anything she could say.

Watching the body language of the jury, hearing their groans and gasps, Gina knew she'd probably need a miracle to get Deke acquitted.

Sizemore followed up on his decided advantage with forensic testimony from Geri Grimester, in particular about the blood spatter patterns found on the ground near Deke's car. Together Sizemore and Grimester reconstructed the two men's positions within the scene, with a heavy emphasis on Deke embracing Thorn while jamming the pen into Thorn's neck.

Most experienced trial lawyers know there is little or no time for fear, and certainly not momentary paralysis. When it was Gina's turn to cross-examine the witness, she exuded a preternatural calm, with no giveaways in her voice or posture that she was concerned.

She rose from her chair, the picture of quiet confidence. No one would have imagined that her stomach was roiling, and her head was swimming. Focus was critical. Everything else was extraneous. Her client's life was in her hands.

When it came to details about a particular event, Gina had mastered the art of focusing on what a witness did not know, did not see, and did not hear. With a forensic expert her approach was the same, but she also knew to hone her attack on what the investigators and the forensic specialists had failed to do.

In this case, Gina's questions for Grimester focused on the failure of the police and the forensic team to perform more sophisticated kinds of blood sampling of the victim to further explore both long-term and short-term probabilities of regular drug use. All that had been done were basic routine tests to determine what was in Thorn's blood at the time of the incident. The point of attack Gina was building the case around was Deke telling the arresting officers that Thorn was acting frenzied and extremely angry at the time of the confrontation. There was a long list of drugs, both legal and illegal, that had the ability to cause the kind of confusion and temporary hostility that Deke said he'd witnessed.

Through her questioning, Gina raised issues about the quantity of blood lost at the scene and how the abnormally low volume of blood in Thorns' body could be a factor that caused autopsy blood testing to be inaccurate. She made the time lapse between the incident and the autopsy another point of contention about the reliability of any drug testing at the time of the autopsy.

But below the surface of what Gina was demonstrating to the court was a drastically different goal. Gina's questioning of Grimester was a way to lure Sizemore into calling Angela Thorn to the stand to clear up any questions about Ken's possible drug use. If Gina correctly anticipated what the prosecutor was planning, she would have the opportunity to unpeel another layer of Ken Thorn's backstory. His suicide attempt and possible unstable mental health would become a feature of the case.

Like all chess masters, Deke thought, Gina wasn't playing for the next move, but was looking three and four moves ahead. He knew she was setting the groundwork for cross-examining Angela Thorn over Ken's drug overdose. Deke even noticed Gina averting her gaze from the section of the courtroom where Mrs. Thorn sat.

He would need every trap in his lawyer's arsenal if he hoped to be acquitted. Deke knew how devastating it was having the dash-cam video admitted. Potentially it was a blow from which he might not be able to recover from.

Judge Heath ended the first day of testimony by reminding the jury that they were not to discuss court proceedings with anyone. The judge further cautioned the jurors from doing any investigating on their own of facts surrounding the case.

Then the judge stared down the jury, furrowing his massive eyebrows. "I hope you will heed my warnings," he intoned. "During the course of my career on the bench, I have jailed ten jurors for ignoring my instructions. Rest assured I will not hesitate to do it again if necessary."

Judging from the wide-eyed reaction of the jury, they did not doubt he was telling the truth, and did not doubt that he would follow through on his threats.

36
AND A CHILD SHALL LEAD THEM

What Andy hated most was how his parents and Cara kept pretending everything was all right. From the moment they came home after that first day of trial Andy knew that everything wasn't peachy keen like they were acting. In fact he was pretty sure everything had gone to hell. The more everyone said things were fine, the more Andy knew they were lying. The way all three of them had been so overly polite was like witnessing a bad school play where no one believed their lines.

That had prompted Andy to look on the Internet to see what had happened that day at the trial. He read accounts of some video that was shown which made his father look like some Wes Craven crazed killer.

Yeah, things were fine.

Andy wanted to be in court. He wanted to show his support for his father. But no one but Andy seemed to think that was a good idea. Andy knew his father wasn't a killer. There had been plenty of times when Andy had provoked his old man, but he'd never raised a hand to him. None of Andy's friends could say that. He didn't know any of them who hadn't gotten spankings. Andy thought it was a testimony to his father's patience that he'd never physically disciplined either of his children. There had been a few times when Andy had deserved a spanking, and more. But even on those occasions his father hadn't acted.

After his parents closed their door behind them, Andy went to Cara's room. Physically his sister was doing a lot better. In the past month she'd noticeably improved. Now she was walking on her own, and out of the wheelchair. He gently knocked on her door.

"Who is it?" she asked.

"It's Andy."

Cara came to the door, but only opened it a crack. "What do you want?" she said.

"I want to talk about the trial," he replied.

When Cara didn't answer, Andy said in a voice not much louder than a whisper, "I went on the Internet and read about what happened. I know about that video which made Dad look like a crazy slasher."

Cara opened the door, and Andy could see she'd been crying. "It was awful," she said. "I've never seen anything so awful."

"Then why is everyone in this family pretending all is well?" he asked.

"Maybe because the truth is so ugly," she said.

Cara motioned for Andy to come into her room and then closed the door behind them. She took a seat on the side of her bed and watched her brother fall into a chair.

"I'm tired of being an outsider," he said. "I should be at the trial for Dad."

"You know he's not going to let that happen," Cara insisted.

"I want to help," Andy said.

She nodded and sighed.

"How would you like it if Dad forbade you from being at his trial?" he asked.

"He did his best to discourage me," Cara answered. "I had to remind him I'm an adult."

"I need someone in this family to tell me what's going on," he demanded. "Otherwise I'm going to explode."

Cara could see how upset Andy was. "Okay," she said. "I'll keep you in the loop."

"I want it straight."

She nodded.

"We've got a half day tomorrow," Andy said. "I don't want to wait all afternoon and into the evening to learn what's going on. I want you to call me tomorrow at lunch."

"I don't know," Cara told him. "There's this tough judge. I am sure he wouldn't approve of anyone calling."

"I am your brother. I deserve to know."

"All right, I'll call you," she promised.

Cara sniffled and had to wipe away a tear. Andy gave her a box of tissues and walked out of her room.

The next day Cara was good to her word, and called Andy's cell at 12:45 p.m. "I can't talk long," she said.

But Andy had pretty much already heard everything he needed to know. "It's not going well, is it?"

"No," she admitted. "The prosecutor spent almost the entire morning doing his best to show what a great guy Ken Thorn was. He is way up on a pedestal now, and I don't know how he's going to be brought down to Earth. Pastor Rodney's testimonial had half the jurors in tears."

"Shit," said Andy.

"Maybe it seems worse than it really is, though. Dad said Gina is holding some pocket aces, whatever that means."

"What it probably means is that Dad's whistling in the dark."

"Probably," admitted Cara.

Andy remembered something. It had bothered him when he'd heard it, but he'd never followed up. Maybe it was important. Maybe he could help his dad.

"Hey," he said, "would you mind if I borrowed your car?"

"For what?" asked Cara.

"I need to talk to Delmar Reed."

"Isn't he that boy you had the run-in with?"

"Yeah, but we're cool now."

Cara couldn't think of a good reason to tell him no, so she gave her permission.

The Reeds lived in a giant three-story Grecian palace. To Andy, it sort of reminded him of the house that Tony Montana from *Scarface* had lived in.

The first person Andy saw when he pulled Cara's yellow convertible into the driveway was Mrs. Reed. She was standing next to some flowering plants talking with the gardener.

Andy got out of the car and walked up to Mrs. Reed. She didn't look very happy to see him, and said, "Andrew, this is a surprise."

"Hi Mrs. Reed," he said. "Is Delmar around?"

"I'm afraid not, Andrew," she said. "What is it that brings you here?"

"Delmar and I have a history class together," said Andy. That was true enough. Andy was a B student; Delmar was barely passing.

"Anyway, I've been missing some school because of my dad's trial and Delmar said he'd take notes for me."

Mrs. Reed looked surprised by that news. Andy decided to embellish it even more. "That was nice of him. I'm glad he's gotten over that whole Conquistador thing."

The thought of her son being so magnanimous apparently appealed to Mrs. Reed. "I don't know if Delmar has those notes with him right now but you could check at the parking lot by the school. That's where he said he would be skateboarding with his friends."

Six shaggy-haired teenagers were popping their skateboards off a side cement wall when Andy pulled up in the convertible. They all looked up, and for a second Delmar appeared fearful, but then his face hardened. There was safety in numbers. "What do you want, Deketomis?" Delmar growled.

"Got a second?" asked Andy. "There's something I need to ask you about without your entourage."

Delmar thought about that. Maybe Deketomis was finally going to give him a sincere apology for what he'd done. It would be nice having him grovel a little.

"Yeah, fine," he said, and began walking away from his group with Deketomis.

Behind him Delmar heard Jeff Franken snicker and say, "Someone's got a boyfriend."

"Bite me, Franken," said Delmar. Annoyed, he turned to Andy and said, "What?"

"Why'd you say Ken Thorn was a pervert?"

"What are you talking about?" asked Delmar.

"On the *Catalina*, why'd you call Ken Thorn a pervert?"

Delmar took a furtive look around. "Because he totally was, or at least that's what I heard. I know a couple of the girls on the softball team. They said he was a real perv. Like for example, he'd pretend he was showing them how to bat, but what he was really doing was copping a feel."

"Oh," said Andy, his disappointment obvious. The way Delmar had spoken that day Andy had been all but sure he knew something other than a few rumors.

Delmar didn't like Deketomis's dismissive look. "You don't believe me?" he said. "Well did you know that guy was a traveling salesman? I mean he really was. That's like a punch line to a joke. The guy really was a perv. Kip Tyler and a couple of the guys went to Mobile looking for a little action. They ended up in a real skanky part of town and found themselves at the Corian Hotel. If you want whores or drugs, that's the place to be. Anyway, who do they see there but a familiar face? They stayed in the shadows, so he never saw them."

"Who?"

"Who else but the perv we've been talking about? They didn't know his name, but they did know he was the softball coach for the church team. Everyone about split a gut when they saw he was there looking for a hooker."

"Thanks a lot, Delmar," said Andy, and then sprinted back to the convertible.

Andy stopped home, changed his clothes, grabbed all the cash he'd saved up, and then printed out some pictures from the Internet.

The ride to Mobile only took forty minutes, but Andy found himself in a world far removed from Spanish Trace. Even in the light of day the Corian Hotel looked to be in an iffy part of town.

Andy knew he'd grown up in a sheltered environment, and he'd have been lying to say he wasn't scared at what he saw. The streets were dirty. They were littered with trash and littered with the flotsam of humanity.

Without any clear idea of what he should do, Andy parked down the street from the Corian Hotel. At one time the hotel must have been a grand edifice, but now showed its age. The area was popular for loitering. Andy watched people coming and going; it didn't seem as if they had any clear purpose either.

As the afternoon waned, Andy continued his vigil, even if he didn't know for what. He began seeing women in low-cut colorful dresses. One woman in high heels with fishnet stockings walked his way and looked inside the car where he was sitting.

"How you doin', sugar?" she asked.

"Fine," he said, and turned away, too embarrassed to do anything else. Eventually she kept walking.

In spite of how uncomfortable he felt, he forced himself to get out of the car. He walked down the street to the Corian Hotel and went inside the lobby. The clerk looked as if he'd seen everything, and didn't like much of what he'd seen.

Ken Thorn had stayed here, thought Andy. People would have to know about Thorn, but he'd have to find a way to get them to talk.

"Got a room?" Andy asked.

The clerk, a white guy of around forty wearing an ill-fitting suit, sniffed the air as if he was smelling trouble. Or maybe he appreciated the rank smell of smoke that lingered in the lobby.

"Got ID that says you're eighteen?"

"I have some green ID," said Andy.

"Get lost," said the clerk.

"There's no way you're all filled up."

"There's a reason we don't rent to minors. It's called John Law. They'd love to fine us for violating lodging laws. Or maybe it would be a reason to shut us down. You working undercover? You one of those underage guys who tries to buy booze or smokes while working for the cops? They love handing out those big fines. Now get the hell out of here."

"I'm not working for the cops," said Andy. "The reason I'm really here is that I'm trying to find out about this one guy who used to visit here. If you can confirm that, I'd be real appreciative. I've got some pictures of him . . ."

"I'm going to toss you out on your ass if you don't get out of here in the next five seconds."

Andy beat a hasty retreat. Not knowing what else to do, he returned to Cara's car. Think, he told himself, think. Maybe he should just drive back home. His parents would be wondering where he was.

No, thought Andy. He wasn't ready to give up yet. All of this was definitely out of his comfort zone, but that was tough. This was his chance to help his dad. Someone in the area had to know about Ken Thorn, and maybe they could testify or something. As long as everyone thought that Thorn was some kind of saint, things would be bad for his dad. With darkness falling, the neighborhood seemed to be rousing itself from its slumber. Andy fired up the convertible and began driving up and down the streets. Every time he spotted what he suspected was a hooker, he froze up.

Finally he pulled over and managed to stammer out his request. The first hooker he stopped wanted nothing to do with him, nor did the second or third. Like the clerk at the hotel, the women (one of them might have been a man, thought Andy) seemed to be suspicious of him. Clearly he didn't belong, and more importantly they probably thought he wasn't really interested in their services.

Since he was still without a plan, Andy returned to his vantage point near the Corian.

This time he spotted four women hanging out in the parking lot on the far side of the hotel. Maybe he'd have better luck by approaching a group of women.

Andy made a U-turn and drove up to where the women were congregating.

"Nice car," said one of them. She was young, no more than twenty years old, and wearing a short, shiny blue skirt. "I like yellow," she said, running her hand on the hood.

"H-h-how's it going tonight?" Even Andy knew he sounded utterly lame.

"Why? Looking to party?"

One of the other women stepped forward. With all her makeup it was difficult to gauge her age, but she acted like the queen bee of the group. "You that crazy white boy that stopped Crystal?"

Andy didn't know quite how to answer, not being sure who Crystal was.

The Queen Bee turned to the others. "Crystal tell me that a white boy was hassling her on the street and holding up pictures of Young Stuff."

He recovered from his confusion about what the woman was saying and extended one of the printouts of Ken Thorn. "I've been asking for help in identifying the man in these pictures. Is this man the same person you were referring to as Young Stuff?"

The four women couldn't help seeing the photos, but all deferred to the Queen Bee. "Why you askin' these questions?"

"It's really important to my dad," Andy answered.

The Queen Bee shook her head and looked at Andy as if he was an alien species, but even she couldn't refuse his desperate eyes. "That's Young Stuff, all right. All this time that be all he ever says. 'I want some of that young stuff.'"

"That's right," chimed in the same younger woman who had originally approached Andy's car.

"I need to ask you some questions about Young Stuff," said Andy.

The Queen Bee decided that enough charity had been dispensed for the night. "You need to get your skinny white ass out of here. You bad for business."

"Look," implored Andy, "I can pay you for your time."

The Queen Bee considered that for a moment, but then shook her head. "Don't hassle us no more. You a cop magnet, and you trouble. You think the po-pos aren't watching you? Hell, you be a fifteen-year-old white boy driving a yal-low car 'bout as bright as the sun."

"I'm eighteen," said Andy. Or he would be in six months. "And I really need to know about Young Stuff."

"This our corner, Justin Bieber," said the Queen Bee. "Get the hell outta here."

"I'm not leaving," declared Andy, "until one of you tells me about Young Stuff."

Queen Bee shook her head. This crazy white boy had no idea what was what. She looked down the street, and then made a gesture with her hand. A moment later, Andy heard a heavy percussion coming from speakers. He looked back through his rear view mirror and saw an older Cadillac driving towards them.

"I'd get the hell outta here if I was you, white boy, 'cuz you about to meet our business manager."

Andy froze, unsure of what to do. He knew answers were almost within his grasp. The Caddy's lights came closer and closer.

It was old Detroit metal, weighing in at more than two tons. What Andy wasn't expecting was bumper cars. The heavy Caddy nudged his sister's car from the rear, but that was enough to throw him forward, and for him to hear the crush of metal. When Andy raised his head and looked back in the mirror, he saw the face of the driver, and felt the malice radiating from the man's eyes. This was not an encounter that would go well for Andy.

He pulled away from the curb, and heard the hoots and hollers from the women. Andy sped off, afraid that the Caddy might follow him. He made a few quick turns, but saw no sign of being pursued. When he was sure he was safe, Andy pulled over.

Cara's going to kill me, he thought, and went to look at the damage. The convertible was her baby. Andy wrung his hands while looking at a smashed rear light and dented bumper. The night had not gone as he'd hoped.

Andy checked his cell phone. He had missed four calls and numerous texts. He didn't bother to see who the callers were—he knew his family had noticed his absence and wanted to know where he was.

At least I have his nickname, Andy thought. Ken Thorn was Young Stuff.

Andy thought about texting his sister to say he was safe, but then decided he couldn't do that. He knew that his family would insist that he immediately come home, and he wasn't yet ready to do that. He had to get someone to open up about Young Stuff. This neighborhood wasn't like Spanish Trace. His town was busy with people during the day, and it seemed to shutter up at night. In this part of Mobile it seemed to be the opposite. More and more people were now on the streets.

I've got to get one of them to talk to me, he thought. And he set out to make that happen.

Andy decided to concentrate on the youngest looking pros-
titutes that he saw. Ken Thorn had apparently earned his street
name. Andy did his own working of the streets. Over the course
of two hours he approached three young women, but none of them
were willing to hear him out. Andy had to steer clear of the Corian
Hotel for fear of drawing the ire of the pimp in the Caddy—and
that precaution limited his search. As far as Andy could determine,
that was the hotspot for working women, but he was forced to stay
on the outskirts of where the action was.

At last luck seemed to go Andy's way. He spotted the young
prostitute that had first approached him near the Corian Hotel. This
time she was by herself. When Andy pulled up next to her, though,
the woman turned around and began walking the other way.

"Please," he said,. "I really, really need your help."

The woman reluctantly stopped.

"You knew this Young Stuff, didn't you?" he asked.

She nodded. "He was a regular at the No Tell."

"What?"

"The Corian," she said. "Everybody here call it the No Tell
Hotel."

"Were you ever," started Andy. "Did you," he continued, but
couldn't think how to phrase it. Finally he asked, "Was Young
Stuff one of your clients?"

The woman opened her mouth to answer, but suddenly turned
around and began walking away. "Wait," begged Andy, and then
found himself blinded by a police spotlight. He raised a hand to
ward off the light.

"Out of the car," said a commanding voice.

Andy did as asked and found himself looking into the stern
face of a Mobile policeman. "Turn around and put your hands on
the vehicle."

When Andy complied he found himself being frisked.

"Is this vehicle yours?" the cop asked.

"It's my sister's," he answered.

"I want your license," said the cop, "and I want the car's registration."

After Andy was able to produce both, the cop told Andy to stay put. Then he returned to his squad car where he sat for a minute, apparently inputting information. Should I tell him why I'm here? Andy wondered. Would the cop be willing to help him? A lot of police didn't like lawyers, Andy knew. It wasn't cold, but Andy found himself trembling.

The cop came back and handed Andy his license and the car registration. He noticed Andy was shaking.

"You're not one of those rich kids with a habit, are you?" asked the cop.

"No sir," Andy said. "I've never used drugs."

"You been drinking tonight?"

"No, sir."

Andy wished he could stop trembling. He knew it made him look guilty. But he couldn't help but be scared.

"Want to tell me what a seventeen-year-old kid is doing out at night in these parts?" he asked.

Andy wanted to confess everything. He was in way over his head, and he knew it. "I," he started, and then found himself choking up, and even worse, he found tears welling up in his eyes.

Here he was shaking like a leaf and crying. Andy lifted up his hand and angrily wiped away some tears.

"This isn't a good place for you to be," said the cop, "but you're going to need to get control of yourself before you drive back home. Not too far away from here is a diner. You think you can follow me over there? I want you to sit down there and get yourself something to eat. You got money? Good, then, after you get something in your stomach I want you to drive home. Does that work for you?"

Andy nodded. He was glad the cop wasn't waiting for him to speak because at the moment all he was capable of was nodding his head. He felt like a shaking, sniveling little kid. Andy wiped the tears from his eyes and the snot from his nose. And then he dutifully followed the cop to the diner.

It was midnight when Andy put in his order for a cheeseburger and fries. He was too drained to be able to think clearly. His food arrived, and even though Andy didn't feel hungry, he soon finished everything on his plate.

When he finally looked at his phone he saw that he'd missed thirty-six calls. He knew he couldn't put off calling his parents. They'd be worried sick by now. Andy just wished he had a better explanation for what he'd been doing. He had wanted to save his father, but hadn't really gotten the dirt he wanted on Ken Thorn.

A short, squat Mexican woman came up to Andy's booth and stood there looking at him. She was wearing a lot of mascara and makeup, and had on a tight green dress. There was no mistaking her profession, even though she had to be in her late thirties. The woman spoke to Andy in Spanish, and he assumed she was propositioning him.

"No gracias," said Andy.

His answer seemed to frustrate the woman. "Ken Thorn," she said. That was enough to make Andy sit up straight, point to the open space in his booth, and say, "Por favor."

After five minutes of trying to talk with the woman who identified herself as Lucia Torres, both Andy and Lucia were frustrated. Neither was able to communicate very well with the other. Lucia's

English was about on the same level as Andy's Spanish. Languages weren't his thing, but he knew someone fluent in Spanish.

"Hey Sis," Andy said when he called her. "I need you to translate some Spanish for me."

"Andrew Deketomis," said Cara, sounding just like their mom. "Everyone has been going crazy here trying to find you! Dad was afraid you had been abducted! We've called the police. We've called everyone!"

"Look, I'm sorry," he said. "I wasn't thinking. But I really need your help. It's important, and I think it can help Dad."

"Wait a second," said Cara.

Even though she held her hand over the phone, Andy could hear her yelling to their parents and telling them he was all right. That was apparently not reassurance enough.

"Dad wants to know where you are," said Cara.

"Tell him I'm in Mobile. Tell him I'm fine."

As Cara was forced to relay questions and answers Andy finally said, "Enough! Tell them I'll be home soon. But right now you need to translate for me!"

Cara was surprised at how forceful her younger brother sounded. And suddenly her hovering parents were quiet as well.

"I'm all ears," Cara told him.

37
HOMBRES MALOS

Andy drove home with two passengers. Lucia Torres had insisted her daughter, Sunny, come with her. During the drive Sunny and Andy talked. Because he hadn't been able to follow everything that Cara and Lucia had been saying, Sunny was able to make everything clear to him. Even though Andy had suspected some things, getting the full story was still a surprise.

"Wow," he kept saying.

When Andy pulled up into their driveway, everyone in his family came running out. Andy was smothered in hugs. For the first time in his life he didn't feel like the family joke. He felt like a hero, or at least he did until Cara noticed the damage he'd caused to her beloved convertible.

"What happened?" she yelled.

"It's a long story," Andy replied, "but first you need to hear a few other long stories."

It wasn't only his family that was waiting. Gina Romano was also there. "I think I better hear those stories," she said.

It took almost a full two hours for Gina and Deke to get all their questions answered. During that time Gina filled two legal pads full of notes.

Sunny was the first to tell her story. It was an age-old account of a predator taking advantage of an innocent.

"I met Ken a year ago," she said. "He stopped me while I was walking down the street and told me how beautiful I was. I tried not to pay attention to him but he kept following me and saying nice things.

"No boy had ever called me beautiful before. No one had ever paid so much attention to me. He asked me how old I was. I said I was eighteen, but I was really fourteen at the time. I lied because I wanted to see him again. I gave him my phone number when he asked. I didn't think I'd hear from him, but he started calling and texting.

"Ken said he was a salesman, and I knew he traveled a lot. We talked almost every day and every few weeks he'd come to Mobile. He always took me out to nice restaurants and told me he liked me a lot. And then Ken told me he loved me. I was sure I was in love with him even though he was so old. He said he wanted to marry me and I was so happy. After that I started seeing him at his hotel."

After Sunny stopped talking, Lucia picked up her narrative. With Cara and Sunny translating, the mother described her horror at finding pictures of her daughter with that "que mal hombre" on Sunny's phone. Determined to end their relationship, Lucia admitted to sending pictures of Ken with her underage daughter, along with the demand that he give himself up to the police.

Everyone heard about Lucia's dilemma; she was an undocumented immigrant who was in fear of being deported as well as separated from her daughter. As much as she wanted to go to the police, she didn't dare. At the same time she had to make Ken Thorn pay for what he'd done to Sunny.

That was when the other man promised to help Lucia. That was when she met with Darl Dixon.

Sunny translated for Gina and her mother. "Tell me about your meeting with Darl Dixon," Gina requested.

"He told me Ken Thorn would never bother my daughter again," said Lucia. "But before he could arrest this man he said he needed evidence, and asked for all the pictures of him and Sunny."

"And did you give him all the pictures?" asked Gina.

"Not all," admitted Lucia. "In my country the police are not to be trusted."

"So you didn't totally trust Darl Dixon?"

Lucia nodded. "He said nice words, but his eyes were mean."

She was worried he might be yet another "mal hombre." For almost all her life Lucia had only known bad men.

"When Thorn died Dixon probably never gave another thought to Sunny and Lucia," said Deke. "He just assumed all his problems had gone away."

"Or what's more likely is that he planned on having Lucia deported," Gina responded. "Only he hasn't gotten around to doing that yet because he's been too busy with the trial."

"I think I smell the brimstone of Pastor Rodney in all this," Deke said. "I'm betting Ken was too much of a narcissist to try and commit suicide, but Lucia's note and the pictures got him scared. Pastor Rodney wanted me to blow up, and Darl was happy to go along with that plan. But neither Rodney, Darl, nor Ken could have guessed how everything could go so wrong."

Lucia understood enough of what was being discussed to say, "Hombres malos."

"Si," said Deke, "bad men."

"That's it, isn't it Dad?" asked Andy. "Doesn't this show you're innocent of murder?"

"It's a little more complicated than that, Andy," said Gina. "First evidence needs to be admitted, and Lucia's status as an undocumented worker makes things more difficult. Besides, I don't want a 'he said, she said' situation, at least if I can help it. But I don't want you to worry about your dad. Over the last two days I've been laying cable for what's about to happen and tomorrow I promise you will be a very different day in court."

"Are you tired of playing rope-a-dope?" Deke asked.

"Tomorrow we come out swinging," promised Gina.

She looked at her watch, and sighed. "I should have said *today* we come out swinging. We're supposed to be back in the court-room in five hours."

"A strong double expresso, anyone?" asked Teri.

38
LAMB TO THE SLAUGHTER

There were a thousand ways that Gina could play all the new information that had been brought to her. She and Deke discussed their alternatives. As usual, both were considering the endgame. They were looking beyond the trial. True justice often doesn't get dispensed in a courtroom. Getting Deke acquitted of charges of manslaughter was only part of the justice they wanted.

On the way to the courtroom counselor and client continued to talk. "Sizemore is going to bring Angela Thorn to the witness stand today," said Gina.

"The safe move is to not have her testify," said Deke. "The smart move is to not have her testify. But I agree with you. Orville is greedy. He's looking for overkill. And he thinks this will be the final nail in getting me convicted."

"I'm inclined to stay with our script," agreed Gina. "By not showing our cards now, we can cast a wider net in the days to come."

"That's easy to say when you're not wearing a bull's-eye," said Deke, but with a smile.

Both of them were totally sleep deprived, but both of them had reason to smile.

Suddenly Orville Sizemore announced, "The prosecution calls Angela Thorn to the stand."

Angela Thorn was clearly a reluctant witness. She unsteadily rose to her feet and made her way to the stand. Once again she was wearing a plain black dress. Her hair was drawn back in a tight ponytail that looked like a concession to a bad hair day.

Poor woman, thought Deke. Now that he knew what a predatory ghoul Ken Thorn was, it was hard to imagine anyone being married to him. From all accounts, Angela Thorn was a devout woman. But as Gina had pointed out, this wasn't a case of judging Angela Thorn's character, but of learning how much she knew about her husband's crimes. If the defense could show Ken Thorn's dissolute lifestyle and criminal behavior, the prosecution's case against Deke would fall apart.

Angela Thorn promised on the Bible to tell the whole truth. Under her breath, Gina muttered to Deke, "Let's hope she's the rare bird who actually means it."

"Have a little faith," Deke whispered.

In a court of law, less is often more. You don't keep going to the well if you don't have to. Apparently Orville Sizemore had never accepted that tactical theory. He didn't want to bury Deke with a shovel; he wanted to bring in the backhoe.

The prosecutor did his best to treat his witness with kid gloves, speaking softly and gently while making sure he kept her on script. "Mrs. Thorn, I know it must not be easy talking about your recently deceased husband, but I am hoping you will allow me to ask you a few questions."

She nodded for him to continue, perhaps not trusting her voice.

"In some of its questioning," Sizemore said, "the defense has suggested your husband might have abused drugs. Did you ever see any sign of this?"

Angela shook her head and Sizemore reminded her, "Please speak for the court record, Mrs. Thorn."

"My husband didn't abuse drugs," she said.

Sizemore asked a few general questions, but even then her answers remained guarded. Angela said they'd been married seventeen years and that she'd met Ken at a church social.

"As far as you're aware, Mrs. Thorn, did Ken know the defendant Mr. Deketomis?"

"No," she said.

"Much of this trial is about establishing a timeline," explained Sizemore. "Prior to his death, when was the last time you saw your husband alive?"

"About two hours passed from the time he left the house to the time he died."

Sizemore could tell his questioning wasn't going well. Angela Thorn wasn't engendering any sympathy for her husband. Her terse answers and lack of emotion suggested a troubled relationship, and it didn't help that she was studiously avoiding looking at the jury. But he'd brought her on the stand for a specific purpose. She was one of the last people to see Thorn alive, and Sizemore wanted her to debunk the notion that her husband had attacked Deketomis under the influence of drugs.

"You couldn't have known it was your final farewell," said Sizemore, "which I'm sure in retrospect makes you sad to think about. Still, the jury needs to hear your observations of Ken as he left your house. Did he look like he might be on drugs?"

"I didn't see any sign of that." Her delivery again was flat. "There was nothing in the way he looked or talked that indicated he might have been drinking or using drugs."

Sizemore was pleased that he'd managed to get in Angela's testimony without Gina Romano objecting. In fact if he wasn't mistaken, there had been a few times when Judge Heath had looked up as if expecting to hear her object. But it was fine by Sizemore that she'd been quiet as a church mouse. It was a nice change of pace, actually.

With a few more gentle words, Sizemore finished up with Mrs. Thorn. She hadn't exactly aroused the jury's sympathy, but at least she'd stayed on script.

Gina looked very tentative in her approach to Angela Thorn. She didn't want to appear unsympathetic to the widow. Gina began her cross-examination by saying, "First of all, Mrs. Thorn, I would like to say how sorry I am for your loss. I know how hard it must have been for you to come to testify today."

Angela nodded at Gina, surprised by her unexpected kindness. Deke knew that what he was witnessing was a lamb being prepared for slaughter because Gina immediately dispensed with her warmth toward her witness and proceeded to put her on the defensive.

"Mrs. Thorn, isn't it true that your husband was hospitalized on February 9th of this year?"

After a long hesitation, Angela said quietly, "Yes, that's true."

"And isn't it also true, Mrs. Thorn, that your daughter made a call from your home the day of that hospitalization and asked for an ambulance because your husband needed emergency medical treatment?"

Unlike her earlier seemingly scripted testimony, it was clear that Angela Thorn had not been prepped for this line of questioning. After what seemed an eternity, she said, "Yes, Kimberly called 911 for an ambulance that day."

"Mrs. Thorn, was your husband rushed to the hospital that day because he had taken an overdose of drugs?"

Orville Sizemore was on his feet with a series of objections, all of which Judge Heath overruled without a moment of hesitation.

"Let's be clear, Mrs. Thorn," Gina said. "In your earlier testimony about your husband, you made no mention of that event. Isn't that true?"

"I didn't lie," Angela replied. "It didn't seem important, and Mr. Dixon and Mr. Sizemore never asked me about it."

"Yes, we all noticed that Mr. Sizemore didn't ask you about it, and that you didn't volunteer it," Gina said. "But nevertheless, you did say to this jury that your husband didn't have a drug problem. Isn't that so?"

Angela looked toward Judge Heath, her eyes beseeching. Heath stared back without a word being spoken. Finally she tried to clarify her testimony. "I don't think my husband had a drug problem, even though the morning he was hospitalized he did take drugs."

Gina pretended to be puzzled by that. "What was it, do you think, that made him take drugs that morning?"

Sizemore again stood up to object. By now he clearly recognized what a mistake it had been to call Angela Thorn to the stand, but once more Judge Heath denied his objection.

"I guess he was upset," offered Angela.

"Upset about what?"

Sizemore was up on his feet again objecting. "How can she know her husband's state of mind, Judge?"

Gina clarified her questioning based on her knowledge that Lucia Torres had told her about mailing Thorn the pictures of him with her daughter, along with her demand that he go to the police.

"Did you see anything that morning that might have upset him?"

Instead of directly answering, Angela said, "Ken was a weak man."

Gina nodded sympathetically, and seemed to back off from her line of questioning. "Mrs. Thorn, please tell the jury about the sales route that your husband would take in selling his medical products."

Orville Sizemore again objected. He had the sense that quicksand was about to swallow his witness, but he still wasn't sure how or why.

Judge Heath was part Solomon and part street fighter. This dual personality had made him an intuitive trial lawyer long before he became an intuitive judge. He recognized this testimony was potentially highly relevant, but even Heath believed that Gina's focus was still about drug use. Sizemore was overruled.

Angela spoke about Ken Thorn's sales territory, how he covered a wide area of the Southeast while selling pharmaceuticals. While offering utterly banal details about Ken's job, her voice nevertheless signaled a reluctance to discuss the subject.

That's when Gina asked, "Mrs. Thorn, do you happen to know if your husband stayed regularly at the Corian Hotel in Mobile?"

"I guess he did," said Angela Thorn, remembering the letterhead that had accompanied the pictures of her husband.

"Why was that?" asked Gina, her voice gentle.

And that's how a bear trap gets sprung, thought Deke.

"When it came to matters of the flesh," said Angela, "my husband was weak."

"Are you aware that your husband regularly entertained other women at the Corian Hotel, Mrs. Thorn?" asked Gina.

Up until that moment most in the jury had assumed the defense was trying to link the deceased with drug use. The turn of events had left many with their mouths open.

Sizemore screamed, "Objection relevance, your honor!"

"Overruled!"

Judge Heath was pushing his judicial discretion to the limit by not demanding a clarifying explanation from Gina.

"I didn't know," Angela said. "I only learned on the day Ken went to the hospital."

"What did you learn?" asked Gina.

"There were pictures," she said, and then began crying and was unable to say more.

Gina spoke for her. "There were pictures with your husband and a young girl, weren't there?"

Angela nodded, and then whispered, "Yes."

"And there was a short note sent from someone using the Corian Hotel letterhead, is that not true?"

Through her weeping Angela answered, "Yes."

"And that note said your husband had to turn himself into the police for his crimes, is that not true?"

Gina brought Angela a glass of water and waited while she regained her composure. Finally the witness nodded for her to continue.

"That must have been extremely difficult for you, Mrs. Thorn."

"It was terrible," she admitted.

"And what did you do?"

"Ken repented for his sins," she said. "But I still didn't know what to do. I did go to Pastor Rodney, and we prayed for Ken's soul. And we also prayed for that girl, the one who was in the pictures, the one he was at the hotel with."

"Prayer is good," said Gina. "But your husband didn't turn himself into the police, did he?"

Angela shook her head. "He told me that he was working things out with Darl Dixon."

Sizemore jumped to his feet. His mouth was moving, but he was producing no discernible words.

"You mean Prosecutor Darl Dixon?" asked Gina.

In the face of these revelations, the entire courtroom forgot about all of Judge Heath's admonitions. Everyone was abuzz. People couldn't believe what they had heard.

"This court will come to order!" The judge's bellow tempered the uproar, but didn't totally quiet it.

But Orville Sizemore had heard enough. He screamed, "The state requests a mistrial!"

Judge Heath was well aware of the consequences of granting a mistrial. The prosecutor's request would provide Deke with the immunity of "double-jeopardy," meaning he could never again be tried for the death of Ken Thorn. But the judge didn't even hesitate.

He brought down his gavel, and then he announced, "Mistrial granted, Mr. Sizemore."

39
THE AFTER–TRIAL

In all of his years behind the bench, Judge Heath had never lost control of a courtroom. But this time, with a little smile that he managed to keep hidden, the judge decided it was okay for bedlam to rule for a minute or two.

Everyone was still wondering exactly what had occurred, and no one was hearing a good answer. The courtroom quieted down when they saw Judge Heath approach Angela Thorn.

He gently patted her on the arm and then said quietly, "You can leave the stand, Mrs. Thorn. I imagine you're tired and could use some rest."

She nodded to him gratefully and tried to muster up some dignity while exiting the courtroom. As everyone watched her departure, the room fell eerily silent.

The judge looked out to all the courtroom observers. "All of you are free to leave as well," he said, "except for Ms. Romano and Mr. Sizemore. I'll need to talk to both of you."

Judge Heath was surprised when no one in the courtroom made a move to leave.

"You mean you actually want to hear about mistrials and the like?"

All the nodding heads seemed to tickle Judge Heath's fancy. "Okay, I'll give a little talk in a minute," he said, "but first I need to thank the jury."

He turned his full attention to the jury. "Ladies and gentlemen of the jury," he said, "your service here this week has been extremely important. Not only did you do your civic duty in agreeing to sit as a juror in this important case, but in a broader sense you allowed our American civil justice system to work exactly as it should. The reason a mistrial was granted in this case is because the State of Florida, by way of their attorneys, requested a mistrial. That was their right, and I am not in a position to second-guess their decision."

Judge Heath paused as if he were teaching a law class. "When you leave this courtroom, you are free to speak to the attorneys who tried this case or to the media if you choose to do so. But I caution you to remember that at this point Mr. Deketomis is an innocent man."

He wriggled his formidable eyebrows. "In closing, I once again thank all of you for your service. I hope it has been an experience that's as memorable for you as it has been for me."

The jury, like the rest of the courtroom, stayed behind. And then the judge opened up the courtroom to questions.

After the mistrial was declared, Darl Dixon did what he usually did: he ran to the press. This time, though, Darl wasn't sure of his best strategy. In Angela Thorn's courtroom testimony she had linked her husband to him, and she'd also opened the can of worms about the girl.

Maybe he could say Mrs. Thorn was so agitated she couldn't be blamed for her misstatements. He'd look magnanimous that way.

Darl was also considering throwing Orville Sizemore under the bus. Although Orville had probably done the best thing possible for himself personally when he'd asked for a mistrial, maybe he should publicly second-guess him.

It went without saying that Darl would say that he still had doubts about Nick Deketomis's innocence.

What Darl had to do most of all was to try and control the situation. Luckily there were plenty of other issues to grab people's attention. And Darl needed to remember the bigger prize: He was running for office.

But up until now Darl had been dealing with a sympathetic Fourth Estate. When he stepped up to the microphone all his friends seemed to have vanished and been replaced by rabid wolves. Everyone began shouting questions about Ken Thorn and the mysterious pictures of him and the girl.

Even Fox TV reporter Mindy Marin, who'd always been Dixon's stalwart ally, now turned on him. "Did the prosecution know about Kenneth Thorn's sexual connections?" she asked.

"We had no knowledge of Mr. Thorn's apparent misconduct," Dixon answered. "Mrs. Thorn was clearly distressed and misspoke."

With those words Dixon committed himself to the big lie. Up to that point in his career, he had always gotten away with the big lie. It had never come back to bite him, and Darl prayed he could get away with it one more time.

But Darl also knew trouble when he saw it. He excused himself from the press, saying he had business that he needed to attend to in the courtroom. The truth was he knew the media still wasn't being allowed in the courtroom, and he needed a port in the storm. Darl went out but he didn't return to the courtroom. He went through the building and out to the back parking lot where his car was. Then he drove away, much faster than usual.

Only after court security escorted the last members of the courtroom outside did Judge Heath ask Gina Romano, Orville Sizemore, and a court reporter to follow him into chambers. Even though Deke had wanted to be a part of this proceeding, the judge had told him to go home with his family. In this instance, Deke believed the judge did know best.

Once everyone was seated in chambers, the judge instructed the reporter to record every word being spoken. It was evident that Orville Sizemore was expecting a spanking, and he got one.

"Mr. Sizemore," said Judge Heath, "do you understand the laws in regard to prosecutors withholding exculpatory evidence from the criminal defendant's lawyer?"

Orville Sizemore pretended righteous indignation. "Your Honor, I've been practicing law as a prosecutor for fifteen years. I'm well aware that I could lose my license and possibly be prosecuted for withholding evidence from the defendant, so that is something I would never, ever do. I'm not even sure why you're asking me this question, because I knew nothing about the new information that surfaced today."

Gina sat quietly; Sizemore was doing a good enough job digging a hole for the entire state attorney's office by himself.

Judge Heath said, "To be clear, Mr. Sizemore, you are telling this court that you personally had no knowledge of Mr. Thorn apparently having a sexual relationship with a minor?"

Sizemore held his ground. "I knew nothing of that. And even if I had, that still would have had nothing to do with the manslaughter charges pending against Nick Deketomis."

"I'm also interested, Mr. Sizemore," the judge continued, "in whether or not your office had information about Ken Thorn's attempted suicide and failed to disclose that to the defense."

Sizemore looked from Gina to the judge. "As Ms. Romano can tell you," said Sizemore, "the individual who organized and directed all the pretrial discovery was Mr. Darl Dixon."

"Go on," said Judge Heath.

"If the court would permit, I could better answer the judge's questions if I were allowed a few days to conduct my own personal investigation."

Both Judge Heath and Gina understood that Orville Sizemore was saying he needed time to get the goods on the only individual who could have purposely concealed information. Judge Heath went along with Sizemore's proposal to be a reasonable one, and everyone agreed that they would gather on Monday morning to continue.

"I would ask that *everyone* here be in attendance, including the Sunrise County Prosecuting Attorney," said Judge Heath.

"I will notify Mr. Dixon," Sizemore promised, "and I'll make sure he's here."

40
TURNABOUT IS FAIR PLAY

Orville Sizemore was accustomed to turning the screws on people, but not having them turned on him. Though he hated to admit it, he was scared. All his adult life he'd been prosecuting criminals, but now he was being made to feel like *he* was the criminal. It was even conceivable that a prosecutor from his own office could soon be coming after him.

Could have, should have, would have, thought Orville. He had accepted everything that Darl Dixon had presented him and not questioned it. And while it was true that he was Dixon's subordinate, some of the so-called evidence hadn't been looked at under a microscope like it should have been. Sizemore was experienced enough to have a "smell test." In prosecuting Deketomis he hadn't used his sniffer like he usually did.

And now it was up to him to try and make things right, while at the same time hopefully saving his bacon. It wasn't going to be an easy juggling act but one thing was sure: There was no way he was throwing himself on a sword to save Dixon.

It was almost eight o'clock when he drove over to the Thorn residence. Sizemore had tried calling Angela, but the phone had been taken off the hook. A light rain was falling as Sizemore parked. Naturally he hadn't brought a hat or a raincoat. It was that kind of day. Since he wanted to make it look like an unofficial visit, Sizemore left his briefcase in the car.

As he made his approach to their porch, the sky opened up. The rain that fell on Sizemore felt like a punishment. He pressed the doorbell and waited. Angela's daughter Kimberly opened the door. She was made of sterner stuff than her mom, and stared Sizemore down.

"I'm Orville Sizemore," he said. "You don't know me—."

"I know you," she said, her words an accusation.

Sizemore tried to smile, but the girl's baleful expression didn't change even an iota. Luckily for Sizemore, Kimberly didn't get the opportunity to give him the bum's rush because her mother appeared behind her.

"Mrs. Thorn," said Sizemore, "I am here to apologize more than anything else. May I please have a few minutes of your time?"

Angela nodded to her daughter, who gave Sizemore one last hard look and then walked away. Mrs. Thorn opened the door to Sizemore. He tried to shake the water off his body, and made sure to wipe his shoes on the doormat, before stepping inside. Then Sizemore followed Angela to the living room. As the prosecutor took a seat, his clothes squeaked.

"Let me start with that apology, Mrs. Thorn," Sizemore said. "When I put you on the witness stand, I had no idea of the—" he struggled for the word, "*entirety* of your husband's situation."

"*Entirety*," repeated Angela. "What a strange word to use. If only it covered all my husband's sins."

The woman Sizemore was now facing no longer seemed to be the listless wallflower he'd had on the stand. Mrs. Thorn was tired of being a prisoner of her husband's misdeeds. And it appeared she was also tired of being a pawn.

"I am surprised Darl Dixon didn't tell you about Ken and his *situation*. How is that for another strange word?"

"If you don't mind, Mrs. Thorn, maybe we should dispense with the wrong words," said Sizemore. "I came here hoping I could find out everything I should have known before taking this case to trial. It's ultimately my fault that I didn't know about your husband. If I'd asked the right questions, then maybe I would have gotten the right answers. I take responsibility for not getting those answers and for making you suffer."

Angela nodded, apparently accepting his apology. "I don't think Darl Dixon did either one of us any favors," she said.

"Amen," said Sizemore, and then added, "No offense."

"None taken."

"When that woman lawyer started going after you," he said, "and I heard some of the things you were saying, I knew we'd lost the case. Maybe I panicked. Maybe I was afraid of looking like a worse prosecutor than I was. By asking for a mistrial, I took away your chance of declaring the truth. At this time I am hoping we can get to that truth."

"The truth is supposed to set us free," said Angela. "That's what the Bible says. But lately I have been plagued by doubts, and wonder if my own church is practicing what it preaches."

"I'd like to hear about those doubts," said Sizemore.

Slowly, painfully, her story came out. Angela recounted how after Ken's overdose she went to see Pastor Rodney in his office, and how that led to Ken going to talk with the preacher.

"Afterward, Ken came home and said he'd prayed with Pastor Rodney, and the pastor had offered him a road to salvation. I asked what that meant, but he didn't say."

"What do you think he meant?" asked Sizemore.

With her voice shaking with emotion she said, "I don't know. I do know that Pastor Rodney arranged for Ken to meet with Darl Dixon. The two of them had a few meetings, and I know Ken had some outings with Darl, even though I have no idea what they did."

She shook her head, and a bitter note crept into her voice. "I am as guilty as anyone ever was of 'Don't ask, don't tell.'"

"On the witness stand you said that on the day your husband overdosed you saw some pictures and a note."

She nodded. "That's the first time I heard of the Corian Hotel," she said. "It was on the letterhead. I didn't know its reputation, though. Now I have no doubt that Ken stayed at lots of places like that on his sales route."

"Did Mr. Dixon know about those pictures and that letter?"

Angela remembered her breakfast with Dixon, and recalled the conversations she'd had with her husband. "Oh, yes," she said. "Ken said that Pastor Rodney had passed on his *situation* to Darl, and that he was 'handling it.' I think Ken said that Dixon had personally intervened."

"You mean Dixon met with the girl in the pictures?"

"That was my understanding. But to tell the truth, Mr. Sizemore, the whole topic sickened me, and I had no interest in knowing what was going on."

"I think I was guilty of that as well, Mrs. Thorn," said Sizemore. "And since I have bothered you more than enough, I am going to take my leave. Thank you for seeing me."

She walked him to the front door where she said, "Do the right thing, Mr. Sizemore."

"Better late than never, right?" he asked.

Both of them managed a small smile.

Sizemore's cell phone rang during his drive home. That wasn't a surprise. His phone had been ringing pretty much nonstop since the trial's dramatic ending, but he hadn't been taking any of the calls. This time Sizemore took the call. The name coming up on his car's display was not anyone he wanted to duck, at least not now.

"Mr. Deketomis," said Sizemore.

"Everyone says I should be celebrating, Sizemore," said Deke, "but that's not how I see it, especially after you subjected me to two days of character assassination."

"I apologize—"

"Save it," interrupted Deke. "Gina told me what went down in chambers after the trial. The bottom line is that the state attorney's office is guilty of criminal conduct. At this time I am not convinced that you aren't a part of that criminal conduct."

"I swear—"

"Convince me in person," said Deke. "I expect you at my house tomorrow morning at eight. Gina Romano will be joining us."

"Yes, Mr. Deketomis, eight o'clock . . ."

Sizemore realized he was talking to a dial tone.

At five minutes to eight an exhausted looking Orville Sizemore arrived at Deke's house.

"I am glad you look like someone who needs coffee," said Deke.

"I didn't sleep," admitted Sizemore.

"Gina's out by the pool," said Deke. "I'll bring you coffee. How do you take it?"

"Black is fine."

A minute later Deke joined the other two attorneys. He put down Sizemore's cup of coffee and then eyeballed his adversary. Deke and Gina had agreed to play "good cop, bad cop." He was going to be the heavy.

"You need to convince me that I shouldn't be suing you both personally and professionally, Orville," said Deke.

"I can understand your anger, Deke. It's justified, that's for sure, but you need to believe this: You weren't the only one that was strung out. I was strung out right alongside of you."

Deke looked doubtful. As planned, it was Gina's turn to start talking. "Orville," she said, "you need to understand that this is your one opportunity to save yourself from losing your license to practice law, which would then be followed by a long list of criminal charges."

Sizemore wiped away some beads of sweat forming on his forehead, and nodded.

"The criminal charges I don't need to describe for you," Gina said. She sounded a bit bored, as if she could not care less whether he was sent away. "You understand what it means to tamper with evidence in a criminal trial. And then there's perjury, and you are well aware of what the criminal code says about covering up crimes committed by a sexual predator against children. That's just the short list of personal disasters you need to bear in mind during this morning's discussion."

Their double-team continued, but it was Deke's turn. "We have an affidavit signed by Lucia Torres. She's the mother of the girl Thorn molested. In that affidavit Torres says she provided information about that sick frigging deviant's crimes to the State Prosecutor's Office. That's the same place where you work, Mr. Sizemore."

Deke stared at Orville. "I'm ready to burn you and your office," he said. "But Gina doesn't want me to throw out the baby with the bath water."

He turned to Gina. "Those were your words, right counsel?"

She nodded. "I hope my faith in you is not misplaced, Orville. I have told my client that I don't believe you are complicit in all of this."

"And I told her your stupidity, if nothing else, makes you complicit," said Deke.

"He did say that," said Gina, "but I have advised my client against acting, at least pending what you bring to the table on Monday."

Sizemore let out some pent-up air and nodded gratefully. "I don't think you'll be disappointed," he said, and then told them about his previous night's meeting with Angela Thorn. What he told them didn't seem to surprise Gina or Deke.

Without missing a beat, Deke jumped in. "At Monday's hearing we expect you to provide an airtight case against Dixon. We believe Dixon has in his possession pictures of Thorn molesting Sunny Torres. Those pictures might be in a file on his computer, or they might have been printed out. By tying Dixon to these pictures, he will have no wiggle room. Those pictures will serve our purposes, but they'll also serve your own. They will prove you were not complicit with Dixon in withholding evidence and covering up crimes."

"At the same time you're presenting the pictures," said Gina, "you can present the affidavit signed by Lucia Torres."

"Understand this, Orville," Deke said. "Your office, together with a couple of other bottom-feeders, placed my law firm in jeopardy and put the safety of my entire family at serious risk. You have jeopardized my professional relationships and reputation all over this country. This will not end well for you unless you do as you're told."

"I understand," said Sizemore.

"If you comply with what we've asked," Gina said, "and you see to the filing of charges against Darl Dixon, then following Monday's hearing we will hold a press conference where we are prepared to stand by you and say you were not culpable for anything that occurred."

"I am going to have to hold my nose in order to do that," said Deke. "I think you were sloppy, Orville, and in your rush to judgment all you could think about was convicting me, whether or not I was innocent. But I'll forever hold my peace as long as you admit that I was wrongly prosecuted, and you make a heartfelt apology to me and my family."

Deke stared at Sizemore, and under his gaze he found himself squirming. "I thank both of you for the chance to make things right," he said. "I won't let you down."

"Are you ready to go on national TV and admit that justice was abused by your office?" asked Deke. "And will you promise to the world that nothing of this kind will ever happen again?"

"Yes," he said.

"Then you had better get ready for your close-up, Orville," said Deke. "Come Monday, you're going to be a star."

41

AN IRONY NOT LOST

At the start of the week Orville Sizemore had been doing everything in his power to put Nick Deketomis away. At the week's
end he had completely reversed course. From constructing his
case, he had gone to deconstructing it. At the behest of his boss
he'd been a pit bull; now he was going after that same boss with
even more vehemence.

The irony was not lost on Sizemore, but if he'd had an opportunity to sleep during his long weekend of preparation he might
have appreciated it even more.

That irony was compounded by a message Sizemore received
from Dixon. On a few occasions, just for his amusement, Sizemore
had played back what Dixon had to say.

"Orville, this is Darl," the message started. "I'll see you at that
hearing on Monday. From what I've heard, you haven't been com-
menting to the press either. That's our best strategy. Of course on
Monday I'm going to have to say that I disagreed with your call
for a mistrial, and that as far as I was concerned we were ready

to proceed with our case. But I'll categorize it as something on which we just agree to disagree. Then we'll say we want to refile on Deketomis because of special circumstances. Anyway, I think things are already beginning to blow over. I'll bet by next week most everyone will have forgotten what happened. That's how it is, you know."

Sizemore spoke to the recording. "Yep, that's how it is."

Of course by that time he had what he wanted. It helped that Darl Dixon was lazy. Having worked for Dixon for years, Sizemore knew this. He also knew where Dixon was most likely to store any electronic evidence or pictures. It had been Sizemore who personally set up the office's network file sharing system using software called File Drop. Since its installation attorneys had been able to work on cases together, and could send and receive information from their cell phones.

Because Sizemore had put the system together, he knew it better than anyone. Unbeknownst to his peers, Sizemore regularly monitored the contents of File Drop. He never revealed his findings, but was privy to an assortment of embarrassing personal information being transmitted by the lawyers. Much of this entertaining material ended up in File Drop.

Sizemore had begun his search by going through the few prosecution case files that Dixon had opened in his role as state attorney. Dixon rarely ever handled a case himself. As far as the other prosecutors were concerned that was a good thing, because in addition to being lazy, Darl had no talent as a trial lawyer. Because of both of those factors, Sizemore only had forty-eight case files to choose from.

He began with the files containing photographs. It took twenty minutes to find what Dixon had certainly thought he had hidden. The pictures showed Thorn molesting a teenage girl in a variety of positions.

Sizemore downloaded the pictures to his own phone, making sure it would be clear that they had come from Dixon's file. He preserved the chain of evidence just as he would have preserved evidence in any criminal case. The time of the downloading to his phone was recorded, as was the date and time stamp entries in Dixon's case file, along with no less than four signature entries made by Dixon. It would be all but impossible for anyone to argue that the pictures Sizemore was prepared to show to Judge Heath on Monday morning had not come directly from Darl Dixon's case files.

Even with the pictures in hand, Sizemore was not content. With his career on the line he knew that he had to nail everything down. He barely slept, eating takeout pizza and nuking frozen meals. By the time Monday morning arrived, Sizemore was ready. He had affidavits, pictures, and supporting evidence.

This time he was much surer of his case than he had been on the previous Monday.

42
MONDAY, MONDAY, CAN'T TRUST THAT DAY

Darl Dixon walked into Judge Heath's chambers two minutes later than the appointed hour of nine o'clock.

"Sorry," he said to Gina and Orville. "I couldn't get out of an important call."

The truth of the matter was that he had stopped to look at samples of campaign buttons for his upcoming race. He was particularly enamored with one that had said, "Oh, my Darlin'!"

Dixon was dressed in a seersucker suit and wearing an orange and blue Florida Gators football tie around his neck. That combination might have worked had his tie not been knotted about eight inches too short.

Smiling at everyone, Dixon found the one open seat. He had no idea it was about to turn into a hot seat. Darl thought they were there for a little housecleaning, something not atypical at trials.

"Where's the judge?" asked Darl.

As if to answer, a member of court security appeared at the doorway, and asked everyone to follow him to Judge Heath's inner chambers. The three attorneys complied with the request. Darl looked a little surprised to see Judge Heath wearing his robes, and a court reporter apparently there to take a record of their proceedings. In an informal affair judges don't wear robes, nor were words recorded. But Darl decided he might as well use the opportunity of having a court reporter there to take down his words.

"Judge," he said, "thank you for making this time available for us. I want to make it clear on the record that the state intends to re-file charges against Mr. Deketomis under special circumstances, and we will have those pleadings prepared no later than the middle of the week."

With the barest hint of a smile Judge Heath said, "I appreciate the state attorney's gratitude, but you may want to save your thanks until the end of this session, Mr. Dixon. This hearing has nothing to do with Mr. Deketomis and everything to do with the conduct of yourself and the state attorney's office."

"Mr. Dixon," the judge continued, "the issues we will be discussing this morning are far from minor. In fact, if you choose, you are more than welcome to have an attorney present as we proceed."

The prosecutor made an attempt at a ridiculously uncomfortable laugh. Too late, Dixon took stock of the stony faces staring at him.

Judge Heath turned to Orville Sizemore. "Mr. Sizemore," he said, "last Thursday I posed some questions to you about the conduct of the state attorney's office that you promised to research. Do you now have answers to those questions?"

"I do, Judge," said Sizemore. "After conducting a thorough examination into what Mr. Dixon knew about Mr. Thorn's suicide attempt prior to trial, I can assure the court that there was no information in the case file or anywhere on record with our office of this suicide attempt."

Darl looked suddenly relieved, but Sizemore wasn't finished.

"Your Honor," he said, "what I am about to now put on the record is information that I had no knowledge of prior to the time that I began investigating the questions you posed to me last week. It is difficult and hugely embarrassing for me to have to present the results of what I have found."

"Now, hold on," Darl protested.

"Mr. Dixon," said Judge Heath, "please refrain from speaking while Mr. Sizemore tells us what he's found."

"I can speak for the workings of my own office," said Dixon.

"Apparently you can't," said Judge Heath. Then he ordered Sizemore to continue.

"First I'd like to present you with Lucia Torres's affidavit, Judge," said Sizemore. "As you can see, she testified having not only met with Mr. Dixon, but having given him pictures of her daughter's sexual encounters with Ken Thorn."

"She's a liar," Dixon said. "And she's an illegal. Someone threatened her with deportation . . ."

Dixon stopped talking when he saw Sizemore producing pictures of Sunny Torres and Ken Thorn *in flagrante delicto*, pictures he heard had been downloaded from his own computer file. He jumped to his feet, pointed a finger at Sizemore, and said, "You're fired."

"Sit down, Mr. Dixon," said the judge.

"There has been an egregious violation of privacy," said Dixon. "And I have no doubt that this search will be deemed illegal."

"I requested that search," said Judge Heath. "At this time you can either take your seat so that we might continue with proceedings, or we can reschedule it in order to allow you to have a lawyer present."

By that time a court security officer had materialized behind Dixon. With a show of both reluctance and petulance, Dixon sat down again.

"I'm a lawyer," he retorted. "I don't need one present. So let's get on with this little show."

"Please continue, Mr. Sizemore," said Judge Heath.

As Sizemore continued to add to the damning pile of evidence, Darl Dixon sunk deeper and deeper into his chair. When he'd heard enough, Dixon motioned for his former assistant to stop talking. Gone was his outrage. He didn't attempt bravado.

Choking out the words, Dixon said, "Judge Heath, maybe it would be a good idea for me to seek legal counsel, after all."

"I will grant your request," said the judge. "But for the record I would like to know if you have covered all that you needed to in your statement, Mr. Sizemore."

"I have," he said.

"And in order to protect this court record I would also like to ask Ms. Romano whether there is anything she would like to add."

"Your Honor," Gina began, "investigators from our law firm have thoroughly combed through every possible lead and talked to an extensive list of people who might shed light on what the prosecutor's office knew and when they might have known it. We began our investigation with the presumption that Mr. Sizemore was involved with all this, but have since concluded that he was not involved in any way."

Sizemore faced the judge. "I can assure this court that I, in no way, had any knowledge of what Mr. Dixon has done."

With an almost trancelike quality, Dixon tried to rise to his feet, but the security officer gripped his arm and guided him back down into his chair, like a caregiver attending to a feeble, disoriented man.

"Before I put an end to this hearing, Mr. Dixon, you need to know that forthwith I will be calling the governor's office. They will hear my account of the criminal events that I am convinced have taken place, and they will also hear my recommendations. I expect they will immediately act upon those recommendations, the first and foremost of which will be your suspension. I will also be requesting that Mr. Sizemore be placed in an interim position as first in command at the state attorney's office until an investigation is completed."

Judge Heath looked around for comments. There were none. Darl Dixon's head was slumped almost to his waist.

"For the present," the judge concluded, "this hearing is finished. It will resume only if criminal charges are not filed."

Deke would have given anything to be inside the judge's chambers, but it was almost as satisfying being outside them. He let Paul Moses organize his impending press conference, while he gave an exclusive interview to Rick Overbrook, the editor of the *Weekly Breeze*. Overbrook was just about the only journalist who hadn't prejudged him in his pieces about the death of Ken Thorn.

With Moses working his usual magic, a huge media throng assembled at the courtroom for a one o'clock press conference.

In front of a bank of microphones, Orville Sizemore read his statement with what appeared to be genuine contrition. "There will be no refiling of the case against Nick Deketomis," he began, and then offered one of the most expansive and genuine sounding apologies ever spoken by a prosecuting attorney. After referring to Lady Justice, and quoting Sophocles, Sizemore said, "I personally regret the suffering that so many people endured because of events that took place at my office."

Moving on to the red meat topics everyone was waiting to hear, Sizemore recounted in detail what had occurred that morning in Judge Heath's chambers: "Further action by the state attorney's office is likely to result in charges being brought against Prosecutor Darl Dixon," he said. "His actions in the case against Nick Deketomis nearly brought about a travesty of justice for this entire community, and I intend to right this wrong."

Sizemore's statement brought on the same tumult as his call for a mistrial had just days earlier. In the midst of that chaos, Gina Romano took her place at the podium. Her cool, green-eyed stare either intimidated or calmed the crowd, which settled down to listen.

"No one believes Orville Sizemore participated in Darl Dixon's scheme," Gina began. "But there was a conspiracy afoot to have an innocent man thrown in prison. Powerful institutions and adversaries allied themselves in an attempt to destroy a man. We have evidence that links Prosecutor Darl Dixon and Pastor Rodney Morgan as having worked together toward that ugly end. Our investigation is not over. We are still trying to identify all participants. In the days to come you will hear how Nick Deketomis was targeted. It is an ugly and often shocking story. I am saddened to think how an innocent man came so close to being railroaded into prison."

As usual, Gina didn't overreach. She left everyone assembled wanting more, but the press conference was over.

"The locusts will soon be descending," Darl Dixon told his wife.

He wasn't sure whether she heard him, what with how loud she was crying. She had been watching live coverage of the press conference. With all her bawling, Darl had barely been able to hear that Judas Sizemore.

Once more Darl hit redial. This was his third call to Senator Roger Dove. Maybe he'd have the juice to help him. God, he hoped so.

"This is Darl Dixon again, Senator," said Darl. "I really hope you can get back to me as soon as possible. I've got a situation here."

Dixon took a breath. In the silence his wife's crying would certainly be heard, but Darl forged ahead. "I'm hoping you can ask the Swanson brothers to help me," he said. "As you know, I was going up against their enemy. I was trying to help them. Now maybe they can help me. I'd like to discuss this," he continued. "I'd like you to call me."

When he clicked off, Darl had this sudden fear that he'd never hear back from Senator Dove, but then his phone rang. He answered the phone believing it was the senator, and only noticed too late the name on the display. It wasn't Dove calling; it was Pastor Rodney.

Apparently Pastor Rodney wasn't watching what was going on at the press conference. At that moment Gina Romano was telling the world that Darl and Rodney had colluded to have an innocent man imprisoned.

"Do I have anything to worry about?" Pastor Rodney asked.

Dixon didn't answer.

"Do I still have the protection of the state attorney's office?" the pastor asked.

Dixon hung up on the old buzzard. That gave him a little satisfaction, but not much, and not for long. Darl's wife started crying again.

43
THE TAKE AWAY

In the wake of his trial Deke tried to return to life as usual, but it wasn't easy for him. "Even my state of denial," he said to Teri, "is in denial."

One day people were calling him a murderer, and the next day they were proclaiming him a hero. Deke knew he was neither. The experience had changed him, and he hadn't come out of it unscathed. His enemies had been out for blood—his blood. Even now he was wary of the other shoe dropping.

Deke hugged his kids more than he ever had before. Andy pretended to hate it, but Deke said, "Tough," and hugged him all the more. Cara let him hug her and worry about her. No one knew the long-term effects of Ranidol, and Deke and Teri were both concerned that their daughter might be facing some time bomb. If that happened, though, they would face it as a family. And maybe their worry was all for nothing. The doctors said Cara's recovery looked complete. More than anything, Deke hoped they were right. But it was the plight of his daughter, and people like Annica, that motivated Deke.

That was his takeaway from his own travails, and that of his clients. It didn't sit well with him, and never would, that human lives were too often valued far less than corporate profits. His own trials had made clear to Deke his raison d'être. He had to provide a voice for the voiceless.

That's why Deke didn't go on a vacation with Teri, even though Lord knows she deserved one. That's why he didn't make a list of those people who had plotted against him, or abandoned him in his time of need. Life was too short, and besides, he had work to do. When Deke took on a case, he was *all in*. And so at the conclusion of his trial, no one who knew Deke well was surprised when he buried himself in work. To him, the next trial was always the biggest trial, even when he'd been on trial for his own life. And so he threw himself into preparing for S.I. Oil and the Swanson brothers.

"You do your work," Teri told him, "and I'll do mine."

Teri was helping Lucia and Sunny Torres. She was making sure mother and daughter would not be separated, and had set up an educational fund for both women. Like she had done for many other people over the years, Teri made the Torreses part of her extended family.

His wife's answer made Deke feel a little sorry for himself. "They say all work and no play makes Deke a dull boy," he said.

"Who said anything about no play?" asked Teri.

And then she showed him what that meant. Some play was a very good thing, thought Deke.

Only a month after his own trial, at a time when many had thought Deke would be occupying a jail cell, he flew to Texas. It was time to go to war.

Howard Nations had expertly prepared for the case against S.I. Oil. He'd provided the law firm of Backerman & Sharp with enough rope, and they'd used it to hang themselves. Nations had arranged a hearing in Houston asking that Judge Gregory Teal sanction the Swanson brothers and their attorneys for committing fraud in the discovery process. Nations had done most of the legwork in the case, and now Deke would appear with him as co-counsel arguing the sanctions.

The hearing in Judge Teal's courtroom began promptly at 2:00 p.m. Nations and Deke sat alone at their table. Meanwhile, Backerman & Sharp had a dozen attorneys in the courtroom. Even if they lost, their billable hours would be quite the consolation prize.

The opposition's lead attorney was senior litigator Richard Russell, best known in the media for wearing a different pair of custom cowboy boots almost every day of the year. Russell called them his "ass-kickin'" boots. Deke had told Howard Nations that the reason Russell had to wear such footwear was because he generated so much bullshit.

At the commencement of the preliminary hearing, Deke was surprised to notice that Karen MacArthur, Backerman & Sharp's lead negotiator, was seated in the back of the courtroom. Normally big law firms hid away their negotiators until the end of trial. They were only too aware that any early settlement would put an end to their firm's huge cash reserve.

Deke stood up and faced Judge Teal. It was up to him to explain the reason Nations had called for this hearing. For an instant, Deke flashed back to his own trial. It was much better to be presenting another case than to be a captive witness to his own.

"Your Honor," Deke said, "in the pretrial discovery process the Swansons and their attorneys have denied that the documents I am about to present to the court ever existed. Those documents are in front of you now. I think it will be clear that someone also directed three key witnesses to lie in their depositions about the very existence of at least a dozen critically relevant Swanson documents. I have those depositions right here and I'd like to go through—"

Richard Russell jumped to his feet. It looked like he was doing a two-step with his new boots. As was usual, Russell feigned outrage. "Judge, it was just an hour ago that we first saw four of these documents they want to discuss in this argument. What I'd like to know is where these documents came from."

It didn't go unnoticed by anyone, including the judge, that the cowboy-booted lead Swanson lawyer was focused on the wrong issue. At the moment it didn't matter where the documents came from. More important was the question of what was contained in them and whether or not they were hidden during the discovery process.

The defense lawyer continued with a more desperate argument, "Possession of confidential reports is certainly illegal and a violation of the lawyer's code of ethics, Your Honor."

Deke laughed out loud and said, "The defense's argument reminds me of the boy who shot his parents and then asked for the court's mercy because he was an orphan."

"That's enough, Mr. Deketomis," said Judge Teal, but he couldn't help offering the mild rebuke with a smile. "As for you, Mr. Russell, you will have your chance to argue, but right now I want to hear all the details about this motion."

In a PowerPoint presentation to the judge, Deke displayed emails from Swanson Industries' employees that denied the existence of documents repeatedly requested by both the DOJ and the FDA. The criminality on display was blatant; several of those documents that employees had sworn didn't exist were not only evident, but were signed by those same employees who had disavowed their existence. Juxtaposed on the screen were lists of times and places the documents had been requested. Deke began focusing on a document that was titled "Toxicity and Disease Potential."

"Your Honor, this document is dated in 2009," Deke said. "Three names appear on it. One of the names is Charles Randall, a nephew of the Swanson brothers who served as Senior Vice President of Operations for Swanson Industries. The two other names are in-house lawyers directly answerable to Anton and Kurt Swanson, including Spence Turner, who has been chief in-house counsel for the Swansons for thirty-five years. This document shows that in 2009 two scientists who had been subcontracted by Swanson Industries to study toxic environmental impacts of the S.I. Oil plant had delivered to the company alarming data about the environmental and human health harm that chemicals from the plant were causing to communities around the S. I. refinery."

A new document flashed on the screen, and Deke continued: "Within a week of S.I. Oil receiving their environmental report, Your Honor, this document was created. Please allow me to read from it."

At a nod from the judge Deke read, "Tell these pinheaded bastards their career is over if this half-assed report isn't made to look better."

Russell jumped up again. He tried to do his lawyerly version of Nancy Sinatra's "These Boots Are Made for Walkin'," but Judge Teal wasn't going to be walked over.

"Be seated, Mr. Russell," he said, his voice sharp. "As you have already been reminded, you will get your turn."

Another document appeared on the screen, and Deke spoke to its contents. "What the report said, Judge, was that the S.I. Oil refinery plant was leaking—and is presumably still leaking— deadly toxins such as benzene into tributaries that run into the

Alamo River, and also directly into three major aquifer sites that provide drinking water for three counties.

"And then, Your Honor, there is this." For the benefit of the Backerman & Sharp legal team, Deke slowly and painfully read a fourth document, this one created by a research firm called Groundswell Inc. That document told Swanson Industries management that the synergistic effect of at least three of the toxins had the capacity to cause neurological diseases similar to multiple sclerosis and Parkinson's disease. Additionally, the high amounts of benzene would inevitably promote the development of blood-borne cancers ranging from leukemia to Hodgkin's disease. In the report, those projected numbers were off the charts from an epidemiological standpoint.

Deke paused in his explanation, gave Russell and his team a pointed look, and then turned back to the judge. "The common thread that each of these documents have is that this very information was requested by the DOJ, the EPA, and by our trial team on no less than a dozen occasions."

It was that immoral arrogance, thought Deke, which infected so many that came in contact with it. In this instance the contagion started with the Swanson brothers and was embraced by their legal team—they seemed to assume that laws and rules weren't something they had to live by.

Judge Teal came from a corporate pedigree where the interests of consumers and virtually everyone else outside of the corporate world were regarded as an aggravation when they got in the way of profits. Greg Teal had never actually worked as a trial lawyer. Most of his career had been devoted to pushing paper relating to mergers and acquisitions between US and international corporations. As was the case in many judicial appointments in the Southern states, Teal had worked his way up through the political ranks of the Republican Party during a time when Republicans could relate more to the image of Teddy Roosevelt than Donald Trump. Even he understood that the party had fallen into an abyss ever since it had joined forces with the radical tea party.

Remarkably, the Swanson brothers, Roger Dove, and their attorneys had all misjudged Teal. They assumed they could manipulate his moral compass at will. They estimated that he was truly a corporate loyalist in every respect. Teal's record might easily lead someone to that belief. He had rarely ruled in favor of injured consumers or individuals who had been harmed by the misconduct of corporations.

But they had failed to notice a few pertinent facts. Judge Teal had come up through the ranks of the Republican Party during a time when Republicans actually held some high ground with regard to the environment, and he had never been asked to make any significant rulings on environmental cases. Further, Backerman & Sharp's overpaid hacks missed the key fact that Judge Gregory Teal's youngest son, Greg, Jr., had died just five years before from leukemia. And perhaps most importantly, they overlooked the fact that Judge Teal had made it known that his retirement was looming not far off. That allowed him impunity from outside interests; he could rule with his conscience and not have to worry about fallout.

Deke was hoping that every one of these variables would impact the judge's conduct. Whether that was unfounded pessimism or optimism, Deke wasn't sure, he just felt the cumulative impact of the sanctions presentation could not be overlooked.

Every lawyer in the courtroom understood what Deke and Nations had just done to both the Swanson brothers and Backerman & Sharp. These documents were now officially part of a court record that could only be kept confidential by Judge Teal's gag order, or by an agreement between the parties requesting that the contents of the record that day be a part of subsequent review in camera by a judge only. But even that would be an extraordinary step for Judge Teal to take to protect the Swansons.

After the presentation, Judge Teal frowned as he looked at lead lawyer Richard Russell. "Mr. Russell, I am allowing your response to be delayed for twenty-four hours. At that point, I want an oral argument and a written memorandum showing cause as to why Swanson Industries, its lawyers, and *its owners* should not be sanctioned. It is clear in my estimation that this case is rapidly moving into extremely troubling territory. I'm suggesting, Mr. Russell, that serious efforts to resolve this entire dispute might be appropriate within these next twenty-four hours."

No one in the courtroom doubted that Judge Teal wanted to avoid having to make any rulings about the conduct of Kurt and Anton Swanson, the sixth and seventh wealthiest people in America, so he did what he needed to do: He adjourned court.

It wasn't actually sanctions and problematic rulings by the judge that the Backerman & Sharp lawyers were worried about. The series of documents presented in court had criminality plastered all over them. Two of the dozen Backerman & Sharp lawyers in court that morning had actually helped direct the document destruction program that was run out of their main office in Washington, DC. Deke's opposing counsel no doubt thought that if he had acquired these specific incriminating documents, it was fairly logical to assume that Deke and Nations possessed dozens of others that they believed had been destroyed. The cowboy had personal knowledge that during the same years outlined in Deke's PowerPoint presentation, the Swansons had done far worse things. He couldn't help being afraid they might surface too.

Judge Teal's warning had noticeably deflated Russell and his cohorts. The swagger and air of confidence was summarily sucked out of the $5,000-an-hour suits sitting at the defense table. Richard

Russell was muttering under his breath; Deke heard some choice, but muted, curse words.

Deke and Nations packed up their briefcases and began making their way out of the courtroom. Each of them knew they'd had a very good day in court, but neither was about to prematurely celebrate. Still, they carried themselves with quiet confidence, and they made no moves to engage in discussions with anyone at the Swanson defense table. Their body language suggested they didn't have to, and that they were more than willing to see the case through.

Backerman & Sharp blinked first, and blinked hard. Even before they exited the courtroom chief negotiator Karen MacArthur called out to them: "What? You don't want to talk?" MacArthur had to know with that approach she was dealing from a position of weakness, but faux pas or not, it did stop Howard Nations long enough for him to say, "You're in the hole right now, Karen, not us. You need to grab a shovel, not us."

Deke and Nations walked by her and out of the courtroom. The lawyers were hoping for what was known as a "Take Away," a situation where one party is desperate enough to pay an exorbitant amount for closure. From experience, Deke knew that a white flag was only waved when one side didn't want to deal with the nightmare of potentially catastrophic litigation. Given that scenario, some companies saw the sense in settling, even for what, on the face of it, might seem like wildly unfair terms. Immediate closure meant avoiding projected and imagined chaos. Deke hoped Karen MacArthur was worried sick that her opportunity to settle was disappearing; that was the take away that he and Nations had done their best to deliver. By not dangling any settlement number on the table they had tried to maximize their position.

"The clock is ticking," Howard told Deke.

"I think they're more aware of that than we are," Deke commented.

"Do you think they're going to play hardball," he said, "or lowball."

By not trying to settle with Backerman & Sharp, they'd given them no opportunity to counteroffer for less. It sounded as if Howard was assuming they'd try to negotiate a low offer.

"I think right now Karen MacArthur is shitting bricks," said Deke. "It's not only the Swanson brothers on the hook; so is her firm. Both are facing huge PR problems. And for once it looks like the DOJ can possibly show some courage."

"So no hardball?" asked Howard.

"I don't even think she's going to try and lowball us."

"I'm guessing we'll know for sure in about five hours," Howard said. "That will give Karen enough time to talk with all the powers that be. If they're going to settle, we should know by then."

As it turned out, Deke heard back from MacArthur only two hours later.

"What about just the two of us meeting, Deke?" she asked.

"I'm already on the way to the airport," Deke told her. "You might have heard that I've been a bit occupied lately, and that's meant I haven't been able to spend much time with my loved ones. Well, that's about to change. I'm heading out on a father-son fishing trip."

"Jesus, you're not making this easy, Deke," Karen responded. "Look, I'll leave for the airport right now. I need you to promise me that you won't leave without our getting the chance to talk."

"Please be there within the hour," he said."

Their face-to-face took place next to the regional airport's vending machines and coffee dispenser. The two of them pulled up chairs. There were no negotiations. Deke dictated terms and she took notes.

"I won't spend any time stating the obvious about just how bad this is for your pathetic clients."

MacArthur didn't demur; she was stone-faced and silent.

"This is your ticket out of an impending disaster for you, your law firm, and those two Swanson freaks," Deke informed her. "You will get possession of all copies and the originals of those morally repugnant and damning documents you saw displayed in Judge Teal's courtroom this morning. We will jointly agree to an extraordinary writ by the judge to seal the record of everything that transpired in court today. Obviously I can't speak to whether or not Judge Teal will agree, but I am inclined to believe that he will do so based on what I observed this afternoon. Of course you would know better than I since he's part of your Grey Poupon crowd."

MacArthur offered a hint of a smile, and Deke continued.

"I will sign a confidentiality agreement with you on behalf of myself and everybody involved on my side. And we will dismiss our suit immediately upon your closing down the refinery operation at S.I. Oil."

"Fine," she agreed immediately.

"I knew that one wasn't going to be a problem," said Deke. "That refinery is well over fifty years old and has fallen far below state of the art production capabilities, so that's a win–win for you, Karen. Word is your evil corporate overlords are already negotiating a deal with the State of Alabama to open one of the most advanced, high-volume refineries in the world near one of their coastal ports. Let's just hope the Swansons take a little more care with the environmental laws on that one. It might help them avoid the kind of payout they are going to be forced to make today."

"Save your morality lecture," she said, "and get to the point."

"Sure, *the point* is you will pay a total of $5.2 billion over a period of three years. Part of that money will be used to medically monitor the people who have been exposed to your profitable poison. Part of it will be used to begin cleanup of the aquifers most seriously affected, and part of it will be appropriate personal injury and wrongful death compensation for the individuals whose families have suffered for decades from your toxic sludge. In addition, separate and apart from that money, you will pay Howard and my law firms a fee of $200 million by the end of this year. Of course there are the fine points and details to put on paper, so you can get all your billing machine pinheads to work out those problems."

MacArthur said, "Well, that won't go over well. But we'll hold our nose and pay you bottom-feeding sons of bitches a substantial amount of money, but only if—"

Deke stopped her. "You don't understand Karen. There *are* no ifs, and there are no *maybes*. None of this is negotiable." Deke held his finger to his mouth, directing her not to speak. "Trust me when I tell you that this is the end of our conversation. I expect it will be Howard in court when the agreement is announced on the record."

MacArthur was well aware that both Nations and Deketomis had reputations for being uncompromising and deliberate in the way they brought closure to a case. That didn't make it any easier for her to concede. In her thirty years of practicing law she had never been so completely mauled by a negotiating opponent.

Deke looked at his watch. "Time's up," he said.

"Deal," she said, extending her hand.

Deke pretended not to see it. He had made deals with the devil before, and probably would again, but that didn't mean he had to press flesh.

"Deal," he agreed.

The intellectual wordsmith types on the Backerman & Sharp team went to work and delivered a signed document to Howard Nations at his granddaughter's birthday party. There was no hearing because Karen MacArthur had met alone with Judge Teal, calling in significant favors. The judge assured her that he would see to it that the settlement was approved and that all the blood left on his floor at the last hearing would be quietly cleaned up. They were friends again. This was the kind of justice that the Swanson brothers were used to seeing, the kind that Backerman & Sharp was used to promoting.

44
FISH TO FRY

This time Senator Roger Dove knew to arrange his own transportation to the Swanson brothers' estate in Palm Beach. Once more, the brothers kept him waiting. Dove was ostensibly there to give them a recap on the upcoming election and how the brothers "political investments" were panning out. He also had the unfortunate task of discussing what needed to be done in the aftermath of the S.I. Oil refinery agreement.

You had to give it to Nick Deketomis, thought Dove. The man had more lives than a cat. They'd had him dead to rights, and not only had he survived, but he'd turned the tables on them. Instead of becoming a senator, their candidate Darl Dixon was certainly going to jail. What was a bit disconcerting to Dove was what Deketomis's counsel had said: Gina Romano had promised they'd be tracking down everyone who'd crossed the line in trying to put her client away.

Dove was pretty sure he had insulated himself enough to not be liable, but that didn't mean he wasn't feeling some prickles of anxiety. He hoped she wouldn't be able to connect him to the dump truck, and a few other dirty tricks. It had been payback time, thought Dove, for Deke's getting him voted out of office. Now his attempts at revenge didn't seem like such a good idea.

After waiting more than an hour, the brothers must have decided Dove had waited long enough. When Dove was finally admitted to their study, he couldn't help reacting to the change in Anton Swanson's appearance. His double take didn't go unnoticed.

"What's the matter, Dovey?" asked Anton. "Never seen a dying man before?"

Dying or not, Anton hadn't lost any of his vitriol. He had oxygen tubes running into his nostrils, and caked blood had collected all along his upper lip. His eyes were bloodshot and swollen to the point that he gave the appearance of a primitive, deep-sea fish. Standing behind him was a white-suited male nurse.

"Doesn't Anton look marvelous after his bone marrow transplant?" asked Kurt.

Dove wasn't sure whether the sick psychopath was serious, or if he was actually making a joke about his dying brother. What quickly became evident was that Kurt seemed to have taken on his ill brother's role as head asshole.

"Although we are enjoying your being speechless," said Kurt, "we assume you're here to provide us with your usual glad tidings."

Dove tried to focus. His wavering attention wasn't helped by the appearance of a Swanson grandchild who looked to be about three walking around the room yelling, "Bomb, bomb, bomb, bomb, bomb!" What made it even harder for Dove to concentrate was the smell that came with the grandson. He was walking around with a full diaper.

"Hello!" yelled Kurt Swanson. "Anyone home in that tiny head?"

"Yes," said Dove. "I have mostly good news about our candidates. We fully expect to win upwards of 80 percent of the races we targeted. Our only significant loss will be in Florida. You might have heard about Darl Dixon. It appears our candidate will be going to prison instead of the state senate."

"Ha!" That got a snort out of enfeebled Anton. "Why bother electing these damn politicians and then sending them to prison? We should send them to prison right away!" He laughed again which then evolved into a coughing fit. His nurse stepped forward and adjusted his oxygen. Instead of being grateful, the skeletal man slapped him away.

"Bomb, bomb, bomb, bomb!" yelled their grandson. Over his noise, Dove tried to continue.

"Dixon was not the only fallout," said Dove. "The televangelist Pastor Rodney Morgan was also arrested as being part of the conspiracy against Nick Deketomis."

It was Dove's intent to use Deketomis as his segue into S.I. Oil, but Kurt interrupted him.

"Phew," he said. "I thought it was the senator stinking up this room, but that's you, isn't it Louis?"

The grandson answered, "Bomb, bomb, bomb."

"Yeah, that is a bomb you got in your pants," Kurt said to him. Then he turned his attention from his grandson to Dove. "Got a job for you, *Senator*. I can't think of anyone more uniquely qualified."

Dove wanted to believe Kurt was joking, and he joined in with Anton's laughing. But it quickly became clear that if this was humor, it was all at his expense.

"After you finish with Louis," Anton said, "I might be next. They got me in diapers too."

Dove tried to ignore the directive. "In the case of S.I. Oil—" he started to explain.

"Deal with the fertilizer first," instructed Kurt, "and then the oil."

The half-dead Anton broke out into peals of laughter.

"Bomb, bomb," said Louis.

The brothers stared at Dove, waiting for him to do their bidding.

"Fuck both of you," said Dove.

He knew the two dysfunctional inheritance babies cared a lot more about humiliating him than they did about losing five billion dollars. To them, that was chump change. They still had another hundred billion or so. And they could care even less about the suffering and potential poisoning of thousands of men, women, and children. To them, human life was cheap. And they had insulated themselves with politicians, prosecutors, and judges to run interference.

"For once," said Dove, "you can clean up your own shit." He stood up to leave.

The brothers had never looked surprised in all the time Dove had known them. Now they finally looked surprised.

"Looks like the senator is finally growing a pair of balls," Kurt remarked. "Of course he's going to need them now that he's no longer on our gravy train."

Dove flipped them the bird as he walked out of the study. Maybe that was the first time anyone had ever dared do that to the Swanson brothers, he thought.

And come what may, Dove was sure he would always be glad he'd done it.

The Vermont fly-fishing trip had been Andy's idea. Father and son were working a stream about half an hour outside the Green Mountain National Forest. Deke and Andy both looked at peace. That was what special places like this did.

"Brook trout are the only native trout in Vermont," Andy reminded his dad.

"Tell those native trout they need to start biting more," said Deke.

"They need cold, clear water like this to survive," Andy told him. "I sort of feel the same way."

Deke just nodded. It was clear his son was leading up to something. "I know you want me to go to the University of Florida in the fall, Dad. But I don't think it's for me, at least not now.

"Not that far from here is a program Martin Bergman told me about. They bring in kids from war-torn areas like the Gaza Strip and Burma and Africa. Anyway, they have year-round programs for these kids. Martin described it as being part therapy, part learning, and part a helluva lot of fun. He said they need counselors, Dad."

"And you want to be one of them?"

Andy nodded.

Deke had wanted Andy to go to college, but thought about this alternative. Maybe it was the detour Andy needed. Maybe it would be more than a detour. It could just be a starting point. The previous six months had helped Deke make peace with many of the realities of the world.

"Whatever you decide, Andy," he said, "I am all for."

"That's good to hear. And what I didn't tell you is that I'll also be doing research for you."

Deke looked puzzled. "What kind of research?"

"You know how I said these trout need cold, clear water?" said Andy. "I've been reading about this proposed big development that they're trying to get put in here. If it goes through, it would mean the destruction of lots of streams. They say this area we're fishing right now won't be able to support trout. People are up in arms about it, but the developer has supposedly bought off all the local politicians."

"You seem to know a lot about this," said Deke.

"I was hoping to land a big fish," said Andy.

"And here I thought this was catch and release."

Deke reached out and hugged his son. Soon enough he'd be releasing him out into the world, but not today.

Today they had to do some more fishing.

ABOUT THE AUTHOR

MIKE PAPANTONIO is a senior partner of Levin Papantonio, one of the largest plaintiffs' law firms in America. He has handled thousands of cases throughout the nation involving pharmaceutical drug litigation, tobacco litigation, securities fraud actions, and many of the nation's largest environmental cases.

"Pap" is one of the youngest trial lawyers to have been inducted into the Trial Lawyer Hall of Fame.

In 2012 Mr. Papantonio became President of the National Trial Lawyers Association, which represents forty thousand trial lawyers nationally.

For his trial work on behalf of consumers, he has received some of the most prestigious awards reserved by the Public Justice Foundation,

The American Association for Justice, and the National Trial Lawyers Association.

He is an author of four motivational books for lawyers. He is also coauthor of *Air America: The Playbook* listed by the *New York Times* as a "political best seller."

Mr. Papantonio is the host of the nationally syndicated radio show *Ring of Fire* along with Robert F. Kennedy, Jr., and Sam Seder. In addition to the radio program, Mr. Papantonio hosts *Ring of Fire* on the Free Speech TV network and America's Lawyer on the RT America network.

He is also a political commentator who has appeared as a regular guest on MSNBC, Free Speech TV, RT America Network, and Fox News.